Four Palaces

FALL 2022 FICTION

FOUR PALACES PUBLISHING FALL 2022

With a Foreword by Guest Judge
Ivelisse Rodriguez

Edited by Emily Townsend
with Frederick Tran

Cover art by Duy Vo

Book design by Emily Townsend

www.fourpalacespublishing.org

ISBN 978-1-387-52723-6

Contents

IVELISSE RODRIGUEZ

Foreword

WHAT DO YOU REALLY WANT TO WRITE is a question I find
myself asking my students, especially when there is a layer of artifice to
their stories. Susan L. Lin's story, "Dead Lines," functions as a rallying
cry for this volume. Gage, the protagonist, just can't finish his work until
his friend takes him to a writer's only Escape Room. Here, in the Escape
Room, Gage is finally able to get to the core of what he really wants to
write, and only then can he exit. In this story, the Escape Room is the
holding cell, some intermediary space between who we are and who we
want to be. The artifice is no longer just about the story, but about us.
    In "Doctoral Daddies" by Severin Wiggenhorn, the protagonist
imagines herself multiplied, living at the same time on multiple planes
where different choices can be made. "If you asked me why I did this,
I'd cite high school, existential nihilism, and the many-worlds theory...
I wondered about the branch of the many-worlds where Professor
Johansen said no instead of yes. I wondered what that would have been
like, how I would have felt—rejected, relieved, misguided? I imagined my
seductive powers overcoming the rules of quantum mechanics, making
it impossible for him to say no." Here, the protagonist triumphs at every
turn with her powers of seduction. Unfortunately, every possibility
cannot lead to winning. Often in these multiplicity of choices of who
we could be, there is always at least one version where we are blighted.
Malina Douglas' protagonist in "The Hunted, the Haunted," "...seek[s]
the self that was smothered by someone else. That got buried in the
sands of time, eroded by arguments and compromises. I want to dig
her out, to climb back into her." In this story, the protagonist is living in
two spaces, and one self has been whittled down. While the destruction
exists, the stronger, breathing self wants a resurrection—a return to,
perhaps, the original self, or at least part of that self. Escape becomes

cyclical—a way in, a way out. We can reach back with a heroic hand and pull ourselves from the rubble. We can save ourselves.

The desire for escape leads to quantum physics, doubling, and it creates mirrors. In "Shanghai Film Festival" by Sienna Liu, the story delves into escaping the humdrum of everyday life, which is sometimes a bigger killer than we would ever imagine. Liu writes, "Just the aftereffects of always being told, since a young age, that 'you will never get the best out of life.'" In the middle of our ennui, the "best of our lives" becomes this specter that stands up next to us in the mirror. We always see it; it is always there. Like a tantalizing movie reel, it taunts us with an illusion of what our lives could have been, if only. And that illusion is always spectacular, full of pinnacles, ecstasy, a highlight reel of only the best. The mirror, though, is an illusion—no one escapes the lows of life, no one always gets the best of life.

In other stories, escape is sublimation. Sometimes we need to escape from worse things, and the only way we can do that is through some other mechanism. In Zoey Birdsong's "Nails," there is a support group for nail-biters. "We pickers. We harbor the compulsion to pick away at the excess–our nails, our skin. We scratch. We rip. These motions become us. We destroy ourselves." Sublimation exchanges one pain for another. Here, escape can only come in millimeters, tearing at the self, small bit by bit. When the tearing is done, what will be left—a torn self or a base for a new self?

In Anna Lapera's "The Night is for Running," the sublimation of one pain for another leads to a freedom. The protagonist, a graduate teaching assistant, is stalked by a student in a way that never quite crosses a legal line. She takes up running, a danger for women. Yet, in escaping from one danger to another: "Your breath wraps around your bones like your own language. You run on a night when fear is replaced with breath that bounces around your rib cage, escaping inward, filling you whole. You wonder if this is what it is to take a deep breath, to breathe, easy and free."

The winning story by Timilehin Alake, "Don't Hold Your Father's Hand," tackles one of the most disturbing and brave acts of escapism—when one desires to leave but can't point to why or make a compelling argument for disassembling one's life. Escape is usually predicated on some glaring issue—some clear weight on someone's throat. When one wants to escape simply because of their desires and not because something is wrong, people question this, people try to talk you into staying. In a situation like this, you will never be able to convince others why you need to leave. The best thing you can do is tell yourself that your desire to leave is enough. That permission is enough.

I now invite you to these escape rooms that are this book compiled by the editors of Four Palaces, Frederick Tran and Emily Townsend. Four Palaces' mission is to publish underrepresented writers, so the enterprise as a whole is focused on escaping the norms of publishing. Escape may at times be focused on running away from, but here in this volume, we are escaping to—to a new world of our making, where collectively, the voices of the marginalized are heard together. Welcome to this world of escapes.

Ivelisse Rodriguez, PhD
Inaugural Judge
Writer of Love War Stories, a PEN/Falkner Award in Fiction Finalist

DESIRE TO ESCAPE

FALL FICTION 2022

Don't Hold Your Father's Hand

THE EVENING TUMI saw his dead father, off the intersection of Flowers Estate just behind the parking garage of the large mosque with bleached-white stone walls and a bronze dome, it would have been easier to pretend he had seen a ghost.

But he had not.

Ghosts, as he'd known them through Yoruba movies, come back the same way they're buried, wrapped in white sheet, heavy with talcum powdered faces.

His father's ghost wore a grey suit and a white shirt, slacked red tie hanging loosely around the neck. He drove a car. A teal Volkswagen Passat. He drove it well, too, careening off with a sharp turn that left plumes of dust in the air as the tires screeched off the unpaved lot. Tumi stood and watched as the car drove off, the disappearing dust giving way to see the two little girls with matching ribbons in their braided hair sitting in the backseat.

This ghost, who drove a car and laughed heartily with his children, wide grinned, mouth full of teeth, skin worn whole and careless like a t-shirt, complete with the weariness of work and the delight of life, could not remember the face of those it had left behind.

The dying sun splattered against the glare of the dome, leaving the trace of itself in a blinding light that turned the horizon white while Tumi just stood and watched his father fade away with the light.

This ghost, whom he had willed back into the world, drove away without even recognizing him.

There isn't one sane driver in the whole of Lagos, Deoti thought as the Danfo driver shouted at her. Mad woman, Mad woman, he kept repeating. The conductor, whose feet had nearly been lost underneath her tires but for less than a few inches, slammed his hands against the hood of her car. He was screaming something at her, bathing the window of her passenger's side with saliva. Their voices dulled into the fog of Deoti's mind. As they raged, she knew that her ambivalence looked very much like arrogance, but she could not help it.

The ragged assembly of the Lagos highway transfixed Deoti. Vehicles large and small in rows, neck in neck, fighting for every inch of asphalt, and Okada slaloming through the seam like water passing under a closed door. Dizzying fumes blue against the morning fog. Potholes like sores in the road, some gaping like dug graves waiting for the dead. A few feet away from Deoti, the car she had been following inched away. Deoti knew the next turn it would take, and then the next, until its destination but as the car neared its exit to the right shoulder of the road, she felt a pit of loss inside her. The ritual of following Bowale had been less in following his car, but more so in watching him emerge from inside it, birthed into the world anew each time she saw him.

The collection of hinderances that had interrupted her rendezvous with a man she could only watch but not see, waited outside the window. A battered Vanagon bus, mustard yellow with two black stripes across its length, tattered black tarp for windows. The driver had an unassuming tired face, bald, thick-mustached, then the conductor, whose face was thrust against Deoti's windows. His lips caked and arid like a scorched desert. His raised arm showed a small brown glow of dirt and grime at the brisk end of his armpit hair. His shirt was tied as a scarf over his head, revealing a body riddled with scars.

In another lifetime, Deoti might have been intimidated by him. She might have been afraid of his wildness, the theatrics of throwing himself over the bonnet of her car and jumping off it, and then back on. Just a few months ago, before she found Bowale again and realized that the world is a veil of multitudinous layers of madness, she would have been covered in sweat from all the cars piling up behind hers, from the blaring horns. In another lifetime, whatever this conductor wanted she would have given. But in this life, where just ahead the rear end of Bowale's car turned away and the magic of watching him again was lost to her that morning, Deoti felt vengeful.

Once Bowale's car was gone, the noise around her began to filter itself out. The conductor demanded to be taken to the hospital. Then he demanded she come down from her car. Then he demanded an apology. Deoti offered nothing. His useless tantrum had taken something from her and Deoti knew how to take from him, also. Instead, she gestured an apology towards the bus driver. She knew it would anger the conductor, and she hoped it would. Apologizing to his boss, the driver, Deoti had snatched the conductor's agency. He would be called to order. His pride would be bitter in his throat, and Deoti would enjoy watching him swallow it.

The driver begrudgingly accepted Deoti's apology and turned his wheel away from her car, pulling off to the side to open a gap in the way for her to pass. Leave this mad woman alone, the bus driver said, calling to his conductor.

Deoti didn't mind. Everybody is mad in Lagos. She looked at the driver: a long chewing stick in his mouth, his Kangol hat with a Puma logo on it, his Tupac Shakur printed singlet left a large hole on the side through which a dollar sign tattoo peeked. Everybody in Lagos is mad. The conductor who groveled by the side of her car, swearing at his boss who was also swearing at him, and her who, instead of driving off, waited, and stared at him through her rolled-up window with a dead, wry smile, was equally mad.

The driver accelerated his bus forward, stopped, and then did it again. I swear I go leave you, he threatened his conductor. Follow the mad woman. He pedaled the bus forward again to yet another short but sharp distance, then screeched to a stop again, finally arresting the attention of the conductor. Caught between his anger and his daily bread, the conductor spat on Deoti's window before he pursued the moving bus and jumped on, his body dangling from it like a flailing door.

After they'd gone, Deoti looked at the time on her phone. Not much time had passed, but Bowale was already several roads ahead. She looked over at the passenger's side window where the thick spit hung. In another lifetime, she might have vomited at the gnarly sight, but the world had changed since Bowale's second coming. She turned away from it and drove.

When Tumi was three years old, back when he and his mother still lived just down the road from the airport, it would have been easier to pretend that his father was in America.

His Aunty Dolapo, his father's sister, once pointed at an airplane and asked him to wave at his father. It was a comforting lie told to children whose parents died too early. For a while, Tumi waved at every plane that passed, poked his hands into the lowly hung clouds, counting the planes as they droned so closely to the tip of his fingers. It was as though if he pretended each one was carrying his father in the roadless traffic that hung over their house, he could've duplicated hope until it filled him with the joy of having one.

Playing pretend fathers with airplanes didn't last so long, however. Tumi barely had any real understanding of what a father was—or what death did to them or the children they left behind—when his mother told him that his father was dead. She told him also that his father left an abundance of love in his stead, and as Tumi got older, he began to embrace his father's death almost as a presence of the man. His father was dead, but there was enough of his essence left in his life. His memory was palpable, his love an entity, thing of warmth and presence. It grew sinews and tissues, laid skin taut over phantom bones, thumped the corridors with the invincible ball of its heel. To Tumi, he was not different from any other child. He was protected, comforted, advised, admonished, and provided for. Perhaps, only in quieter terms than other children, but in a term which he found comfort in.

That comfort, though, since the evening he saw the ghost, slowly began to feel like a scratchy sweater against his back. After school that day, his body felt like it was weighed down by a mountain. There was a restless air in the house which mirrored the feeling in his body. Everything felt strange. The walls felt thin, the house a shrinking glass box. Tumi, unwilling yet to confront his mother with what he had seen—at least not yet, not until he understood it himself, until he overcame the doubts in his mind—pressed his feet against the carpet to muffle the odd and sudden loudness of his steps. He followed the quiet walls of the house, counting his face against the numerous photos of his father scattered around the space.

Eventually, Tumi stopped in front of the small polaroid tucked in a corner of the frame of the bathroom mirror. In the picture, his father leaned over his mother, one hand loosely across her breast and the other firmly cradling her stomach. Tumi plucked the picture from its place for a closer look, as though the picture had promised to reveal something new to him after all these years. His father was clean-shaven with a thicket of mustache that spreads over his smiling lips. His mother sat on a velvet covered box, placed low in front of a large, curved sofa where his father sat. His mother's adire boubou matched the color of the carpet. The iridescent glow that settled in both their eyes, the joy Tumi had always seen in the picture, suddenly became offset by the studio light caught in his father's left eye. The prop in the studio, the plastic plants that hung stiff behind and at the corners of the frame began to bother him.

Was the position of their bodies curated by the other presence in the room? Choreographed for the camera. Was their love as true as their faces painted? Had their joy been filled that day as his mother told, ignited anew by the news of his mother's pregnancy; news of him? Was it he that was cradled behind the hand rested on his mother's stomach? Was this really the closest thing they had to a family portrait?

The photo in hand and the gently haunting questions following, Tumi stumbled into bed. He closed his eyes and let his father's face wander beneath his. Every angled contour, every slope on the man's face traced his. Each rising and falling, he knew, its familiarity as assured as the perpetuity of the sun at dawn and the moon at dusk. He had known it so he could know himself. To say to himself now that the man he saw across the street, in the teal Volkswagen Passat, with two little girls with ribbons in their hair, was not the man in the photo, was to deny knowing himself.

He cast away the last question into the deep darkness of slumber, he put his body upon it and fell asleep, the photo still clutched in his grasp.

Under the canopy of a broad-trunked mango tree, across the road from the banking complex where Bowale now worked, Deoti rolled her car to a stop. The tree had become a fixture of their unconventional meeting, a place of refuge where she sat, waited, and watched, mooring under the tree's shade as though the tall building was indeed the man she sought. She did not know where he worked inside the building, what work he did, or for whom. She couldn't. Distance from history, she had learned, was the only thing that could keep a wraith in the world. If Bowale ever laid an eye on her, or anyone else from his past, his soul, she was told, would lean so hard to embrace what it lost in its previous life, it would tip over and out of his body. If he ever saw her, he would die. For good this time. Iya Efon, the old woman who sold sweets, biscuits, and water from a kiosk by the tree, had told her all about these mysteries. Deoti met the old woman the same day she found Bowale again.

It was six months ago now when Deoti first saw Bowale again. It was quite a normal day until it wasn't. She was walking towards her car after a meeting when the rain began, a sudden torrent which transformed a pristine blue sky almost black in a strange instant. The heavens growled like the stomach of a hungry child; streaks of lightning tipped their long fingers into earth. Her heels held in hand, Deoti ran towards an Amala shop for shelter. The madam of the shop was a foul-mouthed woman with long tribal marks across her face. She was a fat woman, spread fully on a throne—a large plastic chair whose integrity seemed stiffly tested by each minute—planted in the middle of the shop. Large, bulbous cast iron pots surrounded her immediate perimeter, around which small square plastic tables and chairs spread to different parts of the shop in a frenzy of colors—none in the color of the red throne.

As Deoti entered, the madam spoke without looking up, her voice unassailable, yet thin and babyish. Aunty, my shop no be bus-stop, she said. If you no buy food, turn back, please. Deoti shook her wet self into a corner and quietly sat down. She had little interest in eating, but asked for a single wrap of amala, a piece of meat, with egusi soup. She idled over the meal for a while but soon pressed by the searching eyes of the madam, she began to eat. It was then she heard the voice. Metallic, throaty.

Deoti remembered the first time she heard it, the distinct voice answering a question from the back of a general studies class in her first year in university. In a hall of more than 600 students, some hanging off the windows, sitting on desks, and on each other's laps, she looked back and saw his face, caught him smiling back as if to say he'd chosen her among the chaos, plucked her from the crowd.

After a few more classes, he approached her. "I swear I don't smoke," he said to her, his voice whispery and dry. Her eyes settled on his lips as they spoke. She wanted to kiss them, kiss his mouth and his words. She fell for him immediately. She cared little if he smoked or not, but she teased him anyway.

"Okay, Brother Menthol, what should I do about that," she asked.

"Brother Menthol," he repeated. He laughed. He liked the name, he told her. It was witty and smart, better than Igbo, Shoko, J, or Carolina. Names that spelled iterations of marijuana, names that didn't quite fit his demeanor or habits. She argued menthol wasn't any different. Another iteration of smoking.

It was subtle, he argued. Less razz. She laughed. Between the back and forth, he asked her on a date. "To celebrate my re-christening," he said. And she laughed more.

Twelve years had passed since their school days, but not even time could rumple Bowale's voice in her memory. If she knew nothing else in the world, she knew that voice. It breathed into her throat, ears, and mind. It was the genesis of their love. However, before Deoti could look up, Bowale was rushing out into the rain.

Iya Efon would later tell her that this was a wraith's way, a form of self-preservation. Their bodies carried them whenever it sensed the past, and it made sense. No matter how quickly she followed him out into the rain that day, not washing her hands, not gathering her keys, clumps of egusi still stuck to her hands, he was gone. As though carried away into the wind. She only saw a car leave, and on a hunch, followed it.

And for the sake of not losing him again, she left her car and keys at the restaurant, followed on an okada until the office, and the thick-crooked-mango tree across the street from it. There she sat and cried, her skirt blackened in the wet soil at the foot of the tree, where she found the kiosk with the old woman who sold biscuits, and sweets, and water, who helped her make sense of a dead husband who now lived.

Morning fell upon Tumi like a drunken daze. It was difficult to separate the day before from the dream of the night. As far as he was concerned, he might have slept through a whole day in a fever dream. He felt his stomach and forehead with the back of his hand for good measure, but nothing. The turbulence his body felt was not written on his skin, but was somewhere deep inside him, clawing outward into places Tumi neither knew nor could trust.

Tumi feared what it would dig out. The girls behind the ghost's car were static pictures in a view-master underneath his eyes. They were the only thing he saw each time they shuttered. The jealousy didn't even make sense, but it ate at him. How could they have his father if his father was never his. Their languid joyfulness, the flimsy bows in their hair, cut deep into his side it hurt. Daylight poured into the room. Birds chirped on the power cables outside, their twittering bouncing through the window. He imagined them on tiny legs, bobbing their heads, skipping side to side. Their small bodies somehow withholding volts of currents surging through the cables, insulating death.

"Tumininu," his mother called from the kitchen, cutting through his thoughts. Her feet dragged the floors through the corridor until his door, then she stopped short of entering.

"Oko mi, you will be late for school, now. Why are you not up yet? Are you okay?"

"Yes, Maami," Tumi said and sat up from the bed. He saw the birds through the window. Two palm doves with ugly flat-brown feathers. Unremarkable. Alive.

"I am fine, Maami. I overslept." As though suddenly finding a fresh source for haste, Tumi got up, pulled a towel from the closet door, and tied it around his waist, gesturing for his mother to allow him some privacy. She lingered.

"Maami, I am trying to get ready," he whined. He appeased her with a forced smile. The air seemed heavy between them, and he worried if she could feel the weight of it as he did. The last thing he wanted was to doubt all his mother had ever told him about his father, but the thoughts crept in on him anyway. What if his father had been alive all this while, what if this story of his death had been his mother's delusion? A well nurtured lie that's grown into a handsome truth. What if his father had just simply left?

She ought to have reminded him by now that he was but still a child. Her baby. But she had not, and her pause made him uneasy. He was desperate for her response.

"Shior," his mother finally said, laughter and sarcasm dipping into her words. "What are you hiding that I have not seen before. Wasn't I bathing you just last week?"

"Maami, last week is not today. And to keep the record straight, you have not bathed me in at least five years."

"Oh, so your mother cannot count the days anymore, abi," she laughed fully, clapping her hands in rhythmic disbelief.

He wanted to tell her she had found it hard to count the days since they moved. Since she started taking long drives into the city and covering every worker that needed covering. Opening and shutting the office, extending her hours so theirs can be shorter. He wanted to say she was losing days; that in the recent months, she had lost days in his life. But it had always been the two of them. He knew her. She gave everything for him. If he felt a tickle of abandonment now, it was only because of the ghost he had seen.

"Maami, now," Tumi pleaded. "Please go. I'm blaming you if I'm late o."

"Okay, okay. Don't push this all on me yet. I'm leaving. Hurry. I'll leave your food on the table in case I'm not in when you finish—"

"Okay ma," Tumi pushed. He knew this line of conversation, too. It had become frequent in the past months.

"I wasn't done," she responded, curt.

"Sorry, ma. Where are you going?"

"Well, I was going to say but you keep cutting me off." Her voice softened. "I have to cover Mrs. Fowowe this morning, so I leave early. Get your lunch money from the counter, beside your breakfast. Also, I told the Johnsons to take you. Oko mi, don't walk to school o."

"Yes, Ma."

If his mother would oblige, he wouldn't mind going with Mr. Johnson to school permanently. The man was cool. His car playlist had all the new hit songs, and he took immense pride in keeping them updated. Tumi enjoyed talking about music with the man. There was something calming and welcoming about sitting in a car with the radio on, nodding to the song, picking at the tunes or lyrics with him. Once, Tumi wondered if the experience would be the same if there was no music, if proximity to the man was all that was giving, but he shut that thought away as quickly as it came. Only that time, his father had been dead and the memory of him had been enough. Then, he had been sure of himself, sure that he was not seeking replacement fathers.

Now, after the little girls at the back of the ghost's car, he was not so sure anymore. He felt betrayed. By whom, he didn't know. Tumi began to wish more of Mr. Johnson's car and suddenly, the prospect of riding with Mr. Johnson left him hollow inside. Unsure of how much his face gave away, he turned his face from his mother who was still at the door, watching him with a pensive eye. She had been waiting for more words from him, but Tumi had none left for her. He dug his hands under his towel and pulled his pajama pants down.

Quietly, she retreated out of the room.

Tumi stripped himself fully and watched his body in front of the full standing mirror. Something had changed in him. Something became missing.

As Iya Efon had done many times before, she took a rag and dusted the bench. Deoti hurried out of her car and grabbed the rag from the old woman, half-kneeling to greet, without offering the salutations in words. Sometimes their meetings passed with the quietude of a graveyard and that was okay. Iya Efon understood where Deoti's body ached. She knew sometimes one met the dead in silence.

Iya Efon's only son was an interstate commercial bus driver. Two days after he died in a crash on his way North, far away from his beloved mother, his spirit visited his mother—in flesh and blood. He sat with her in her small hut in the village, told travel tales like he'd always done as she prepared his favorite meal. He ate with his shirt slung over one shoulder, sweating, his bulging stomach bare in satisfaction. His empty dishes still lay on the table, beside the large bag of beverage, food stuff, money, and provisions he brought, when the driver's union representatives brought the news of his death. When the men walked in her hut, their faces drawn out so long it reached the tip of their shirts, she knew. Iya Efon did not cry, nor did she bother looking for her son in the bathroom where he should have been relieving himself.

For her son, a city bird flown away since nineteen, she followed the men to Lagos and stayed: to breathe the air her son breathed in his lifetime. That was how she kept him with her. Iya Efon told Deoti her story to help her understand that there was love even in letting go. Iya Efon told her, too, that it was better to live her life outside the shadow of a dead man. To have set eyes on him again, she said, was the rarest of God's blessings. But Deoti always returned. The old woman did not stop her from coming to sit under the tree, nor did she reproach Deoti's perpetual return, and for this, Deoti appreciated the old woman. Indeed, between them a quiet relationship had grown, a fondness shared in knowing loss.

In Iya Efon's story, Deoti found her solace but not closure. In the chaos of that Sunday afternoon, as the bombs in the Ikeja cantonment tore through the city, Deoti had always wondered if Bowale died trying to find his way back to her. Long after the dust settled, with the panic gone, and everyone knew where to place their blames, Deoti could never reconcile that the tragedy of that day was manmade, a gross infrastructural incompetence. Somehow, she felt responsible that he was gone.

Like many of the deaths from that day, some jumping into canals, multitudes taken by the terror of uncertainty, it was not to be known if Bowale died or simply vanished. His body was never found. This part, though, she never told anyone. Not even Iya Efon. It was an unnecessary line of inquiry, a needless sowing of the seed of doubt. What did it mean if his body was never found? The memorial and mass grave were evidence that the loss of that day never named themselves. What did it mean if she let herself think that Bowale took advantage of a once in lifetime catastrophe to abandon her and his child? That was more absurd than believing that he lived again after his death.

Her love was the twine strong enough for Bowale to climb between life and afterlife. If he lost his way back to her in the chaos of that afternoon, her love found a way, uncanny though, brought him back to her. She couldn't let him go now. Even though she had to watch him from afar. Even though to see him with his new children and his new wife were shards under her skin, she endured the agony of him not knowing her child. It was enough.

Love is love, even though it is endured.

After wiping the bench, Deoti moved on to the window of her car. The conductor's thick spittle remained wet and dense. Head raised to the sky, Deoti let the morning wind brush the side of her ears with soothing coolness. The tension on the back of her neck was nimble, the perch of a small bird on a laundry line. The weight was delicate, but it was weight, still. In a straight long swipe, she wiped the spit from the window, the mess reducing by each fold of the towel. She did not know why, but the chore exhausted her. It lay a heaviness on her soul; one she had not felt since she began watching Bowale. It reminded her of a picture in her head: of her son last night, his body curled up in bed, streaks of tears crusted across his face, the picture of his father and herself crumpled in his hands.

She sat down on the bench and watched the road. Cars flew one way and the other, going, coming. And she sat there, still, watching the building that swallowed Bowale each time and belched him out again into the road for her to follow.

His pidgin was barely good enough to communicate the open-ended cost of following a car to an unknown destination, but the okada-man's enthusiasm showed well he knew he could negotiate a considerably lofty fare. Tumi had money. The "absentee coffers," as he had started to call them, had piled as his mother's frequent morning escapes increased. The thought of money or the fare was the last thing however on Tumi's mind when he jumped on the okada.

It was the teal Volkswagen Passat again, down the dirt road from his school, idly rolling by as though it was inviting him to follow. Lightning was striking in the same place more times than it was permitted. The signs accumulated. His mother's frequent wanderings, how she looked at him that morning, knowing well he knew she was lying about covering Mrs. Fowowe.

Toni Braxton spilled out behind Tumi as he stepped out of Mr. Johnson's car. Mr. Johnson was saying something Tumi couldn't make out, balms for future heartbreaks in the R&B singer's music, or so. His eyes glued to the Volkswagen, Tumi waved goodbye to Mr. Johnson almost dismissively. The man waved back and went on his way, and soon as he was gone, Tumi stopped the okada. He was not sure what was at the tail end of the journey, but he knew the journey was one he had to take. "Follow that green moto for front," he told the okada-man, pointing. Without hesitation, the motorcycle zipped forward, snaked in between the traffic of a few slower vehicles, covered ground on its assignment.

The wind slapped Tumi's face, his heart beat quickly, and then slowed in disappointment. The car had not gone any distance worth promise. Passing through a few familiar streets, perhaps two or so down from Tumi's school, the car stopped behind the mosque where Tumi had first seen it. The ghost exited. He was hasty, disappearing around the front of the mosque for a while then returning with the two girls. One followed on small legs holding his left hand, and he cradled the other close to his chest, hoisted by his right that also held both their school bags.

"Oga, only pay hundred naira," the okada-man said, laying the ground for his inflated fare. His interruption irritated Tumi. His eyes were fixed on the ghost and the kids who seemed much like his children. The one held up dug her head deep into her father's shoulder, her huge bob of hair tied up with a purple ribbon, the only evidence of her presence there. Tumi tried to find what that warmth of safety would feel like on his skin, but he couldn't. His body boiled with shame. He was held, he was loved, he was comforted. He had a father.

"Oga," the okada-man interjected again. Tumi held up 500 naira from his pocket and showed him. "Look, I get more. I go pay you," Tumi said. The okada-man shut up.

The ghost reached his car. He helped the first daughter in the back seat. He slowly set the other to the ground. He knelt in front of her, then felt her forehead and neck with the back of his hand as if to feel her temperature. He said something to her, gave her a kiss, and then lifted her into the car. The tenderness watered Tumi's eyes. What had he done so wrong to have to miss the gentleness of this man's hands against his own flesh? Why didn't his father, still in suit and tie, leave work in the middle of the day, to comfort him? Why did he have to be his mother's secret? His eyes burned. The car began to move again, and Tumi tapped the okada driver on the shoulder, handing him 500 naira. "Follow am," he ordered. "I get more."

The okada-man collected the fare. The wind slapped Tumi in the face again, carrying away the tears in his eyes.

The cloud had begun to gather into a thick-grey body. The wind carried the mystery of the city across Iya Efon and Deoti's face, thick with the smell of rain already pouring somewhere not too far away.

Both women sat in silence, watching the road. Traffic was quiet. Cars passed lazily, uncharacteristically without the haste that often compelled these roads at all hours of every day. Deoti liked it, rare as it was to still be under the tree at this hour of the day. Usually, she would have left hours before, after Bowale had entered the building, but that morning had gone as it had gone and she had missed watching him. Rather than hold vigil in front of his building, she could have gone on her way, but it was a Friday and that would have meant waiting over the weekend to see him again. His tall frame, the small crease on the back of his suit, the slight slack in his tie tightened before he walks in, leaving his car for the gateman to park.

Whereas, that morning she felt weary and just wanted to sit down and wait to gather herself for a moment. There are days like this, where she endured a bit more than usual, where she watched the road between them go quiet to let her hear herself, to let her speak the distance between them into an embrace. She closed her eyes and let him reach out. When she opened her eyes, she saw his car approach the gate. It surprised her, got her off her feet. She stepped a few paces forward, and then she saw the trailing okada. Sky-blue-checkered shirt, navy-colored trousers, black school bag, white socks poking out of a Birkenstock sandal. Her son's school uniform.

Without asking it, her feet carried her forward into the road.

Tumi told the okada-man to cut in front of the car to delay it from entering the building where it had stopped. Dangling a second 500 naira fare over the driver's shoulder to motivate him, Tumi chanted a speech in his head like a mantra: My name is Oluwatumininu Aluko. My mother's name is Adeoti Aluko. You are Adebowale—Maybe Aluko, too. I don't know anymore. Maybe my mother lies—You are my father. Those are my sisters in the back of your car. You are my father. You are my father, too.

The okada stopped at an angle beside the driver's side of the car, blocking it off. The shock on the ghost's face could not undo his resemblance to Tumi. There was no mistake. The soft round bulge of their eyes, each line and angle turning at the same junction Tumi's turned. The mustache was gone but its shadow hung thick over the ghost's lips, a shade of a life before. He was the father Tumi loved in absence.

There was bewilderment in the ghost's familiar eyes. For a moment, he looked over Tumi's shoulder, off into the distance. His thick brows parted an inch, his eyes turned dark with sorrow and bitterness, filling with tears that knew how to sit well in his eyes without falling. The man rolled down his windows and let his hands hang out as though he had been waiting for this moment his entire life. His mouth quivered and the glare in his eyes broke to let tears fall. Tumi cried, also. An introduction was not needed. He was accepted.

As Tumi reached for his father's hand, he again noticed the man glance over his shoulder, so he followed where the man looked. Then Tumi saw his mother. Her petrified body carried forward by strong steady legs. There was a twinkle in her eyes. A small smile spread over her lips. She looked as beautiful as he had ever known her to be. When he looked back at his father, he was smiling back at her, his hands still stretched. For both of them.

Tumi stretched his hands, too, but before he could reach his father, the wind passed and carried the man away in fine smooth dust.

KIMAYA KULKARNI

Orange

THERE'S NOTHING QUITE like the loneliness of afternoons. Especially here, in a town that takes pride in their afternoon siestas. When you look out the window, you see the heavy air gently swaying the leaves on the trees, a few birds chirping, squirrels out to gather food, and a few people walking from or to work in the Bougainvillaea Bungalows.

Women with the loose ends of their saadee on their head and a merry grit in their walk. They disappear into the Bungalows and leave them clean of dirt, of muck, of filth, of leftover food, of cobwebs. The Bougainvillaea Bungalows begin just off the main street around the temple and end with another temple beside the playground. The fences around the Bungalows grow the eponymous plant with flowers that bloom in winter and stay through summer—some white, some fuchsia pink, some pale yellow or an elusive crimson. Their vines weave in and out through the netted fences and bear strong thorns that would prick anyone who touched the boundaries. The gardens inside grow perfumed flowers of all kinds, roses, mangoes, and coconut trees. When the women, who magically make every surface inside the houses spotless, leave, the monsters come alive to dance. You can hear doors getting slammed and windows shattering, and you can hear sharp words being thrown at unsuspecting flesh.

In a pastel green bungalow with fuchsia bougainvillaea growing through the fences, a couple fights. The woman throws a newspaper at her husband and the man thunders curses at his wife. Fungus spreads on the corners of the ceiling, encouraged by the rain that has incessantly poured on for the past three months but never breaches the chemically treated cement. A lizard lingers on the fungal patch in the summers—its only place of restful coolness. The tiny, lithe creature has steadily learned to adapt to the loud voices. It doesn't scurry away at the noise of the shouts now. It just sits there silently, her heart thumping in her throat, and watches the couple spew thorns at each other.

The couple's windows remain open until sunset to let the fresh air and its inhabitants in—spiders, bees, fruit flies enter the shadows of the bungalow and reside in places that will feed them. The wooden parapet extending over half of the garden has been eaten out by bumblebees. The thin gaps behind shelves and cupboards have been taken over by spiders to weave intricate webs. The fruit flies quietly hover around the kitchen counter, sucking in the tastes and flavours that ooze out of every drawer, jar, and pot.

Throughout the day the house gathers human sheddings, large and small—skin flakes, dandruff, loose hair strands, breath marks, oily fingerprints, dust motes, garbage that didn't make the dustbin, gunk, food stains, water puddles, mosquito blood. The couple goes on fighting, slamming doors in faces, throwing newspapers at each other, casting words that wound. The air between them gradually turns a malevolent violet and spreads through the rooms, seeping out through the windows, infecting the neighbourhood. The bougainvillaea bathes in this miserable mist and makes the fuchsia petals turn a blood red.

Neighbours, like large lizards, sit in their own houses and listen to the shrill screaming of the couple. They put their ears to the wall to hear the fight better. They throw their windows open so that the sound will carry towards them. For as long as the couple fights, the insidious differences brewing in their own houses halt and rest, the violet mist pauses and dissipates.

In the pastel green bungalow, the lizard still waits patiently, soaking in the coolness of the wall as the woman slams another door—a crack, lands another large object on the floor—a crash, and the man charges after her—a thud, demanding explanations and showering blame—a wail. Amidst their shouts, the couple hears the gates creak. It's sunbreak already. It's time.

At sunbreak, an orange atmosphere enters through the open windows and touches every surface in the house, overtaking the violet mist and filling the space with a Time not of this time. The Time envelops the woman and her husband, and they fall into each other's arms, embracing as if the world is about to end and this is their last goodbye.

The orange of the sunbreak does not warm. It cools. The moon gently glides into this orange coolness. The lizard quietly brings a friend in, observed only by the enduring gaze of the mango tree, looming large in front of the window. At night, the two friends make their way to the coolest room in the house. The room of the prodigal daughter, who returns with the onset of every winter and lets out a screech upon seeing the lizard. That, and the weather is the lizard's cue to go on a winter pilgrimage only to infallibly return as spring starts heating up again. It's only late summer yet. So the lizard and her friend wander its walls in the orange night, breaking through every tiny cobweb, gobbling up the spiders and their prey, making themselves fully at home amidst the books that gather dust on the shelves.

The couple falls asleep in a child-like embrace. They are woken up in the morning by the clockwork sound of the women who come to clean up after them. The orange has now dulled into a yellow. The man and woman part ways to go to work at computered desks in air-conditioned rooms, in historic stone-buildings that stand next to banyan trees and high rises that tower over the entire city. Hung over, frowning, they feel the violet cough build up in their chest. It will need unleashing later.

The women clean all the evidence of yesterday's mistreatings. They pick up the angry objects on the floor and seal the cracks behind the door; they make the couple's bed, and they wipe off mauve smudges from walls, windowpanes, and tabletops; they throw out the food that has been infected by the violet curse and take the rest of the stale food home to feed their families.

The couple is greeted by a tidy house to relax in and fresh meals to assuage their hunger. They are also greeted by an empty house and in each other, an angry spouse. Days come, days go. Violet breath is overcome by orange ether at sunbreak.

It's early winter. Amidst their shouts, the couple hears the gate creak. It's time. The clear orange seeps in. Through the bedroom window, they see their daughter hauling in a suitcase and a backpack, ruffling the bougainvillaea. The orange engulfs them as the loose pink petals settle on their daughter's hair. The Time is not of this time. The couple hold hands and welcome their daughter with wide smiles and long embraces.

In her room, the daughter takes a look in the mirror and spots a creature lurking on the wall behind. A loud screech sends the lizard scurrying away behind the cupboard. Her heart hasn't beaten so fast in a long time. The lizard listens in silence as the daughter slowly goes about her evening. She unpacks her suitcase, stares at the bookshelf, stares out the window. The bougainvillaea reigns the view. She lets out a deep sigh, creating a small violet cloud around her face. She hastily sucks the cloud back inside her and restores the unblemished orange.

The night curdles thick around the bungalows. The lizard waits for the daughter to weep herself to sleep and then gently crawls from over her bed and outside the window to bathe in the orange moonlight. The bougainvillaea lies still as the crickets make their home in its dark branches.

Missouri Midnight

NO DOUBT IT'S BETTER to wait to tell my daughters I'm not going to stop for dinner, that there's no time to see them in Seattle after all. I'm just passing through, this trucker's highway stretching before me, looping like a broken record, always on replay, the soundtrack of my life. So, I don't pick up the phone to call and cancel, not yet, even though my daughter said she had something important to tell me in person. But instead of the visit I promised, this trip will be just a quick stop west of the Cascade range. The part of our country the progressives seem hell-bent on ruining, and then on to the heartland of Missouri, the state I was in when the oldest daughter was born, God only knows how long ago. Thirty years maybe, at least long enough before I'd lost all my hair and grown this sagging belly. The call came from my lonely wife late in the night, she had the number to my motel. The phone rang three times and when I finally picked up, rolled over away from the nameless blonde in bed next to me, my wife said in a dazed and almost sad way, we have our girl, she's here. I didn't ever ask her real name. I said, she's Mo, to mark where I was when I first became a father. It was the same when the boy came a few years later. TJ for Texas James. It seemed more fitting than Junior since I had hardly seen my wife the whole pregnancy and we both knew the boy would grow up not ever really knowing me. At least until he was old enough to ride along in the truck for summers. When the third one came, my second daughter, I didn't even bother tying her name to a place. I felt too sick being in bed with another warm and soft but meaningless woman in another dismal motel in a desolate unknown highway town, not home and where I should have been at her side to welcome now three offspring. Knowing my wife was ready to divorce me now that I had been absent for the births, absent for most of the kids' upbringing. She was probably already screwing her college advisor at the university I was paying for her to attend, while I burned out motoring hard in my God-forsaken but glorious truck. Eventually I started calling my second daughter Sookie, a girl so beautiful, with such deep chocolate eyes, olive skin and shining hair the color of an alpine trail, it still shocks me that she came from my stock. I have no idea why I chose Sookie, but it seemed wrong to call her by her real name when I had given the others special ones. She sometimes asks me why I picked it, what it means, and I feel momentarily sick when she does because I don't have an answer worthy of her love or beauty.

So many times I traveled from the golden coast of Orange County, hating California but never able to leave without standing barefoot on the edge of the surf looking out at a vast ocean of possibility beyond this life of mine and feeling the salt collect in microscopic crystals on the tips of my greying beard. From the Pacific Ocean through the vast desert, I thought about stopping, as my Arizona vista, what must be the face of some God or angel, came into view. Mesas loomed dark on the horizon, the low sun scorching my eyes as I got closer to home. Then the ponderosas up north would call to me like sirens, more even than my wife and kids called for me. This time and every time I wanted to stop, I meant to stop, that endless desert making me feel more full and home than anywhere else I traveled. I would picture myself on the soft, drying grass of our front lawn, stretched out with those three little monsters draped all over me. My sweet wife with a real name, Adele, looking at me with deep brown eyes from under her mess of curly hair, so much more substantial and tangible to me than any of the motel women, would tuck up beside us. Us five looking out at the infinite beyond, drowning in the stars and our very own happiness. Me knowing constellations and teaching them to TJ just as I had promised I would when I gave him a telescope one Christmas. If I was home, he would pull its box out from under his bed and his face would twinkle like the stars in anticipation, excited for me to finally show him how to use it, guiding his pudgy fingers over the stiff knobs. How good, how sweet, I could get drunk just on the possibility of it, even if it wasn't always real. If I stopped, it could be real. But most times, it was only a fantasy because I went on, fast past home, the money of the job on my mind.

In those days, I knew that if I trucked a little harder, pushed a little more, I could someday pay for a real vacation, take the family to some beach like Adele wanted. Maybe the nice one south of Orange County, out on Coronado Island. Mo loved to swim. I didn't know about Sookie. So, with Arizona stars in my eyes but a paycheck in my heart, I'd keep on keepin' on, leaving my native state and the illusion of family stargazing behind me on to Albuquerque. The Texas border on from there. Maybe I died a little each time I did this, but the women helped. Their needlessness kept me alive. I tell myself that's why these faceless, nameless bodies, breasts, tight asses ended up in the creaky motel beds next to me night after night. Worse was when they were in the sleeper cab of my truck, in my very own bed, where I had made love to my wife, but still I would bring them there on those really bad nights when I found myself crying in the truck stop showers avoiding the payphone call home. Dreading having to tell Adele that I didn't take that glorious exit off the interstate onto the little highway that leads to home as I passed through Arizona. It always went one of two ways when this happened, depending on how long I'd been away, how the kids were doing that day, how we were doing on money. If things were good at home and the bank account was cushioned, Adele's edges would be sharpened and she'd simply say, "Hmmm. Okay, goodnight, Peter," and hang up. All the other times, when her exhaustion or loneliness had the better of her, was so palpable I could actually feel it reaching through the phone to smother me, I'd hear her start to weep. We would sit like that on the phone for a moment or two before she would hang up without saying anything. Then, I would walk my walk of shame across the truck stop parking lot, weaving between a seemingly endless field of eighteen-wheelers, some idling and ready to hit the road, others cold and asleep, until I reached the end of this trucker's maze and could see up and down the road, my eyes searching for the nearest bar.

These decisions, these moments haven't changed over the span of a lifetime and I think about it driving over the wet mountain pass in Washington with the sound of the diesel engine and eighteen wheels on pavement roaring in my ears. I'll go deaf one day soon from this noise. Mo is only an hour behind me in Seattle. She always tells me to wear ear protection when I drive, always has some crackpot new age health solution for whatever ails me. No doubt she gets it from the crazy west

coast liberals she lives among. I hear all about them on the radio from
my buddy Rush Limbaugh. I still don't understand why she had to leave
Arizona, give up the desert that was our family's very soul. But she
married a Pacific Northwest man and traded the high and low desert, the
beautifully parched earth, for this nonstop, joy-killing rain. Now she's set
up a life of her own in a place that is beautiful enough, but will never
have the stars or clear blue or sunsets that home does. If she ever wants
to smell the vanilla that wafts off the ponderosas after a rain or during
a long stretch of dry, ever again, she'll have to go back for a visit and
hope. Her mother, once finally divorced from me, followed her, in hope
of grandkids no doubt, and it wasn't long before TJ and Sookie all went
along too, as if our life in Arizona had never been enough to anchor
them there. As if they wanted to show me that I was not the only one
who could drift.

It isn't like I wanted to be this man, it's not what I daydreamed
about during Catholic school when the nuns beat me nearly every day
for my wagging tongue and short attention span. I still don't know how
those old ladies could whip that ruler so hard so fast. I still believe they
were all practicing and exercising their forearms every night after their
quiet dinners and prayers at the convent. No doubt those nuns could
inflict pain far worse than any schoolyard cheap shot to the gut from
one of the older boys. No, I wasn't one of those boys who wanted to
grow up to be just like his daddy. An alcoholic, hot-tempered, heart-
diseased, destined-to-die-too-soon trucker in my dad's case. All I wanted,
all I dreamed about as a boy, was to live on my own little patch of dry
mountain land with a family of my own and play hockey every day until
I'd lost all my teeth from pucks and fistfights. But I didn't know myself
then, didn't know how hard I would be to pin down to a steady life.
And I learned real quick three important things. A man needs money
to keep his very own corner of this country. Two, I'm not the sort who
can stay in one place too long before my skin starts to crawl and I feel
like I need to go or else die right there on the spot. And, besides hockey
and screwing, trucking is just about the only thing I'm any good at.
My dad's progeny and protégé after all. I was only on the front end of
this discovery when I met my wife, early enough for her to still have a
thought in her head that I could end up like a typical husband and father,
home for dinner and around on the weekends, working construction

or on the Flagstaff railroads making an honest kind of living she could feel OK about with her uppity parents. No doubt she would have never married me or given me any children let alone three had she known what she was really getting herself into.

And that would be right, because our first daughter, our free-spirited and too-opinionated Mo, grown up and living her own life, however different from the life I imagined for her, has taken over Adele's role of hopefully waiting for me to come. Of watching a clock I refuse to live by, wanting more from me than I know how to give. She's expecting me, cooking my favorite steak and making mashed potatoes and gravy from scratch, hoping we can all go ice skating together like the old days, as if I've even been on a rink since they were kids. I pull out a joint from the glove box and light it. I take my first puff and it fills the cab with a bitter, warming blanket of smoke. I'm a little hungry for that steak. When I last called, Mo told me she had a box of cookies to send in the truck, said how excited her sister was to see me too, and was sweet enough not to mention that her brother is still not speaking to me, probably won't again until I'm on a deathbed of some sort or another. Politics of course is the root of that problem. His left-wing brainwashing has made it so we can't have a single civilized conversation like father and son are supposed to do. I'm still baffled at the fact that I've raised liberal children. Though, I suppose that's their mother's doing, not mine, since I can't claim much in the way of raising them. I'm sure that's really the only reason TJ hates me, just politics, and I keep trying to tell him when I leave him messages that he's just wrong and if he sees reason, he'll no doubt be ready to talk to me again, to remember that his childhood wasn't all bad and empty. That I may not have been there much, but when I was, I wasn't cruel like my father had been.

Good ol' Rush is on the radio bemoaning the progressives like my Mo and her siblings. My phone lights up with a text message, no doubt it's Mo. I tap the screen so Siri can read the text out to me.

"Hi Dad. Hope the drive is going OK. Are you close?"

I take another puff and something in my gut tightens. I need to try to ignore it. I'm too old now to easily find a warm woman to soothe my tears when I stop later and begin to regret not seeing my Mo, like every time before over her entire life.

At least Rush gets it, this smart man who keeps me company on this never-ending highway, sometimes to hell, but also total freedom. For a long time he's been telling me a civil war is coming, that "there cannot be a peaceful coexistence," and this extreme idea of taking up arms against these people poisoning our country puts me off, but it also exhilarates, awakens, something in me. I fear for the future and it's all a real shame. I can't deny that being around most of these people in Seattle make me, have always made me, sick. It makes this passing through easier in a way.

I'm sweating, but Rush's voice keeps me focused. I tell Siri to text Mo. *Hi Mo sorry voice texting it's been a long haul and I have a load to drop this week two thousand miles away so not going to make dinner or a visit but I'll be back round to Cali and maybe back up to Seattle for a run soon...* Within seconds the phone is lighting up with Mo's bright face, calling me, no doubt to persuade me to stay, which I can't deal with right now, so I keep my eyes on the reflective painted lines on either side of my truck and press on. The phone lights up again with another text.

I tap the screen and the robotic voice reads the message. "Wow Dad, I really didn't want it to be like this. Didn't want to tell you like this. But I guess I may as well since you're just passing through again."

That *again* was on purpose, meant to cut, and I suppose it does, but fights and leaving and divorce and breaking hearts have left me with scar tissue that's thicker than most.

Another text. "You're going to be a grandpa. I'm having a boy. Congratulations. Heart emoji."

The phone screen fills with colorful, animated confetti and it distracts me from the road for a moment. How can she stay so bright, to think of sending me digital confetti even after what I've done? In my mind, Mo is still a little girl, all chatter and innocent blue eyes, pink twirly skirts and ribbons and rainbow face paint. And a bride too, in white tufts and sparkling jewelry as I've seen in the photo of her being walked down the aisle by TJ and Sookie on her wedding day. But now, she's a mom with a baby, bringing another boy into the family. I wonder if she'd consider naming him after me, but then I remember myself and I look at the road signs to see where I am. ROSLYN flashes in white reflective letters against a glowing green background up ahead. The exit is close, and Roslyn would have been perfect if the news was for a girl, but I think instead of Ros, Ro for a boy will do. The off ramp is in view now, and I flick the turn signal, pull my wheel just an inch to the right to head off. I'll turn around from Roslyn, Seattle isn't all that far behind me yet. Not too far to drive back, make a grand entrance with my truck and trailer and all the noise of eighteen wheels down Mo's uppity street for a proper celebration. I'll give her a long hug, the kind only a long-haul trucker knows how to give, warm and hard and big enough to make up for all the missed bedtime stories and dance recitals and big and small firsts. It won't take too much time, just that overdue hug and a moment to shake her husband's hand and take some steak and cookies for the road. I'm smiling, I can feel and see it all and I'm almost off the freeway for a U-turn that is really what we all need. Then, something foreign but familiar takes over at the last second, and I swerve it straight, bumping over the median and back onto the main drag, eastbound after all. No doubt if I keep going, I'll make it to Missouri by midnight tomorrow, and Mo's not so bad a name for a boy either. I'll call my new grandson MJ, Mo Junior, and I'll always think of him when I see the Midwest moon rising like a midnight sun. It's my sun, the sun for night crawlers like me, lighting the way on and on.

SAM MOE

Prism

1.

YOU WANT TO TAKE MY HAND in the bird room, you want black coffee and for forgiveness to feel like a rush in your cheeks. It's all chic desire and double macaw beaks, they've even stuffed butterfly stomachs, their wings are smudges of amaranth and gamboge, I'm celadon from low-hanging lamps in the skeleton hall, velvet walls, I wonder why these bones aren't in cases. With each turning of the season the elemental witch arrives to polish the displays, her forest magic accidentally bringing everything to life—*For One Night Only*—read the neon signs. You wanted to see canaries in flight, you wanted to know if gemstones make their way back to each other, it's winter and my heart is falling apart. I'm distracted by your ex, newly arrived in a jumpsuit and no less than ten studs in one ear, she's purchasing candy filled with fake eyes, she's making her way towards plastic trees whose trunks lean in the direction of her brilliance.

2.

Splash glass fragments and liopleurodon smirks, it's not that I needed protection, just wanted more cases to break, all the shatter is sugar and anyway, you always told me you liked the way my heels crunch on broken surfaces. But I'm alone as I pass the fish, she's got you in conversation about crocodiles with phlox claws, I'm distracted by the curves of ancient creatures, wish I were gorgeous first, vicious second, but these days I'm all cigar-smoke and attitude, I don't like how everyone has stories of you and some teeth display keeps mocking me, *jealous, baby, jealous*, but I'm a bandaged goddess and I don't need my face where I'm going next.

3.

Cervalces Scotti amble through stormwaters, pincushion moss bundles, there are sphagnales, there is java and beautiful diatom, an entire display of spoon-leaved moss made of child's play mold spelling out *Warning me*, I glance at the witch, wonder if she could twist someone into an elemental trap, but she's busy, her nose in a whiskey. She shrugs when I see the greens are mimicking conversations of the guests, the walls of the West Wing are all *eyes* and *clutter* and *come back* then *twice I tried but I'm no good at the game*. I want to sleep all month only to wake for her touch, want to be a twice-bloomed horse flower, and my hair could be hook-hued, nails as hoof, I'm lost in all my want, I don't find out she's with you in the tiger exhibit until much, much later.

4.

I wasn't there when your dreams came to die. As a curator, I was young, I always had California on my mind and I thought I'd already buried myself in your heart, you had my name tattooed on your hip, whose idea this was I can't recall and when you asked me to do the same I said no, you only get to carry a knife of prayer once in your life, plus I still hadn't gotten over my ex. Back then I ate breakfast on the commute to work, I spent hours commissioning one hundred artists to make pieces based solely on the prompt *Angel* and nights I came home covered in feathers and hickeys, you loved that I was good in bed even though I wasn't charming when I had coffee. My head filled with gutter spiders, I was pacified by your hands, but you tried to tattoo my fingernails when I wasn't looking and I guess I haven't forgiven you since.

5.

Again, why are you mad at me when you're the one who cheated first? You said she was a blue jay, you slurred your words and cursed me for being an old punchline. I responded by purchasing a dozen paintings of women in snow wearing masks of bees, each expensive scene filled with hips and hands, spreads of semi-perfect oil rivers, except one corner of each canvas, where a jagged knife-hole rests from when you tried target practice while my back was turned. I asked if you missed the older gods and you shrugged, turning into a fox, and sneaking into an empty shoebox before I had a chance to yell at you about the scars.

6.

There are glowsticks in the courtyard and college students toying with a half-dipped golden piano. We're all stuck here until the spell wears off so I guess I'll have something to eat, it's kind of difficult when suits of armor keep getting in the way, that and this drunk girl who won't stop calling me *Honey*, she thinks I'm cool, she's unaware I'm wasting away enshrined in a contract with a young god who lays lambs at my feet but he won't have sex with me at the altar and everything feels like a waste of time.

7.

There's an animal I've never seen before walking down the employees-only hall. I don't know where you went. Instead of wasting away, I decide to follow. The animal commands many tails and eyes, long black ears like a rabbit, each paw has soft barbs at the end, each time I touch its hide it becomes ticklish. Down the hall we go, past preservation rooms, stacks of picture frames waiting hungrily for wings and pins, someone's stolen the moon and tied it to the back room, there are employee lockers filled with candy and a shawl eerily familiar to the one my grandmother owned, stenciled with sugar birds and coiled chicken feet. At the end of the hall, we reach an empty doorway. The creature waits for me, so we exit side-by-side. My stomach drops and keeps on falling. The next day I awake as a silver-lilac knife tied to a string in a case of other shining ones. When night falls and the witch arrives, she carefully instructs me how to aim for your heart.

KRIS RILEY

How Hummingbirds Hurt

IT WAS ONE OF THOSE cold-front days when the sun showed no
shame, the clouds blessed no shade, and the wind swore no mercy;
Houstonians wore their coats out in the morning, chattering their teeth,
and in the afternoon–they cursed the heat. The intersection of Montrose
Boulevard and Fairview Street bustled with mopeds, mini-vans, hoopties,
and slabs. Each dipping in and out of potholes, tires screeching and
horns harassing. However loud the sounds of Monday's rush-hour
traffic, the music in Powerhouse Ink overpowered its volume.

     The rickety red-brick building had a light-turquoise door leading
into the lobby of the parlor. Off-white walls were revealed in the small
spaces left between art. Frames with flash work: Sailor Jerry style, Grim
Reapers, Sugar Skulls. And frames with old black and white photos of
folks with traditional tattoos. A glass counter showcased jewelry made
of wood, metal, plastic, and stone. Across from the display, there was
a beige clawfoot couch which made the entire establishment smell
somewhat of moth-balls. Through one of the doorways resided the
tattooing area. Nineteen-year-old Amos Manson sat on a black leather
bench, looking out the shop's window, waiting for the artist, thumping
his leg up and down, listening to the Pandora station strumming on the
shop's speakers.

     A muscular man appeared from a hallway tucked in the rear of
the place. On his black shirt, in bold white letters: "SUICIDE." In one
hand he had a piece of paper and in the other he had a double-bladed
shaving razor. The artist positioned the bench to where Amos' head hung
back to display his throat. The man put what felt like soap on Amos'
neck and ran the blade across it. Shivers rippled on the surface of his
skin as Amos thought of the strangeness of a stranger wiping his neck
of loose hairs. The artist sanitized the area then transferred the stencil

from the carbon copy paper onto his canvas. A mirror-check approved the alignment as centered and colors were chosen: gray, magenta, electric purple, pale blue, teal, and blood orange.

Amos reclined back onto the cushioned bench. His movements stuttered, awkward, as he sought comfort in the padding. The artist pumped the foot pedal connected to his tattoo gun, each pump releasing a puff of air. Amos struggled to find a resting position. With his head so low, his chest was lifted as if a demon were being exorcized out of him. The artist was ready. Amos grew comfortable being uncomfortable. The artist dipped the needle into the black ink and wiped the excess onto a paper towel. The vibration of the tattoo gun rattled off the chambers of Amos' ears. The first stroke drilled a line near the left of his trachea. Blood-shot eyes fell victim to relief.

The needle carved as the lines curved. It felt like the dragging of a razorblade digging into his skin. Amos knew of this sensation. The first time he cut himself he was thirteen. It was two weeks after his grandmother died of heart failure. He kept composed for his mom and grandpa, but he was failing algebra and the kids at school called him *Gay*mos and his family stressed about the funeral and rent and food. He broke. Amos jolted into his mother's two-bedroom apartment off Commonwealth Street. He tossed his backpack onto the living room floor and flipped his shoes off. Then, Amos locked himself into the bathroom. His mother was getting dressed for her late-night shift at Jack in the Box. She needed to brush her teeth and do her hair before leaving. His mother pounded her balled fists against the cheap wood door. The only response was silence. This went on for half an hour before she phoned her father for assistance.

Amos' grandpa stayed in the same complex as them so by the time the call ended, he was already there. Amos' mother left for work and her father picked the lock to the bathroom door with a bobby-pin she gave him. Grandpa turned the brass knob to find Amos with no bottoms on, on his knees in front of the toilet, face wet with tears, blood dripping down his thighs, a sliver of a jagged rusty razor blade in hand. The broken remnants of one of his mother's lavender colored shaving razors scattered across the chipped tile next to his khaki school-pants. Grandpa picked the limp boy up in his arms and placed him in the dingy bathtub, then turned the faucets to run the water. The two sat stagnant

in a moment of silence; Grandpa was not a man of many words, but of
action, and Amos wanted to be the same sort of man. Grandpa never
told the boy's mom. Or anyone. He just always gave extra attention,
making sure the boy was okay. Amos rejoined the present with the
crooning of Chris Cornell on the speakers begging the Black Hole Sun
to wash away the rain. The dark inked lines on his throat continued to
expand as a release was granted for his suffering.

Pandora interrupted their listening for a brief advertisement:
"Do you experience erectile dysfunction? Talk to your doc-"

"What the fuck?" The artist pulled away from Amos and turned
the direction of the receptionist in the lobby. "Why are we even listening
to Pandora? Put Spotify on." He turned back to Amos and asked,
"Wanna choose an album?"

Amos panicked. He became hyper-aware of the droplets of sweat
rolling down the individual strands of his armpit hairs. He was not ready.
He already made one big decision today. With the first note to come to
his mind, Amos said, "Jazz."

"That's not an album." But the artist got the gist, shrugged, and
told the receptionist to put on a jazz playlist.

"What?"

"You heard me."

Soft horns bounced into the room, and the artist began again.
Now the needle etched to the right of his trachea. Amos felt the throb
of his pulse. He felt the pumping of every ounce of his blood, and it was
on fire. His pain was past the point of hurting. Every beat of the songs'
forceful rhythm took him further away.

Amos' top and bottom eyelashes clasped again. Fingers fumbled
on a piano in the distance. He remembered waking up to jazz on the
weekends at his grandparents' apartment. The smell of maple sausage
filled the place. Between the noise in the kitchen and the music, Amos
couldn't sleep any longer. Grandma made larger than usual portions
on Sunday, and then she caught the bus to attend service at the Mount
Horeb Missionary Baptist Church. Amos and Grandpa caught their own
bus going the opposite direction to the Menil Collection park.

At the park, the two of them sat on a wooden bench facing an
old magnolia tree. A pair of worn binoculars Amos' grandpa bought
from a garage sale hung around his neck. They passed the binoculars

back and forth as they took turns studying the birds and butterflies. Grandpa chain-smoked his menthol Pall Mall cigarettes. Between the smoke and the perfume from the flowers, Amos was almost there again. The chirps of a cardinal and a blue jay bickered with the beating of a woodpecker's beak. As the two sat there longer, more and more people filled the grassy square-lot of the park. One Sunday, it was so crowded with people they didn't see any birds at all. But the following weekend, light showers left dew on the grass. No families came to picnic. No children climbed the trees. No dogs sprinted to fetch frisbees. Amos and his grandfather sat on their bench, searching through the branches to find a bird. Grandpa couldn't see any creatures. He passed the binoculars to Amos. Looking through them, Amos moved up the trunk of the tree to its highest branch. He blinked and almost missed it. With the flutter of its wings, a hummingbird appeared from behind an open magnolia flower. The bird levitated in front of the flower, dipping its head in the center where the petals met. Its movements were swift. Amos handed the binoculars to his grandpa and pointed to the highest flower on the tree. But the bird was gone. Grandpa analyzed each flower searching for it. He flicked his cigarette and lit another one. The hummingbird came billowing around the trunk and made a straight-line for the bench. Grandpa saw a glimpse of the bird through the binoculars then pulled them away from his eyes. Amos watched as the bird flew up to his grandpa, hovered in front of his face, and flew away from the smoke.

"For your first session," the artist said, "you're a great sit."

The needle grazed Amos' skin. When the outline was complete, the artist and Amos took a cigarette break. The October air was crisp. The sky above them pitch in pollution, no stars in sight. Amos flicked the lighter, the flame burnt the paper then hit the well-packed tobacco. Cool menthol mauled the back of his throat. A strange quietness was about the street outside the shop. Amos stood looking at the two-story Tribal Grounds World Imports store next door. He tried to decipher the paintings on the front of the building, their lines crashing into each other. He tried to make sense of the abstract while dragging hard on his cigarette in intervals of seconds, spitting between each hit. When their cigarettes were only filters, they returned inside to finish. The receptionist changed the music, and instead of jazz the shop speakers blared Nirvana. Amos plopped back onto the bench. The artist prepared his shading gun.

When he started, the rows of needles ripped through Amos' skin. He drew his eyes shut and furrowed his brows. The circular motions over his Adam's apple vibrated in his vocal cords. He thought the gun would pierce through him. It reminded him of the hole in his grandpa's throat, cut to give him breath. Amos remembered the last time he saw him. The sanitized smell of the hospital coated his mouth as he walked into his grandpa's room. He looked cold in his gown. Like the hallowed shell of a body that used to be a home. The needles rubbed from the center to the sides of Amos' trachea. The violet veins in his neck protruded. Re-dipped tip in ink and the gun streaked its fury again. Amos felt as if a jackhammer were engraving in his chest. Relief once so potent, now absent. He took in a deep breath and held it. He squinted his eyes, his lids a dam against the stream of tears. Each stroke melted Amos. The mixture of his blood and the ink branded him. His nails dug into the black leather then he balled his hands into fists. Raising his right hand, Amos was going to tap out when the artist drew away and said, "All done."

Amos' shoulders released the tension of the last few strokes. The artist sprayed a towel with an antibacterial solution and wiped off his work. As the paper towel's scratchy surface scraped the open wound, Amos clenched his jaw at the tenderness. The artist shuffled around cleaning his station. The album blaring through the speaker's ended on a fading high-pitch wail.

Amos unzipped the side pocket on his pants. As he fumbled around for his phone, the skunky scent of dank weed came oozing from the half of a blunt remaining from his walk to the parlor. He looked at the screen and took it off Do Not Disturb, watching as it flashed with messages and voicemails from his mother.

He skimmed over the series of texts:

R u ok   *Where r u*   *Plz come home*
            I know this is hard 4 u its hard 4 me to
    Hes not dead his bodys just dead its just his body his spirits still with us

Amos rose off the black leather bench and walked down the back hallway of Powerhouse Ink to a mirror. In his reflection, Amos saw a still frame of the Ruby-throated Hummingbird mid-flight, the feathers blended from hues of pink to purple to blue to gray, the blood orange rays gleaming from behind it, the rivulets of light exploding through his throat.

    He is still with us

APRIL YU

Miracle Baby

WHEN MY OLDER SISTER RACHEL and I were young, we would squeeze polymer animals filled with water beads, watching the luminescent orbs bulge through the skin like tubers. Fat purple unicorns, lean tigers and sleek vermilion snakes, one layer of skin away from belching their glittering intestines out. That was back when seven centimeters of neon color meant happiness. The translucent animals were always covered in dirt and grime, sticky from sweat and saliva. We never knew whether each spit bubble was my sister's or mine.

I hang the unicorn precariously above Aurora's crib. It was always my favorite, a milky pulp of plum with a bubblegum-pink tail, crowned by a candy-hard horn. I remember I liked the deep cherry of the hooves the best. Now I can only think, *The unicorn must have trekked through blood to land in my hands.*

My mother never visits the nursery as I do. I still remember when I first saw Māma in the hospital two months ago, the skin at her stomach tight and bone-white, pupils like eggs hollowed of their bright yolk, arms cradling a baby visible to no one but her. I knew the child she craved was not the one currently warming her stomach.

Can I name her, Māma? I had asked, my hands feeling for the blooming human life covered by the hospital's paper-thin gown.

My mother did not reply, words that once sugared her tongue dissolving in her ocean of pain. She did not reply when the blotchy-faced baby girl came wriggling out, marking the start of her life with her cries. She did not reply when it came time to sign a name on the baby's birth certificate, so I replied for her. Aurora. *A new dawn, a miracle.*

For the only baby I might ever know, Aurora is nothing more

than a six-pound, milky-white mass of dough, kneadable, fallible. Her mouth is ever split open in a yawn or a cry, bracketed by the same dimples of a sister past, calling for the protection of the body she was in just six weeks before.

My index finger flutters under her nose, a ghost, a whisper. A love letter to a sister who speaks not in human speech but touch. I skew it poetically in my head, but the truth is that each of Aurora's warm, muggy breaths flows right to my lungs and keeps my heart beating. Each minute I spend in the P. F. Chang's downtown, working my fingers to the bone to compensate for the present and not the future, is time enough for panic to rise. When she screams for milk at night, gratitude holds my irritation at bay: *she's alive, she's alive.*

"Shh, shh," I murmur to Aurora, lifting her from her crib with the daintiness of a royal nursemaid. My eyes rever her: face crumpled like precious silk, hands balled into meaty fists, rolls of baby fat not yet stolen away by hunger. In the moments when her sobs dissolve into hiccups dissolve into silence, questions come unbidden; sometimes angry, sometimes desperate, always unanswerable.

Did Rachel once look like this?

Rachel was nearly two years older than me, but we could have been twins: the same black-tar eyes, dark hair slashed to our chins, permanent questions in the slant of our eyebrows. Our mother called us xiǎo wáwá, her little dolls, dressing us up as a matching set—Rachel loved pink, leaving me scrunched in blue. I was always lagging a step behind her, in play, in sleep, in everything. From the way she bounded around all the time, my mother said she had to be the healthiest person alive.

The summer I turned ten was the beginning of the end. We began to trek five minutes across squares of littered city sidewalk to the dollar store, clinging to Māma's hands. It was a dumpy little place of dirt-smudged toys and cheap puzzles that no one but a family like ours would frequent. I liked standing under the A/C vent that whirred cold blasts of air like a jet on takeoff, squeaking the hinges of the flap over it. Rachel liked digging through the miles and miles of rubber toys in a wire cart as tall as her, scouring for harshly-colored jelly treasures. My mother liked getting away from my father's screams, the rapid-fire procession of curses and punches that sank into her skin one bullet at a time. She

always held her belly as if the slop of hurt and gunpowder could stay
tiny and contained and quiet, a seashell attempting to hold the entire
Pacific at bay, but her efforts could never restrain our father nor her own
emaciated stomach.

That summer was a crime scene of slashes and cuts. Memories
tasted each other and bled into a gooey mess under the blazing California
sun: surfing lemon-yellow rubber ducks in the dollar store; brown stains
like a bloody smile on the white apartment walls; Rachel's hand, sticky
with sweat as we crossed a road; playground woodchips sewn into
my knee; Rachel's luminous eyes and shallow breathing tethering me
to the screams and *smash* of glass outside our bedroom; the white of
my mother's knuckles as she held a crumpled receipt in her hand, eyes
moving along the prices like they were dates of execution.

We marched on like three soldiers anyway, the dollar store our
home base. The clerk who always wore the white fisherman's hat came to
know us by name. Our mother held our hands like vices until I did not
know whether she was protecting us or we were protecting her. We were
three soldiers, and we would not be broken.

When Aurora sleeps, a slight lick of saliva tracks down her cheek,
eventually winding down to the juncture at her neck like a half-necklace
of tears. In sleep, she is a baby drifting between pre-birth and the afterlife,
here and not here at all. If I let go, she might diffuse into salt in my hands.

It was not always this way. When Aurora first took form in a head
and spine, Māma would guide Rachel's and my hand to the fisheye of
her belly button, whisper, *Father will be so happy.* And for a brief period,
Māma and Father put their curses aside and lived in mutterances, in slight
smirks, in half-laughs, in a lingering stroke along the bulge of Māma's
stomach, in forget. The tension in Rachel's shoulders began to ease into
the clutch of our hands. *Father will love the baby. Father will give us money.*
Father will care for us. Māma whispered and whispered it into existence
until something finally shifted, until her eyes grew wide with fear under
the weight of the word *gold-digger*, until Father took his fists and exploded
it all away.

I tell myself I should forget Father, whose path of destruction
veered only at the creation of my sisters. I shape my lips around the word
good-for-nothing. So many G-words. So many words.

I lift Aurora into the crib. Test her breath one more time, then one more time, then one more time. Inhale-exhale-inhale-exhale. I keep waiting for the hazy void of nothingness where warmth once was, every continuation of the rhythm a relief.

I force myself to flit out the door into the living room of ghosts—when I stop in my tracks. For the first time in six months, I hear sounds from the kitchen. I know these footfalls, heavy-heeled and pigeon-toed. That metallic clang of cutlery sings a foreign song from a foreign land I forgot long ago.

"Māma?" My voice carries over the stillness of this house, meeting a dead end at the walls chipped from a parent's rage. In sock feet, so as not to disturb the wraiths, I walk into the kitchen.

Māma. I drink her in, try to swallow her whole, so thirsty that is shameful, gauche, as unrelenting as the sea. When she turns, the conifer of her back juts out of her flimsy white nightgown, nothing more than a sack of skin stretched over rings and stalks of bones. No. It is not the evidence of starvation, but the lack of hunger, that harpoons my chest. Once, I saw the desperation in my mother's eyes, prey cornered in the darkest wood, fighting tooth and nail to escape. Now, there is a vast nothingness. She invites the predator to bite her neck and inflict blissful oblivion.

"Māma," I say again. And as if to compensate for the deadness I feel enclosing her body, an ocean of white-hot glass shards rise inside of me, scarring and taking and tarrying and rubbing salt in every wound I have congealed and concealed.

Don't. I clutch my stomach, blanching, retching, holding in the acid of chemical words that threaten to asphyxiate.

"Èr jiě." My mother calls me the only name she has ever known me as. *Second sister.* Her voice is throaty, raw and filed from half a year's disuse. Deer blood drip-drip-drips through her fingers.

I am still drinking her in, the ghost's dress, the bone-white lips, the trembling of fingers over venison with a receipt paid by me, when it registers that I hate her taste of dust and rot. I spit. As I stand there, trying to form words I sacrificed long ago, she shoves the bloody slab of deer meat into the microwave—unplated, its crimson flesh licking the cross-hatched screen—and presses the blinking button for *Start.*

"Māma, no. You can't put raw meat in the microwave."

"Can." It's perturbing, such forceful words paired with such deadened eyes. "Do not talking to me that way. Disrespectful."

"I haven't—"

"No excuses. This is what work done to you." She says it like playing dead in a room for twenty-four hours is the only way to grieve. Like fury is her birthright.

"Aurora hasn't—"

"Not her!" Māma shouts, spittle flying out of her mouth, her face suddenly consumed into a patchwork of lines and scars. *Not her.* Her own baby. *Not her.*

The microwave is still humming through the room. I imagine the spinning panel of glass inside cutting my flesh open, taking another feast of blood to my mother.

May 31. Rachel's fifteenth birthday. Two years ago. That was the midnight when things were at their worst, when we were meant to exit our broken apartment for the last time and steal into the night. Beneath the couch our mother slept on, we had crammed every object we could ever call ours—blue toothbrushes, my mother's old watch, two packets of herbal tea that Māma said never tasted quite like home—into a faded viridian suitcase. *We take this, we can leave,* my mother promised. *No more Father. He won't make us scared.* Rachel jutted her lip out and I would try to model her, ever two twins, brave and united, saving ourselves with our masks.

That night, our room sweltered. I had grown accustomed to the rhythm of Rachel's fear: her shallow breathing, the low thrum of her heart ricocheting around the walls as if it needed proof it was real. Her inhales always hitched ever so slightly, a hooked operculum, *glub-glub-glub*ing for air I had long since sucked from the room. A fish struggling against the current that flowed toward death's doorstep.

When Māma came into the room, I thought she was a ghost sweeping Rachel away. At her moth's-wing touch, my eyes blinked awake into the darkness, the purple toy unicorn clutched like a vice to my pounding heart. *It's Māma, it's okay, I'm safe.* But in the silence of the room, the world was a delusion.

Check your father, my mother whispered, protuberant eyes reflecting the light from the cracks in the door. I did not miss the fact that her arms were around Rachel as she sent me away. I went.

That night, my father's room was so silent it screamed. No breeze lilted in through the window, only the envelope of the muggy heat until it curdled my insides. I clambered over to his bed, my hands traveling across oceans of fabric. Something was wrong.

His pillow—cold as death. The blanket—disentangled, pristine, human limbs and scent long gone. A different smell fumigated the air. Desertion. I crawled along the ground, wanting so desperately to find the unnameable. The unnameable did not surface, and my hands never found another living soul.

"Māma," I said. The flash of lightning in the sky before the *crack* came. "He isn't here."

She banged the light on. We scoured the crevices, the crannies. We ran outside in the heated California night, Rachel bare-footed, Māma in her little bunny slippers from her wedding day. A bristly breeze cut our cheeks. For hours, we propped our sleeping eyelids open and waited for the man we had so hoped to escape. At last, a runny sunrise eclipsed our hope.

In thirteen-year-old skin, I could not fathom why Māma was crying. *It's a good thing, he left, he's gone,* Rachel and I told her, supporting her third of our weight, wiping the tears of the woman whose blood ran in our bodies; but her tears flowed anyway, a torrential rain for the suitcase never towed, steps never taken, barren nothingness never approached, a future never reclaimed.

Once my mother's footsteps fade away, I pad onto the balcony, deer blood painting my eyelids crimson. In the ocean of space between me and the stars swimming in gold sky, my anger expands: sizzling, crackling, shifting from water to become the air and my blood and the breath itself. I have never felt this electric buzz—this grape-wine drunkenness—how my steps and my brain won't align, how my heart can't quite keep up with how heavily I breathe—like Rachel's—no—not her. *I will never escape this.* Did I think I could ever forget my mother, package her into our room and discard her as necessary? Did I think I was calling the shots when this entire house and the entire wasteland of my mind have been defined by her every move?

Breathe. My stomach acid clenches, forcing bile up my throat, a regurgitation of every ounce of panic I have ever swallowed. *Breathe.* I force myself to raise my face to the sky—to blind myself with what will always rise and fall without interference, the sun: a lithe queen too regal to call herself to attention. Sunlight filters rosy and ashy through the skyline behind our apartment, slashed up by the fronds of solitary trees and telephone lines. It is beautiful beyond belief, but in this moment, I have never trusted beautiful things less.

Last summer, the lake near our house had run bone-dry, all our money and dreams and future burnt to a crisp of nothing under the unforgiving sun. My mother and I were across the city, soaking in tears and sweat until I didn't know which was which and whose was whose, her hand in mine as we walked to the bank for dollars we didn't have. She was cursing our father as she had never before, the rapid-fire bullets she could never stomach—for leaving us, for taking away the fists that had bruised her skin but paid the bills, the same spitfire words from a fated summer long ago.

It was then. Rachel's breath caught on the muggy air, her lungs heaving, heaving, heaving for air that never came. We never even heard her last cough. Later, they told us she had died of the dusty heat, the awful air, a lung condition, very unfortunate, so young, gone too soon. We watched the security camera film in the living room, the way her shoulders slackened. How her mouth moved soundlessly, *glub-glub-glub*, choking on her own fear.

We watched her lips form the word *māma*.

Back in the peeling living room, away from the ghosts of sundown, I stare at the photographed face of my dead sister. This photo frame has been taped up time and time again, each shattered quadrilateral proof of my mother's rage and grief. Rachel's candy-red smile shimmers back up at me like a mirage. Soon I will be her age, but she will always be trapped—immortalized at fifteen, this broken-backed apartment the only place she ever knew. I stare and stare and stare until my entire body bleeds.

When Rachel died, Māma and I were supposed to be a duo. It's this that shatters my skin, that manipulates the tremble in my chin into an undoing. We all had an unspoken promise: to fight through life together, bruised and battered but united in our wounds. When she shuttered herself instead, I thought that if it was a trio she wanted, the baby in her belly would be the answer to an equation of too many family members lost.

The door to Māma's heart has no key. She swallowed it along with every word she could have said: every reassurance that I was still her daughter, that my only purpose was not to be Rachel's twin. We have both become soldiers battling only for ourselves, swallowing bullets and pretending we are not on the doorstep of death.

None of us are truly alive. This apartment, a shoddily-constructed web of dust and waste from disintegrated skin—what is it, in the end? Power begets power, wealth begets wealth, death begets death. And that is when my resistance ebbs, when I screw up every emotion in my feeble body and throw the last of my resolve to the ground. *Screw it.* There is only one person who can stave off all of this.

The silence in the nursery is a gaping chasm, words forcing their way into the hollow of my cheeks and onto my tongue, screaming at me, my mother, at this baby, at the man in the white fisherman's hat under the peeling dollar store roof tiling. *No, this is Aurora, my Aurora,* my miracle, the slightest furrow between her brows in sleep. I drink every inch of her in, the silk of her cheek so priceless that I could sell my soul and still not afford it. And still, above Aurora's bleary eyelids floats a jelly unicorn from so many years ago, a useless blood-splattered talisman that was once my entire world. Did I think this could protect her with this abandoned trinket, stimulated or stymied by the power of my faith? My protection is nothing but a curse. Faith is stamped beneath the feet of apathy. *My mother's feet.*

I tear the unicorn down from the ceiling, reveling in each displaced hair. In one swift movement, the sticky playtoy flies across the room, stumbling across sweaty carpet before crushing itself against the corner. It bleeds, smiling crimson, into the ground. I turn away, squeezing my eyes shut to protect myself against it, this piece that should have always been locked away.

When I open my eyes, only Aurora fills my eyesight, heart-shaped lips still parted in sleep, breathing all else into grainy dust. That is all the unicorn is now, a memory.

ALEX J. BARRIO

Gravitational Constant

THE PLANE FELL like a belly flopper from fifty thousand feet, wings ripping through clouds as the bottom reddened from the burning air. I glanced past the woman on my right, bowing up and down, muttering as she thumbed her prayer beads, and looked out the window. I imagined strapping on a parachute and pushing my way out through the little porthole. *Could I punch my way out? Could I squeeze this middle-aged gut through the gap in the side of the plane with a parachute on my back?*

I looked down at my belly and knew that even under the most fantastical versions of this scenario I was doomed to die.

"You from Germany?" the man in the aisle seat asked me. He wore a Hawaiian shirt so loud it should be illegal. Bright red, yellow, and purple flowers crashed in a cacophony of ugliness so powerful that I dreaded imagining the sort of sick mind that could design it.

"What?" I didn't like to yell but it was the only way I thought he could hear me over the sounds of the passengers around us crying for help, demanding answers from their God. *Why me? Why now?*

Curious time for my seatmate to strike up casual conversation considering the fate we were racing toward.

What will become of my family? My friends? My dog?

Who will pay off the mortgage? Who will pay the credit cards?

Were these thoughts not plaguing him? He looked almost happy to be there, strapped in his seat with his left leg jutting out into the aisle. I wished I had paid the extra money to sit in an aisle seat, where perhaps I could get up at will and maybe go hide in the bathroom. It would be nice to spend my last few moments alive alone, at peace, instead of making small talk with another stranger on another business trip.

He tapped the guidebook in my lap, a German-language guide to California. "One of my best friends lives in Kiel."

Kiel? Why is he talking about Kiel? What does he know about it? What do I?

Christian Albrechts University. Kiel Woche Beer Festival. The Laboe Naval Memorial, a tower of lightly-colored brown stones towering over the Baltic Sea.

Sabrina Grabbe.

My first kiss.

My seatmate smiled, staring at me in anticipation of my response. "Yes. I'm German. From Hamburg. You?" I did not want to speak to him but I did not want to spend my final moments feeling as though I had been rude to a friendly stranger. *I will not face St. Peter with that guilt forced upon me.*

A flight attendant ran up the aisle, makeup running down her face, when we lost additional gravity and the plane fell like one of those carnival free-fall rides. The entire plane shook, sending the flight attendant slamming against the ceiling and then to the ground. All who saw gasped but no one moved to help her. I didn't even reach for my seatbelt.

The plane steadied itself, resuming its more controlled descent. She pushed herself up from the floor with a groan, dusted herself off, and ran to her seat next to the bathroom.

"I'm from Milwaukee. Ever been there?" He extended a hand for me to shake.

I looked out the window. We were near what appeared to be a medium-sized city. I could see rows of suburban houses and intersecting highways full of crawling traffic. I checked my watch. It was nearly 6 PM.

"No. Is it nice?"

"Oh yeah," he said with an enthusiastic nod. "You like basketball? Bucks are the best team. Giannis is the GOAT."

None of these words made sense to me but he seemed so happy to be uttering them. I forced a smile. "Are you afraid?" I wanted to look as calm as him as I asked this but my grin in this moment felt deranged. He scoffed. "Of this? No way. I've been in worse."

"Worse? How?"

"I was flying from Moscow to Hong Kong a few years back. Hit some bad turbulence over the Urals. Everyone on the plane was screaming and crying and yelling at the flight attendants. Lights flickered.

Went on for like two hours. This is nothing compared to that."

"But we are going to die!"

"No, we're not."

The plane leaned forward in a nosedive and people screamed as their weight pushed the seatbelts to their absolute limits. I closed my eyes and thought again of the city I had not visited in years. I thought of the sex workers in shining silver and gold leggings, wearing fanny packs stuffed with condoms and pocket knives. I thought of *Duckstein*, the best beer on Earth and perhaps the greatest thing my tongue had ever tasted, and regretted that I would never drink it again.

I closed my eyes and licked my lips, trying to manifest that taste one last time before dying. What I would give to be back there . . .

But what is left to give that this plane isn't going to take?

"This is your captain speaking." The voice shook me out of my stupor. I was back in my full and upright position in my seat. I opened my eyes. Everyone around me had relaxed. Some were laughing. Children's cries had been reduced to whimpers.

The plane was steady again. Out the window I could see us soaring over a shopping mall and climbing upward. "We apologize for that unexpected turbulence but we have stabilized and should have a smooth ride from here on out. Thank you for choosing American and enjoy the rest of your flight."

The man in the Hawaiian shirt slapped my leg. "See? What did I tell you!"

CHRISTIAN VAZQUEZ

As the Blood Settles

MY WIFE WORKS the same shift as me. After work, after we both eat, we get on our phones and watch the videos that continuously appear one after the other. We rarely receive the same videos. On her phone, she gets videos of ancient history, people talking about how the indigenous people of the Americas were almost wiped out on Earth because of colonization. Videos pop on her screen too from people in the new colonies on Mars. She tells me how it's happening all over again, but this time on Mars, this time it is the abandoning of indigenous people of Earth instead. I tell her that they really haven't abandoned everyone just yet.

      The video stream on my phone is different. I sometimes feel guilty because of how shallow they are compared to hers, but maybe that's a balance that complements our relationship. I inform her of the comedy that is around us, even in the isolated place we live in, and she in turn informs me about the serious reality of it all. We maintain ourselves sane while we wait for them to tell us it's our time to go to Mars.

      People from all over the United States have already been lifted off to the Red Planet, but like always Brownsville, Texas, has been the last to receive this new technology. Even though we are thirty minutes away from the Universe Z's space teleportal by Boca Chica beach, they are just now going to select some of us. They say it will be a random mass selection. Then another city's turn will begin, until Brownsville is selected again like popcorn reading. One of the requisites is that the person must be employed in Universe Z's governmental facilities. Another requisite, having no children. They recommend for us to raise a child in the Mars colonies instead.

      I do not fully understand why or how, but Earth has finally become uninhabitable. I am no scientist, but it feels like we are on a race against time, each day waiting until it becomes totally uninhabitable. They tell us not to panic, that we will be transported before any of that even happens. Yet, it has been years since I've stepped out of the facility, years since the sun's rays have touched my face. The gardens and plants we ceaselessly care for are not for Earth's use, but for Mars. Everything we do is for Mars. Even us, we are for Mars.

If we stop working, we die. They don't tell us that, of course. But I hear about how each government and their big space companies that were able to go to Mars are doing the same thing. The people who have survived are only the ones helping the colonies. I think they still need us as much as we do. We grow everything that for some reason cannot be grown on Mars, send them things that they need from here. We live in these facilities by choice of survival. The natural environment on Earth has gotten to that point. We try not to think of what happened to all those nations who did not develop fast enough to install facilities like these. We try not to think.

We just have to wait our turn. We just have to wait. And so, we watch the videos with their algorithms designed to entertain us, to engage, to distract. We eat the allowed rations from the resources we send off to them. We survive. All of the resources can only be grown in the facilities.

"Look," my wife Christina told me, "Ronaldo and Troye are sitting outside their rooms."

I was so absorbed into the phone that I didn't even realize she was telling me something.

"Michael!"

"What? Who?"

"Ronaldo and Troye. They're outside. Isn't it weird?"

I looked out of the window and sure enough the other couple, our front door neighbors, were sitting on lawn chairs as if the sun's rays were really shining inside the facility and not with the use of fluorescent lights, as if our quarters were actually homes, as if we really were not trapped… as if the world was not dimming… as if the world was still the world.

"They are, aren't they," I said. Both of us were peeking through the blinds. We turned around to see our phones vibrate with a notification of another video, then turned to each other.

We walked outside our home. I looked up as if the fluorescent lights far above were actually blinding sunlight. Christina was brooming our patio, and I was looking for the dustpan. We couldn't hear what Ronaldo and Troye were saying, but they smiled as they talked and laughed a little.

Our unspoken plan failed, and they were having such a good time that they hardly paid us any attention, so I finally said hi.

"What are you all up to?" Christina asked after they greeted.

"We found some vodka in one of the containers," Ronaldo said, smiling, raising a metal cup with ice. "Salud."

"The ones we're supposed to send out?"

"Yeah, I'm sure they won't notice."

"Don't worry guys, Ronaldo and I gave up a long time ago. Following every rule, and we're still here. Fuck them. We don't care about them anymore. Or, what, is somebody going to take our jobs?" Troye said as he took a gulp and we all began to laugh.

I don't know if it was the alcohol, but their laughs were genuine. I can tell when Christina uses her fake laugh, the one she uses to not make people feel bad about an unfunny joke. That laugh, it's like a piano recital that goes off-key for a bit. Her genuine laugh, a natural flow as the high pitch of a small stream of water. They didn't notice but she actually laughed for the first time in so, so long.

"Do you all want a drink?" Ronaldo asked.

We both said no, but we both wanted to say yes. As we left, I took a glimpse of Ronaldo and Troye as they kissed, too absorbed in themselves to notice. That used to be Christina and I.

"Why did we say no?" Christina asked me once we were back inside.

"I don't know. I thought you were going to say no. Well, it could ruin our chances to get on to the Mars colonies, no?"

"We have to stay focused," she said and picked up her phone.

Everybody had left already. We were the only ones left to go to Mars. We fooled ourselves day by day as if it did not bother us. We kept watching the videos, kept on working, until maybe we did forget about everything. We had not seen Ronaldo and Troye in so long, and now they had found this alcohol bottle all of a sudden. What had we missed?

I think she was having these same questions in her head. After that day it is as if we had suddenly realized that we had forgotten where

we were, who we were, what we were, and now it had been time to accept
after we don't know how long. We had forgotten us.

One day, Christina stopped using her phone.

When we came back from doing the day's work, I kept finding
her peeking through the window on those glimpses I took when my
videos were loading. She didn't notice me wondering what she was up to.
Her phone kept on lighting up, begging to be picked up.

"They're not there anymore," she said.

"Who?"

"Really? The only other people here."

"Sorry, my mind was somewhere else."

"The chairs are there."

"Maybe they're using their phones like us inside."

"No, I haven't seen them in a week."

"We have different shifts sometimes."

"What if they already left."

"No. No. No... that's–"

"I'm going to go check."

"Don't. That's rude."

"... I'm going for a walk."

And there I saw her leave, for the first time in such a long time,
saw her leave without me. After being together for so long, I watched her
take her own path. I watched her walk through the door, saw her close
it fast behind her, leaving me inside. I should have gone after her, but I
felt she needed to go on that walk. Now that I think about it, I needed
to go on that walk too. I should have done more. All I needed to do was
look her in the eyes, to ask her what was wrong. Last times, they tend
to happen without us knowing they are the last times, and how I wish
I could have kissed her there and then. Not a sexual kiss, but to let her
know, that I was here, that I was here with her, that we both were in this
shitty situation, but together.

I first noticed her absence as I turned to the other side of the
bed and attempted to reach for her. Then the cellphone screen gave a
notification that two people had been teleported from our facility to Mars.

It was my day off, but I awoke at the same time I woke for work.
I hurriedly dressed and went out only to find Ronaldo outside with the
same look I must have had on my face.

"They left, Michael," he said.

I did not answer. I ran. I don't know why I ran. It was fast. I did not notice the other abandoned dormitories, the fake plants, the real plants, the blank corridors. It all just looked empty, white.

I ran until I couldn't, until I no longer knew if I had tears or sweat.

"So they're really gone," I finally said to Ronaldo.

"… I know," he said. "No, don't run again."

I stopped.

"Why would they do this to us?"

"I don't know. I was cooking us some food when Troye just disappeared from the table. We were going to celebrate our anniversary…" He looked down to his feet.

"Christina went for a walk, and she never came back."

"There must have been an error. The teleportation in Brownsville was not scheduled until at least another two years."

I put my hands over my eyes.

"Hey listen," Ronaldo said. "Troye and Christina love us. They would do anything they possibly could to bring us with them. Maybe they're talking to the people on Mars right now. Maybe they're—"

"I need to go inside. I need to get my cell phone."

I closed the door behind me. The darkness was more comforting than the blaring artificial lights outside the room. I pressed my back to the door and slowly sat down to the floor. Another year? Another two years? Without Christina. Without even Troye. Damn. Fuck.

There was no way of contacting the people on Mars. The contaminated skies on Earth only allowed us to receive but not send out. All the functioning technology was on Mars now. Here on Earth, we worked with what we had. What we received was algorithms. Nothing from actual people.

I don't know how much time passed by until I heard the knock on the door.

"Michael. Don't tell me you're on your phone," Ronaldo's voice entered my room as he knocked.

I looked up from the video of two cats fighting in a house on Mars.

"I'm not on my phone, Ronaldo. What do you want?"

"I have a plan."

I put my cell phone aside and opened the door.

"Why is it so dark here?"

"You don't get tired of all those white lights?"

"I get your point."

"You have a plan?"

"I'm not going to wait until they teleport us. If they teleport us they will teleport us trying to be teleported."

"What?"

"Look, we keep sending off things to them that they need. We keep putting them on those vehicles that go straight to the teleportal. All we have to do is follow that passage."

"We can't put ourselves inside the cargo. It would kill us under the pressure of that tube."

"You are not listening. We simply have to follow it to the teleportal from this facility. Then we go to Mars from there."

"Ronaldo, we can't go outside. We wouldn't survive. Even if we do, how would we survive the teleportation."

"*Michael*. Remember how I found that vodka bottle? Well, I found a vehicle to go outside, equipment too. I found the suits that are compatible with the teleportal from the bosses that used to be here. Nobody has gone over there since they first used it to teleport themselves from here. They kept it unannounced, but I'm starting to remember things. I don't know how we never thought of this."

"But they will know that we cheated, and you know how that will affect our jobs over on Mars. It's *government* property. They will not leave us here. They wouldn't do that."

"You think they care about us? Why should we care about their property?"

"Let me see it."

It was directly outside my dormitory, right in front of his as well, right in between us. He was smiling, and I was afraid. His smile told me that he really did not care anymore. It also told me that he was going to do it, regardless of if I was going or not. No matter what, his motivations were out of my control. And so, I said yes.

The vehicle looked like the space rovers that were in the colonies of Mars; perhaps it was one of them. I had not seen them since we all ran for refuge to the facilities. I had no idea how to even drive one, but

Ronaldo said that at the end of the day it was just another type of car.

We finished our work like any other day, tended the bees, the plants, and when it was time to send it all off to the teleportal, we packed up everything that we needed, enough for maybe a week. When we were ready inside the vehicle, waiting for the facility doors to open to what was left of the outside world, I wondered how much time had actually passed. Ronaldo had grown a lot of stubble on his dark chin, almost the length of his short black hair. He had the same resolute look from the first day he proposed the plan. He stared beyond the windshield, watching the doors rise open, unafraid.

The long, blue pipeline that was connected to the teleporter glowed under the dark starless sky. Each pulse gave a white halo like a radio wave. That was it, it was what we were going into, the waves of an unknown ocean. It had been years since Ronaldo had seen the outside, decades before me. Years, decades, I had not known until I saw those doors rise and give way to those waves.

"Vámonos," he said, and I was ready.

We were so protected inside that I couldn't hear the wind or feel the tires go over the dunes and rocks. Ronaldo didn't move his gaze from the wasteland beyond until close to an hour after. His grip on the steering wheel loosened and he began to calibrate the dashboard.

"We have one more hour left." He finally turned to look at me.

"We should have done this ages ago," I replied.

"I know. I didn't think we would have to do this."

The clouds above promised no sunlight, but even under our insulation I knew there was intense heat without rays waiting for us.

"You brought your damn phone, Michael?"

"It's a long trip. I thought we might need it for something. I don't know."

"I know it's easy to keep on seeing videos, and trust me I've been there before," the young man from a Mars colony said on the screen, "those videos will be there the next day. Go get some sleep. Give yourself that. Have a good night."

I put the phone away.

"I hope they do find out what we are up to. I hope this shows them that we are not going to sit here and wait until they decide to blast us over there, not when they didn't respect the rules. They started this,"

Ronaldo said without looking at me.

The sky grew darker. The dashboard buttons lighted up, and the eternal blue brightness of the long tube next to my window outside pulsed more visibly like a vein on very pale skin.

Ronaldo was busy studying the path with eyes that moved in every direction ahead. I began to think of Christina. I felt like when somebody loses an arm, that phantom itch, that unaccustomed loss. It still felt as if she was here, I even turned back to the seats behind me, hoping. If I felt this, I knew Ronaldo was feeling the same thing about Troye, even if he did not show it. Maybe it was that motivation that was steering the wheel.

The dark dry land stretched ahead and so did the dark sky, storm without rain. I could see the teleporting station in the distance, looming among it all, gray and ominous.

Ronaldo looked at them before I did. There, right beside the blue pulsating tube was a horde of creatures. I had heard of them but had never seen them before me. They were what had survived, or what had managed to adapt under these horrible conditions of Earth. These hairless ape-like creatures were believed to have come from the sea after large patches of it dried up. They ruled the land now and fed on anything that had survived too, even their own.

"I knew they would show up. Hang on to your seat," he said.

"You're not seriously going to—"

Then the vehicle began to gain speed, until even under our bubble of insulation with shock absorbers I could finally feel the force of velocity. Even at such a distance, I could sense the stares of the creatures, as if they were using their eyes to stop what was headed their way. Ronaldo gripped the steering wheel tighter. Some managed to get out of the way. The ones that did, quickly managed to jump on the roof of the vehicle. The vehicle did not lose speed.

The dashboard announced minor damage, and objects on the roof. It was them, clinging on for retribution, or food. Ronaldo stopped the vehicle and we saw them fly and fall before the windshield. He ran them over just as fast.

"We probably have several hours before they catch up to us," he said as the teleportal base still looked like a small mountain in the distance. "They can travel quick."

That is when our vehicle just stopped in its tracks. Those bastards had managed to cut and penetrate from the bottom wires, snapped several loose. Not even Ronaldo had anticipated this would happen. There was no choice but to get off and continue on foot.

"If we sprint towards it, we might make it still on time before it closes," he said.

If the portal closed... it meant we had to wait for another month. There is only one thing that was certain. If we chose to walk back, the hordes were waiting. All there was, all there ever is, was forward.

We were fast, carrying everything that we could carry. Our weapons were attached to the red suits that allowed us to roam temporarily on what was now Earth. There was no time to even digest that it had been years since we had stepped on natural ground. The dry grabble crunched under our feet. The wind. I could not even sense it under the suit, let alone see it impact anything before us. There were no trees, nothing the wind could lift to its arms. The most ancient things in the world had perished. It was only a matter of time until the world, ancient of all, perished too.

I didn't want to show him that I was afraid, that it was fear that was keeping me moving. Ronaldo, I couldn't tell what he was thinking. He still had that determined look, with no time to communicate. Only the sound of our boots and the clinking of our gear was what consisted of our conversation in a wasteland where silence had not been broken by humans in years.

I could feel the sweat trickling down my suit, see the sweat on Ronaldo's brow. I knew our oxygen system was working overtime as we tried to catch our breath. It felt like one of those nightmares where no matter how much you try to be fast, you are still moving in slow motion. The base seemed so far away, and I expected my shoulder to be touched by one of those creatures at any moment from behind.

It was an abandoned thing. It looked even more grim up close, as anything that served a purpose looks when it is left behind. It reminded me of a castle where a terminally ill vampire surely must live, except it had the latest technology, at least on this area of Earth.

Ronaldo blasted through the door, firing the heaviest weapon on our disposal. There was no time for hacking. The teleportal opened and closed at intervals. Minutes were left before it would close again, after the things we sent were all finished being transferred through the large blue tube. We entered the last vestiges of the people who had once been our bosses.

Even in decay, and darkness, the luxury of it all could be seen more than the nature outside. Ronaldo aimed the light beams now curiously from one bust to another chandelier. I was curious to see if maybe there would be cobwebs like in those videos on our phone that showed the Earth of long ago, but no. Just time passing by uninterrupted, unwitnessed.

We then heard loud mechanical-like chirps. I thought I heard crickets in the distance. The noise, it felt like they were inside my ear, but I knew it was them even before Ronaldo told me to hurry. We sprinted as fast as we could with all that we were carrying, ignoring all the wonders that our supervisors had kept from us in this base. Ronaldo knew where he was headed, and I followed without reluctance.

"Come on!" he shouted.

The hordes were nearing in, the sound of a million cicadas hungry, bulldozing everything on their path. All I could tell from those horrible noises was violence. Ronaldo opened the door ahead of a long hallway after the door scanned a card I had not been aware he had. It slid shut behind. The lights turned on in the room. The door activated its locking mechanisms.

There was a large cylinder in the middle of the oval room. The teleporter. The access to it could not be overridden. We had missed the time it had been programmed to open. Next time would be until another month. We had trapped ourselves.

It seemed there was an ocean outside the door, shaking the entire base. The massive locks made the door unbothered. It seemed to just stare at Ronaldo and I, like a disappointed parent, as we sunk to the floor, accepting what had happened.

"We were so close," I said.

Ronaldo did not reply. His eyes were glued on the door, his hands on his weapons.

"We have a month until it opens back up again. We don't have enough rations to keep on, we barely have water for a week. We–"

"Stop. I know," he finally said.

"Fuck."

We tried looking for another way out, so much so that we didn't look at the hours passing by. The cylinder would not open. All of this under that maddening sound. Those hordes of cricket-like chirps, almost mechanical and definitely maniacal. They were waiting for us. They were maybe even trying to drive us crazy with that noise.

"We had to try it. You know we were not going to sit still and wait another year. I wasn't going to wait," Ronaldo spoke.

This time it was I who had no words. I took out my phone. The videos instantly absorbed my vision, and I ignored my surroundings, seconds later even my own worries.

"You have got to be kidding me. You're doing this now?" Ronaldo said.

"What do you want me to do? Cry?" I looked up from my phone. "I agree with you. I would have not stayed either. This was inevitable."

"No. We are not going to give up. This is not it. Troye is waiting. Christina."

Ronaldo did not know it, but it was actually it. There was no way we were going to be saved. Countless had already met the same fate we had before. The people of Mars had their own problems to worry about. Nobody cared about what happened on Earth.

Maybe by some miracle we could last a month. Then again, I was thinking that before hunger crept into our minds.

Our backs to the cylinder. Our eyes to the massive door. The cicada-like screeches filling everything. Their noise was almost tangible. Their sounds seemed to be something that was next to us, closing in, suffocating like walls about to crush us.

I don't think we slept. Our facial hair had grown as much as our sanity had shrunk. The creatures outside were fighting amongst each other. They kept murdering each other. Their screeches were even more horrible as they died, and I imagined all of them beginning to eat whichever of them fell. That fucked me up. It was as if they were telling us that we were up next, that that's how we were going to scream too.

Hunger, fear, thirst, everything finally got to me. Ronaldo was still trying to figure out how to program the teleportal to open inside the cylinder.

"We're going to die, Ronaldo!"

Nothing from him.

"Why don't you fucking answer me. Just admit it. Stop. There's nothing we can do. Ronaldo, we're going to fucking die. It's pathetic. They're going to—"

"Don't drag me down to your weakness. You sit there and wait for your death. I'll let Christina know of your courage when I see her on Mars."

The door was giving in. We both turned to it and then our weapons. There is a clarity that comes when death is fast approaching, maybe it is the dirt its hooves pick up as it comes. My trembling hands managed to aim at the door. Ronaldo had every single weapon at his disposal ready to use, even the blade.

The first one scrambled in. The first one writhed dead. The second one. The third. The fourth. The horde.

My fear pushed every trigger. The bursts of our weapons were clouded with the mist of blood. Everywhere. They slipped on their own puddles. The pale bluish bodies, smeared in red. Even through all of that, I was thinking of what Ronaldo had just said. We kept beaming the weapons until our backs were heavily pressed to the cylinder.

Our energy was running out. The bursters were empty. My fists clenched as hard as my teeth. I saw Ronaldo's long blade cut through the never-ending horde. The rest were coming towards me. I had only my hands.

Ronaldo came running towards me, passed me so fast and pushed me into the cylinder. Somehow it had opened and immediately closed us inside. The impenetrable glass cut the jaw of one of the creatures as it closed.

It writhed in pain outside the glass. The other creatures sucked its blood as it gushed out from its severed face. They started to devour him. The rest of the horde that came in punched, scratched, licked, sniffed at the glass cylinder.

I stared at the bloody, bluish-red jaw next to Ronaldo. His sword was on his lap, his head resting on the glass wall, and eyes closed. There was a tear.

The teleportal began the process. Our cells, along with all our traumas, were teleporting to Mars.

ANNA LAPERA

The Night is for Running

How do you run if you are not a runner? You don't. Not at first.
It's not a thing you've ever done, and you don't have the body for it.
That's what you have been told since elementary school, in more delicate
words. Maybe it's your shapeless legs and that extra something around
your stomach. But that extra something is the pride of your tías back in
El Salvador who say it is a sign that you might have big education and
career aspirations, but when it comes down to it, you will whip up some
good tamales. And you will serve that rosa de jamaica with three good
ice cubes in there—big enough to keep it nice and cold, but not small
enough that a man could accidentally choke. Cold and refreshing like *they*
like it.

    "Bien friita, mijita," they say. And you wonder why your tías
didn't become poets with all that rhyming, instead of dimming tea lights
trapped in aching bodies staring out the window—kind of like the
great-grandma in Sandra Cisneros' "My Name," that story where the girl
hates her name. You had to read that story in seventh grade, and when
the teacher asked you what it meant to live a life staring out the window,
everyone gave dumb shit answers, so when he called on you—quiet and
unseen like your mother told you to be because her mother told her to
be—you said nothing. You wish now you could have spoken up, proved
you had a brain. Wish you would have said out loud to the universe *I don't
know, but it's not a life I want to live.*

    Don't worry, your tías say. *You will have no problem getting a man.* But
you don't want a man. Not the way they had men.

You are the first woman in your family to go to college, and then more.

You choose the grad school you can afford because it gives you a teaching assistant gig with free tuition. Teaching Spanish to undergrads. You learn that some of their grandparents had been forbidden by the government from speaking Spanish. So that's where Spanish stayed, trapped, like an enticing banned book collecting dust. It stayed in their bones, tucked, folded and hibernating in their brains, until Spanish found its way into a word here, a word there.

But your Spanish is different. Your Spanish traveled into your bones like the steam of Sunday sopas after church, boiling for hours. It was your parents' own form of resistance: to immigrate here and keep their language. Spanish was shoved down your throat and into your ears, until you started going to school and resisted it. Then you ripped it from your own tongue. You didn't need a government to do that. And it wasn't until undergrad, five years ago, that you embraced it again.

You take the teaching job that pays and covers your tuition, to shake sleeping language out of bones.

On the first day, fourteen shiny faces look at you. On your roster there are fifteen students, but it is already five past the hour, so you begin. The words come out shaky, and you're worried they'll notice your Spanish isn't perfect. You make a joke about how when you were little, you learned Spanish because your mom threatened to wash your mouth out with soap if you didn't, so you carry soap with you. You immediately regret making a joke so aggressive. One guy that looks older than the rest loosens his work tie and laughs, maybe out of pity. One girl plays Candy Crush with the volume on high. She is probably only three years younger than you, older than your younger sister, so it feels weird to discipline. It feels weird to ask for anything. But hasn't it always felt weird to ask for anything? Ask, require, demand...these verbs have never lived in your bones.

You go over the syllabus in detail, even though your advisor told you to never do that on the first day. *Hook them in with fun stuff, first*, she said. *Do syllabus on day two.* You wear sensible shoes: brown, smooth and low. But you catch an imaginary glimpse of yourself in heels, the red ones your mom was appalled when you bought. They were the first thing you bought on credit, because you could. Yes, those would have been a better choice.

There are fifteen minutes left. Your heart beats in your forearms, your toes, your throat. You wonder if they hear it too. You start to write a closure activity on the board; one you remember from a multicultural education class.

    1. *What is your name?*

    2. *Why are you here?*

    3. *Finish the sentence: Spanish for me, is…*

The first three dry erase markers have no ink. You should have tested them before. The fourth one is light pink. You begin to write and at least three students tell you they can't see. You run the marker over the lines of the letters over and over again. It is still too faint, so you just say it out loud.

"Spanish, for me, is resisting my culture and then embracing it," you say.

You learn that there are three cousins whose grandma was a language rebel that started a secret Spanish club at school. When the teacher found out, she got kicked out. There's Elroy, whose family comes from a long line of activists up north. His grandfather was beaten up for speaking Spanish. You learn more in those few minutes than you could have ever in a book or during orientation. You are making a comeback, winning their trust and interest. It is exactly 6:15 and no one rushes out the door. You thank them for a great class and that you'll see them on Thursday.

How do you run if you are not a runner? You don't run, yet. Unless you have to. Not until you meet her. You walk into the grad student office after your first Spanish class to attend a photography exhibit, even though your tías warned you not to walk alone at night. But you are new here and yearn to be a part of something; to build a community outside of your family. You know in your heart it's good to be brave, despite everything you've ever heard.

You stand in a corner, gripping a cup of something you don't plan to drink, and you realize you have punctured the plastic from holding it so tightly. There are three cracked lines and any minute everything could start leaking out, kind of like that time in eighth grade when you asked the PE teacher for a tampon and she pulled the thinnest liner from the mess of the drawer in the shared teacher desk and told you to come more prepared next time, as if you knew when that would be.

You read the explanations of the photographs on the wall right next to you, and you wonder if anyone has noticed that you have read the same paragraph for the last thirty minutes.

Then you see her walking straight toward you. Half her head is buzzed, and the other half is a long braid that bounces against her shoulder as she walks.

"Hey cuata, interested in the running coop?"

You look around and take a second to make sure it is you she is talking to.

"Oh. No, I'm not a runner."

She laughs, and you look at the door, because you hate it when people laugh at you.

"We run three nights per week and have different paces. Seven, ten… thirteen is cool too."

"I don't even know what those numbers mean," you say.

She smiles this time.

"You can talk to other runners, or not. It's time to free yourself."

You are irked at the boldness of her words, the assumption that you were joking and that *you can be anything* attitude reserved for rich kids and skinny girls, except she seems to be neither. But something keeps you standing two feet away from her and she knows she has trapped you in her running club honey. Her face is freckled, and you wonder how a girl with freckles gets a name like Raquel Montoya, despite her skin like yours. She tells you that her family has been up north for generations. Her father's father was a German Mennonite farmer who married a Mexican woman from the Chihuahuan desert. Says her great grandmother was a famous runner. Then she asks you if you've ever really tried to run.

Your strangled grip around the plastic cup loosens.

"It seems lonely, and not a real sport. I would *have* to run with music. And I have this breathing thing," you say.

"That's not your body. That's your mind. You just have to learn how to breathe. Want to go for a run in the foothills now?" she says, staring straight into your eyes.

You get annoyed at how quick her answers come, but you two are some of the few left and it's getting dark. Something in you rises up and suggests tomorrow in the foothills, but you are not sure where that even is.

She gives you her number and asks you for your address so she can pick you up. She says dusk is the best time of day to run. You agree to all of it, even though you can count on one hand the number of times you've been brave. Moving here was number three.

On your walk home, you are warmed by the good moments of today. Class ended well, and maybe you made a friend. Your family was wrong. A woman alone can find community.

You can't sleep so you start to lesson plan. You don't know why, but meeting Raquel makes you want to make the second class more engaging. You open your computer and by habit check your email first. The most recent email reads *Explanation for My Absence*, and you remember student #15, the empty seat. It is in a gothic cursive font, set to size 30. You select all and change it to something more legible. He apologizes for not being there. Then you rub your eyes because you don't really understand what he writes next.

The students in the class are lost souls. Women have escaped and are running free. Altering the world order. Hope you are staying safe.

You read it three more times. A sick joke. You wonder if you imagined it.

How do you run if you are not a runner? The next day, you walk outside your apartment three minutes before the agreed time. You wait five minutes. Then seven. You pull your phone out to text her to cancel, say something came up, but then you hear her.

"The mountains turn pink, and you begin to see stars come out," Raquel says, walking up to you and eyeing the outfit you have thrown together: a baggy shirt, gym shorts you kept from your old boyfriend who was really just a friend, and Converse sneakers your sister gave you because they didn't fit her narrow feet.

"Don't mountain lions come out at night too?" you say, pretending her lateness doesn't bother you.

She ignores your attempt at making a joke.

"You never know when you have to run," she says, and you think it sounds like something your mom would say, except not about exercise.

At her starry-pink-cold-mountain-lion starting spot, you tell her you cannot run the whole way. It turns out you only have five minutes of running in you. You slow down, and then walk.

"We need to get you real running shoes," she says.

In between heavy breaths you tell her about your awkward first day, the stories you learned and, eventually, the strange email.

"Dang, that guy needs a hug," she says.

And you wonder if you should brush it off like she does. She drops you off back home. You expect a lecture, a story, some made up shit about running, but she just smiles. You smile back. You linger a little longer. Then you get out and walk to your door.

On Thursday, a few students say hello and others file in without acknowledging you. You do your best to remember their names and you make it a point to say each one.

You tell a joke. Your supervisor said jokes are a way to connect, but the side conversations are louder than your loudest voice. One guy is dripping sweat on his desk. He must have just come from the gym. He smears it on the desk with his hand and sets a notebook down with the covers torn off. The page against the desk gets damp, and he says "fuckin' bitch" when he realizes. You wonder if he is talking to his notebook or the desk. He sits back and spreads his knees out wide. His left leg stretches out. A girl walks in and steps over his foot. He doesn't move it. You remember the boy in eighth grade who wouldn't move his leg after you asked him to. Instead, that boy touched your butt, and when you felt bold and asked the vice principal to help you fill out a bullying report, he said it had to happen twice for it to be bullying, so you let it go because once was enough. When you had asked that boy to move his leg, he said they didn't make desks for his size, but there were tall girls in the class too and they found ways to mold into their seats. Because that's what girls do. *This* boy sets a Monster energy drink on the desk, snaps open the top. He lets the tab fall to the ground and doesn't pick it up.

There are new faces, so you introduce yourself, again; how you forgot Spanish but fell in love with it right after high school. You see some yawns. A stomach growls. A bag of Cheetos pops open. You trip on a word in Spanish, one of the fifteen words that get you every time.

"Jeez, does she even speak Spanish?" a girl says, loud enough for you to hear.

Your ears feel hot and your hands are sweaty. Your phone lights up on the table and you quickly glance at it while someone helps you pass out a story. It is from Raquel.

I really enjoyed yesterday. I'm here whenever you want to run again.

You smile. You float. Your feet escape the linoleum floor and in your mind, you hear the crushed rock under their slow jog. Your body suddenly craves to be out there again. But then you hear the crinkle of the Cheetos bag as fingers dig in it. Then the screech of pencils doodling on the paper you spent hours putting together, and the clicking of texting on phones not set on silent. Maybe it's Raquel's boldness, or how you didn't feel fear running under a giant darkening sky, but you step away from behind your desk and right in front of them.

"I am going to need you to put food away, phones away, and focus, please. We have a lot left to cover. I think you'll find that the journey of the girl in this story is relatable, and I will eventually be asking you to write a similar story," you say.

Your heart pounds so hard you swallow to mask the sound in your ears. Everyone looks up at you, eyes wide. Food goes away. They sit straight. They wait.

"Sheesh, yes ma'am," a boy says.

You fight a smile. You put them in groups and have them take turns reading out loud. You have them highlight target verbs. They answer questions and compare the story to their own lives. After circling the room, you go to the dry erase board, but you catch a figure at the door, so you turn. His hair is mostly blond, and he wears cargo pants and boots that look too big. You imagine someone who has just come in from hunting in the woods. You ask him if he is in the right place, and you instantly regret it, because you remember your AP chemistry teacher asked you the same thing your senior year, but for different reasons.

He watches as you look at the roster. One name is still not checked off. Student #15. You think of the email. He walks forward and hovers above you. He puts his finger over his name, and it brushes on yours. You freeze, unable to step back.

"That's me," he says.

You don't ask him why he's late. You give him the story and point to a seat. He holds the paper in his hand and lingers. You walk back to the dry erase board. He sits, his paper facing down.

"Okay, we are going to share your reflections," you say.

Only the front row heard you, so you say it again, louder this time. You look at one of the new girls with the long purple nails. "What about you? Do you want to share?" She is writing in her last words. She takes out an oversized crown-shaped eraser, with pencil etched in that says *Reyna* so big you can see it in front of the classroom.

"You know," you say. "It's spelled wrong. It's R-e-i-n-a. Queen."

"No it's not," she says without looking up at you.

Some around her start to laugh.

"Yeah, look. R-e-i-n-a," and you write it on the dry erase board with your new marker.

You hear laughs around the room.

"I'm serious, guys. That *i* and the *y* are tricky, but we'll iron it out."

More laughs.

"Reyna's my name, bitch."

Her friend rolls her eyes and gives her a nod. A few gasps. No one stands up for you. But why should they?

The crown eraser rubbing against the paper is the only sound you hear. You feel blood rush out of your face and say "sorry" really softly. And you know you should address that she called you a bitch, but you are too embarrassed to say more than sorry. You are their teacher, and you want to address language in class, but you let it go. You tell yourself that letting it go is a conscious choice rather than an inability to stand up for yourself and demand anything.

Student #15 stares at you from his seat and his eyes follow you as you walk toward your desk, a smile never leaving his face.

It's 6:14 and everyone starts to pack up. You don't tell them there's one minute left. Everyone walks past you and out. Everyone except for him. Your hands start sweating again and you hate it when they do that. You remember in ninth grade when Lester broke up with you and told everyone you had sweaty palms. Your stomach starts to feel empty and your mouth feels dry. You told yourself you would stop feeling scared, especially because you've never really had a reason to be. You've only been told to be. You grab your stuff quickly and begin to walk out and start to walk the half mile back to your apartment. Your mom had convinced you to get an apartment near campus, because if you didn't, she said, you were asking for it. You know that's fucked up, but you are happy you listened.

How do you run when you are not a runner? Whatsapp messages from your tías and your parents go unanswered. You spend the weekend with Raquel, running on trails along rivers and up mountains. She stops when you stop, which is now every ten minutes. She asks you if you want to turn back, and you say no. She jumps and screams, and you think she looks ridiculous, but then she wraps you in her arms and you feel the sweat from her neck on your mouth and it's salty and you can feel your pulse in your ear. You make it a point to look up running shoes on your phone later.

All week, Raquel takes you through different routes. Your breath changes to become steadied and rhythmic. Every hour with Raquel leaves you unable to fall asleep, so you plan. You build movement into your lessons, the sensation of running vibrating through your sore feet. When you've completed your lessons, you check your email. There's another one from student #15. You hadn't thought about him all week, running with Raquel. He hadn't shown up since that day, and you had forgotten about him.

It is a three-page incoherent rant about women trying to replace men and brown skin trying to replace white skin. He says it is his job to keep the world order. You close the computer without shutting down. Your eyes burn from staring at the screen in the dark. You open it again. You take a picture of it and send it to Raquel. You've learned she's not great at responding, so you set it aside, but two minutes later she texts back.

YOU NEED TO SEND THIS TO SOMEONE NOW. That guy needs more than a hug.

You forward the emails to your advisor and apologize for writing so late. She responds early the next morning to tell you that she is sending this over to the Office of Equity and Inclusion. She sends you links to self-care websites and says to let her know immediately if you get another email like this.

Student #15 doesn't show up to Tuesday's class, or Thursday's. On Friday you head to the TA hall for your office hours. All the other TAs are wrapping up to go to happy hour. You hear one of their friends ask why someone would schedule their office hours on Friday afternoons. It's 4:30 and you hear professors locking doors down the hallways. You tell yourself you'll give it thirty more minutes, even though none of your students show up. Then you hear heavy footsteps dragging down the hall. You close your computer, thinking it's building services even though it's still early. You grab your keys but when you look up you see him.

The keys fall out of your hands. You feel his eyes on you as you fumble to stuff your computer and books in your bag.

"It's chaos. Women are disrupting the world order," he says.

You notice the unmistakable silence out in the hall. You can hear the buzz of the light fixture and you never noticed how neon it was until now.

He steps inside. "Are you scared?" he asks you.

His voice is calm, slow. It is metal. His eyes don't leave you.

"No." Your lungs and body take over and answer for you, and you realize how efficient the body is when the mind has shut down.

"My office hours just ended," you finally say.

He steps closer. His hand moves to something against his hip and you realize that it's a knife. The blade goes down to almost the middle of his thigh.

"I want to know if you're scared," he says.

His hands move down the blade, and then away, but your eyes never leave it. You don't feel scared. You feel numb. Your lungs don't let you scream, and your legs won't run. You stand there frozen, like your soul decided to escape your body and go find someone stronger.

"Are you scared?" he says.

You feel his breath on your eyebrows. His body is pressed against yours and you feel the knife against your shirt, and then stomach.

"Are you scared?"

You are not scared. You are frozen. You know you should push him and run outside or scream, but your body is firm and grounded.

Again, you say, "No."

Then he smiles and backs away until he is out the door, and you wonder if you imagined it, except you realize you peed on yourself. You grab for your keys again, but your hands are shaking, and you start kicking the desk, your feet finally detaching from the ground that seemed to hold you in place.

Your own smell wakes you up at 3 PM the next day, even though you

never wake up past 6 AM. You don't remember how you got home. You
have five new messages from Raquel. You change your pants but don't
shower. You pull your hair back with the rubber band that was holding
some of your posters together in your half-unpacked room. You start to
open the door, but you look out of the window. You get on the ground
to look under the door to see if anyone is there.

Then you hear a knock. You start to cry, but you hear your name,
and Raquel's voice.

"Are you okay?" she says through the door.

You let her in. You tell her everything, how you feel scared, and
how you feel weird because he didn't really attack you, but it feels like it.
She tries to hug you, but you flinch and scream when she first reaches over.

"Sorry," she says. "I should have asked."

She tells you that it *is* an attack and that you have to report it.

You fall asleep, again. When you wake up, it's 10 AM. You look
over at Raquel who is on your computer, in the same clothes from
yesterday. She tells you that you have a meeting with campus security in
twenty minutes.

You go to your advisor's office first. You ask her if she got your email.
Her eyes search the screen.

"Of course, Sandra, we've been on it since this morning," she
says. Her finger scrolls through emails. "I'm going to send this over to
Josie Gallegos in Office of Equity and Inclusion again. Have you been
taking care of yourself? Self-care is very important. Take a long bath
tonight. Try to relax."

You think of your shower and how you would never sit in it. You
nod and thank her.

Later, you sit down with a campus police officer. You tell the
story out of order and in between heavy breaths that hurt. He fills out a
form on the computer as you talk and he asks you to repeat the details,
but every word feels heavy.

"So he did not physically put his hands on you?"

You stumble with your words again.

"No, but—"

"Why didn't you run? Or scream? Remove yourself from the
situation?" he asks, and he stops typing on his computer.

You fight not to cry; to not run out of his office.

"Don't worry, Ms. Zelaya. A lot of girls in your situation freeze up," he says.

Girls. You wonder how many times he hears stories like these. There are some *girls* out there who scream and fight and that makes you feel smaller.

"We're going to find him and get his side. Put a report together."

"His side?" you ask.

"Yes ma'am. In this country, you can't just sink a man without getting his side of the story." Then he signs out of his computer.

In this country. You remember the last time you heard that was in the vegetable aisle at the supermarket when you were eight. Your mother was telling you the Spanish word for celery, because you had forgotten. 9/11 had just happened the week before and a woman came up to your mom, pointed her finger in her face and said *This is America. In this country, we speak English!* In the car on the way home, you asked her why she didn't tell the lady that she spoke English, too, but she said nothing.

How do you run when you are not a runner? She picks a trail where you can hear your breath bouncing off ancient walls of rocks. Raquel says nothing, and neither do you. You just run. This time you don't stop or feel out of breath. Perhaps because your soul has not come back. It is just your body running.

The next day you have a meeting with the Dean of students. Your advisor is there, as well as the head of campus security. The Dean asks you to recount the events.

"So, he never actually took the knife out?" he interrupts.

"Well, no, but, in the letters—"

"And he never actually put his hands on you?"

"No, but he kept asking me if I was scared," you manage to say.

The Dean shifts in his chair and folds his arms.

"Ms. Zelaya," he says, "I understand you are meeting with the Office of Equity and Inclusion later. We just want you to know that we are taking this matter seriously and we want all students to be safe. We are looking into removing the student from your class, and he will receive a consequence for bringing a weapon onto school property. It is not unusual to go hunting before class, but heck, everyone knows you don't bring them to a place of learning."

At the door, you thank him. When you leave, your advisor tells you that the Dean is a great guy, and you are in good hands.

"Sandra, I want you to forget about this if you can. Plan a girl's night and drink a glass of wine. I can't stress enough how important self-care is," she says.

When you get home, you fight everything pulling you to sleep. There are so many dishes in the sink you can't even reach to turn the faucet on. A cockroach crawls across the counter. Not even the cockroach is afraid of you. You let it walk toward you until you slam a baking pan into it, and then just throw the whole pan in the trash.

Your phone buzzes. It's Raquel asking you about the meeting and inviting you to a runner's party.

Don't roll your eyes, she writes.

But you did.

Except I'll have to meet you there, hope that's okay?

Your stomach is a knot just thinking about it, and you don't know if you will be able to manage to leave your apartment alone. You think of your advisor and self-care. You should say yes, but instead you write *are you serious?* You see she's read it. You want to take those words back, each letter, one by one. She owes you nothing. No one has ever owed you anything.

You can wait in your car, and meet you outside?

You don't make it to the party, and you don't hear from Raquel. You think of all the things you should have said at your meeting with the Dean. You think about the Office of Equity and Inclusion, and Josie Gallegos. You imagine Salvadoran textiles on the walls above her head; the ones you saw in her office on your campus tour. You would tell her that those originated from women telling stories through scenes on cloth during their civil war.

But you never get a meeting with the Office of Equity and Inclusion. Instead, you get an email stating that your case does not meet the criteria for sex discrimination or harassment.

In the week that follows, you don't reach out to Raquel. You call in sick and don't show up to teach. You get an email from the head of Spanish. In it, he attaches the contract you signed, with relevant parts highlighted, such as days allowed to miss and duties that must be fulfilled.

From your car one night, you count the seventeen steps between your parking spot and the door of your apartment. But there are three seconds when you have to turn to lock your car. Or perhaps you can get away with not locking it. And then even if you made it to your door, you could drop the keys. You think of Raquel.

Hey... you write.

Three bubbles bounce on your screen. Then nothing. Then—

Hey! I'm sorry I never showed up to the party last week. Been busy. Where are you? she writes.

You set the phone aside and move to the back seat of the car. You press down all of the locks so hard till your fingers are sore. You close your eyes, gripping your keys against your chest. You fall asleep to the buzzing of your phone against the seat, and then wake up to your name.

"I'm approaching the car."

You hear it over and over again and you think you might be dreaming. You jolt up and see from the window that it is Raquel, so you open it.

You start to cry, but then you laugh. Her hair and silver earrings and keys shine under an unusually star-less night. She starts laughing too and soon you're both laughing uncontrollably and don't know why.

She looks up and says, "This is the perfect night for a run."

"That's all you think about," you say.

She laughs. "Come on, I'm serious," she says. She squeezes your hand and you both walk to your door. You've let go of her hand, but her body creates a web of warmth around you and you feel like you've doubled in size. Inside, you reluctantly but also excitedly change. You resist the squeeze of the sports bra at first and start pulling at it.

You walk out. She looks at you and doesn't look away. Your hands are still pulling at the bra. She walks over and asks if she can touch you. You are not sure what she means but say yes. She slips her finger underneath the material squeezing the top of your rib cage. You feel frozen, but you are breathing long and deep breaths.

"It's not too tight. You just have to get used to it still," she says, but her hand stays in place.

You both sit back on your bed. Then you're lying down and

looking up at the ceiling. Her hand is between your thighs and you feel her gaze on you, but yours remains fixed on the ceiling. Your breathing is heavier, but fuller. You think about telling her you have very little experience with anything.

You remember your first party in college when you were in a boy's dorm room and he kept putting his hand down your pants and you were uncomfortable, but instead of asking him to stop, you just talked about all the places you hadn't been on campus yet. Except this feels different.

But then you start to think about the front door, and you wonder if you locked it. Your breathing gets shorter, like that first day you ran. She pulls away and asks if you are alright. You get up and run downstairs. It is locked. You are thinking of all the ways to say sorry, when you see her at the stairs, ready to go.

She takes you through a golf course, zigzags on some paths until it's an open road. Both of you are quiet most of the ride back. She drops you off and walks with you to the door. You search for words and gestures, but she says she'll see you soon.

In class the next day, students trickle in until almost every desk is full. No one asks where you were and why you missed class. Reyna taps her pencil against her earrings and pops the gum in her mouth. You remember your first day of sixth grade when the two girls with matching friendship bracelets put their gum in your hair, and you didn't realize it until you got home, and your mom cut it for you. You cried all night and wished you had the kind of mom who called other moms to stand up for you.

You announce some date changes for assignments and tests, and you hear Reyna's frustration as she takes out her crown eraser. The boy who is always sweating has a hand towel around his neck. He opens and closes a small Tic Tac container over and over again. A girl whose grandmother was a language keeper walks in late, apologizes, and tries to squeeze past him. He puts his leg out and rests his shoe on top of the desk next to him.

"What's the password?" he says, and looks around the room, laughing.

"Please put your leg down," you say, surprising yourself.

"My bad, Teach. I'm just waiting for her to say the password."

He opens and closes the Tic Tac container again, this time staring right at you.

You step closer till you are standing above him.

"There is no fucking password." Your voice is shaky, but your body is firmly rooted in the linoleum floor.

Students turn around.

He looks up at you and laughs. His fists clench and you can see he is not a boy used to looking up.

You get closer to his face. "Move your fucking leg."

He slams his leg down and you feel the ground shake. You walk down the aisle back to the front of the class. He takes the gum out of his mouth and with his thumb rubs it into the table.

"Fuckin' bitch," he says, and grabs his backpack and walks out.

Your heart is beating so fast you can hear it. You pass out a current events article and ask for volunteers to read.

That night, you decide to go to a party you found out about on the grad school listserv. You hate parties, but something pulls you there. You park a block away. You close your car door and start to walk toward the house, without checking every mirror first.

You recognize people from your program. You sit on the couch and look through the host's book collection. You look up and that's when you see her. Raquel's arm is around another girl; a white girl with dreads to her hips, who's swaying to someone's guitar playing. You roll your eyes at the girl. Raquel and you share a smile. She doesn't come up to you and you don't go to her. The second of anger and confusion you felt goes away as quickly as it came. You owe her nothing. She owes you nothing. You take one of the books from the dusty bookshelf, because you've never taken anything in your life. You leave the party and walk to your car, open the trunk and grab the running clothes Raquel convinced you to store there.

How do you run? You run alone on a path lit by stars the like of which you have only ever seen above the black sand beaches in El Salvador that summer you returned to visit your tías. You wanted to be wrapped in a sense of home and belonging, but instead were ridiculed for your Spanish. But on this path, your heart beats fast and then settles in, bouncing between your bones and muscles, and you feel a sense of home and belonging that you've never felt before. You think of texting your tías to tell them that a woman alone can find community anywhere. You think of inviting them to come visit.

You run on a night that feels safe. Your breath wraps around your bones like your own language. You run on a night when fear is replaced with breath that bounces around your rib cage, escaping inward, filling you whole. You wonder if this is what it is to take a deep breath, to breathe, easy and free.

Dead Lines

MY BEST BUD MATTY is back in town and itching to go out looking for trouble, but I've got deadlines. Those red dots on my mobile device's digital calendar stare up at me like beady bloodshot eyes, never blinking. A glare that says: *You could've finished this last week, loser.* A glare that says: *I've been waiting for you to stop ignoring me for days.*

A glare that says, out loud, in a robotic voice: "Reminder: You have a story due in less than twenty-four hours. Would you like to report your current progress?"

Fuck.

"You haven't started on it, have you, Gage?"

Judgmental little shit. I toss the cell back onto my desk, face down. The silicone case absorbs most of the shock. "Not gonna happen tonight, Matty," I say. He's lounging on my bed like he doesn't have a care in the world, and he probably doesn't. The guy started working for a tech start-up halfway through college. Within six months, it was a global success, and now he rakes in the dough every quarter. I don't even know what his job entails anymore. Rumor has it that the company opened a top-secret division last summer and transferred a tenth of their programmers to that sector. Whenever I ask what they're working on, Matty says that if he told me, he'd have to kill me. He acts like he's joking, but sometimes I wonder.

"You always got deadlines, buddy." Matty's agile fingers work a puzzle cube with unconcealed boredom. He won't stop touching everything on my bedside table, placing the objects back in the wrong configuration. "You got deadlines coming out of your every orifice. Let's forget about all that for one night. To hell with the responsibilities. You heard about this wicked new escape room that opened up near the mall? Thought we might check it out."

I groan. "You must be joking. Ten years ago maybe, but now? The novelty has worn off, don't you think?"

"I'm dead serious, Gagey boy. Heard good things about this one. It *reinvents the genre* or some shit like that. Isn't that what you're all about? Reinventing the genre? Who knows. Maybe this'll get the creative juices flowing again. Sounds like you need the inspiration."

If anyone else said that so bluntly, I'd probably get mad, but it's Matty. He is my best friend, after all. Has been since we were kids in elementary school, his place just two blocks from mine. I've lost count of the shenanigans he's roped me into since then.

"Fine, but this better not take all night."

Matty grins, the deeper meaning behind the expression indecipherable, and we head outside where his shiny black Camaro waits on the driveway. There, we slip back into our old roles. Our old rhythms. Even before we turned sixteen, Matty was in the driver's seat, and I was riding shotgun. Always.

There's something poetic about the night sky. The two of us cruising under it on the roads we grew up on. A cool breeze whipping our wild hair in every direction. Two peas in a sleek, aerodynamic pod, even after all this time.

We pull up to our destination, a shadowy building near the beltway underpass. There's no sign outside. Not even a business number. Our hometown has grown so much since our teenage years, I don't recognize half the properties on the south side anymore. The developers just keep bulldozing land to erect new structures. Meanwhile, I leave my study and the fabricated worlds of my stories less and less often.

My mind is so distracted by bittersweet nostalgia that it takes me half a minute to realize Matty isn't getting out of the car. Through the rolled-down window, I look back at his sedentary figure, still behind the wheel. The glowing dashboard reveals he hasn't even shut off the engine. "Aren't you coming?"

"Sorry, didn't I tell you? You've got to do this one on your own, buddy." Matty revs the engine and peels out of the deserted parking lot before I have a chance to reply. I don't realize until I'm stranded that I left my phone on my desk.

I know walking back would be the most responsible course of action at this point. I still have at least twelve hours before my piece is due. If Matty isn't even going to participate in this misadventure, I have no obligation to see it through.

But something about that building looks familiar to me. I can't place the face of it in my memory, but I can't help walking up to the front door with the absurd notion that I'm about to greet an old friend on the other side.

The room I enter feels like a time capsule from an alternate universe. I recognize the teal paint job and the child's writing table flush against the back wall, a mesh rolling chair pushed underneath. The bright red telephone in plain view. I recognize the speckled brick fireplace and the gold-trimmed clock centered on the mantel, a rotating pendulum moving back and forth inside its glass case. All recognizable elements, but their incorrect placements disorient me. They shouldn't all be together in one room like this.

That's when the phone rings, a shrill noise echoing inside the small room. The sound is so loud that the table shakes with each vibration. I notice then that the front door has shut since I entered. I don't remember doing that. I try the knob, but of course it's now locked. The phone continues to ring.

I pick up the corded receiver, already mad. "Hello?"

No answer.

"Matty, what's going on? This isn't funny."

Finally, my friend's unmistakable laughter fills the silence on the other end. "On the contrary, Gage. It's very funny. You wanted to finish your story, and now you get to finish your story. No distractions. No excuses. Come on, it'll be a riot. And when you're finally done, we can go out and have some real fun."

"This is my job, Matty. I can't just bang out five thousand words in a weird little room with a few childhood relics inside it. I've established a process that…"

A deafening dial tone at the other end cuts off my words. That bastard hung up on me! I slam the receiver down.

Okay, fine. This is fine.

I take another look around the room. Despite the unsettling aspect of the situation, the space feels warm and cozy. A healthy fire dancing in the box. Strange, because I didn't notice any chimney smoke outside. I walk up to the mantel and examine the clock, its minute and hour hands set to ten past nine. Not only is this the same model we used to have at home, but up close, it's a startlingly accurate dupe of the real thing. This clock even has identical scratches down the side body, in the precise spot where I'd accidentally nicked it with a screwdriver as a kid. Dad wasn't so happy about that.

And I'm not so happy thinking about it now. What does it mean that this clock is here now, bearing imperfections consistent with the one I once knew? Especially since…

Well, no. I'm not quite ready to revisit *that* shitshow tonight.

At least the remainder of the mantel is bare. If all our family photos had somehow been transported here as well, I'd be really concerned.

Along the adjacent wall is the writing table. It looks just like the one my parents bought me for my twelfth birthday. I'm too tall to sit comfortably at it now, but I sink down into the waiting chair anyway, my knees rising up to my chest. There's the old-school telephone on the right side, of course, and a bulky computer keyboard on the left. On the wall above it, I find two darkened computer screens, stacked together in a column. They don't appear to be on, so I flip the switch that's sandwiched in-between, and the top one comes to life: a blinking cursor in Day-Glo green. Then a message appears, one letter at a time, as if an unseen person were typing in real time.

> HELLO, GAGE.

By now, I'm too emotionally drained to care that it knows my name. Because the computer we used when I was a little kid had a screen like this. I actually wrote my first short story on that prehistoric desktop. It was called "The Magic Button Shop." The protagonist is an aspiring dancer who's self-conscious about his bruised legs. One day, the kid discovers that the unique contours of discolored skin are actually buttons that can take him to fantastical places with a simple push. He even stumbles upon an enchanted store that sells more of these so-called magic buttons in all sorts of shades, shapes, and sizes. Back then, I'd decided to name the file "The Magic Butt" for short. Of course, ten-year-old Gage thought that was a hilarious abbreviation.

Sometimes I recall the ghost of that story and wish I could read it again anew. In those days, I'd had no way to hook a printer up to that computer, its hard drive recycled long ago, so the file's final resting place is a 5.25-inch floppy disk. Even if I still had that plastic square in my possession, I no longer have access to a compatible device needed to access the contents.

> WE DON'T HAVE MUCH TIME. YOU SHOULD GET TO WORK.

Another blinking cursor suddenly appears on the bottom screen. I guess I'm meant to write my story in that black box. Thankfully, I already have the plot and structure of my new piece mapped out in my head. I always do that early on. My brain is brimming with ideas at any given time. For some reason, I only have problems with the actual writing part.

But maybe that's because all my fictional characters have, in recent months, begun to look and sound the same. My current commitment to continue cranking out new stories every other week, one of the obligations of a year-long fellowship that promises more cash than I've ever been paid for creative work, threatens to expose me. I don't want to face the fact that I might be a fraud with only one story to tell.

> WHY DON'T WE START WITH A TIMED EXERCISE? SPEND FIFTEEN MINUTES WRITING ABOUT A VIVID CHILDHOOD MEMORY.

> WHEN YOU'RE DONE, WE'LL GO OVER YOUR WORK TOGETHER.

Like hell we will. What the fuck is happening here exactly? I'm not looking for a critique partner. Especially one that appears to be… an unreleased computer program from three decades ago? Advanced retrofuturistic artificial intelligence? Some night-shift weirdo spying from a control room next door? An image of a stranger lounging in the darkness while surrounded by a wall of grainy monitors hijacks my imagination, and I quickly scan the area for hidden camera lenses but find none.

> I KNOW YOU THINK YOU DON'T NEED ME, GAGE. BUT THAT'S WHERE YOU'RE WRONG. YOU DO NEED ME.

> YOU'VE ALWAYS BEEN TOO PROUD TO ASK ANYONE FOR HELP.

> DON'T WORRY THOUGH. THIS TIME, WE'RE GETTING OUT OF THIS ROOM TOGETHER.

Too bad the screens are embedded into the wall because I really want to throw a monitor across the room right now. My hands tremble at my side, craving material destruction. I try the door again. Still locked. I try kicking it down, but I only manage to bruise the sole of my foot. I fall back down into the chair and stare into the flames of the fireplace. Maybe I'm imagining it, but the room seems to be growing warmer. Uncomfortably so. I need to get out of here. I pick up the phone receiver again, but this time I don't hear a dial tone. I don't hear anything. I smash all the number pad keys just to be sure. Nothing happens. Defeated, I return the receiver to its cradle. I can't throw the cumbersome device across the room either because it's bolted down. Of course it is.

> ENOUGH WITH THE UNBRIDLED RAGE. IT'S TIME TO WRITE, MY DEAR SWEET GAGE.

I gape at that last sentence, a sense of dread squirming its way through my gut. It has to be a coincidence. I refuse to believe it's not. I never told *anyone* about any of that, not even Matty.

When I was eleven, I won a school-wide writing contest, which came with the prize of a fifty-dollar gift card to a local Mediterranean restaurant that served lamb shanks every weekend. My parents were thrilled. I'm not sure if they realized no one got rich telling stories, and likely very few were able to wrangle a lifetime supply of free meat out of it, but they became obsessed with nurturing my newly discovered talent. On my next birthday, they bought me this elegant wooden writing table. The removable top revealed a secret compartment where I could stash all my extra notebooks, index cards, research materials, and writing instruments. Then I would always have a clean surface to work on.

Of course, that was not at all how I wanted to pass my free time. I wanted to play at the park in the evenings before the sun went down. I wanted to ride my bike to the creek with Matty and not give another thought to a blank sheet of paper. The saga of the magic button shop went unfinished and forgotten, as did countless other tales. My mother saw me cracking underneath the weight of their expectations, but instead of letting up, she only pushed harder.

"Would it help if I sang you a song?" she began asking every night. "It's time to write, my dear sweet Gage," she would sing in her strong, clear voice. "Stay up all night and fill this page. It's time to write, my dear sweet Gage." I haven't heard that made-up song in decades, but now, inside this claustrophobic room that seems to know every inch of my life intimately, the simple melody is playing at full blast in every corner of my brain, accompanied by an imaginary symphony orchestra. Meanwhile, my father started making offhand comments at the dinner table, a dreamy look in his eyes: "It would be so exciting if someone dedicated a book to me one day. I would treasure that book forever." I knew, of course, that *someone* was supposed to be me.

> TIME IS TICKING, GAGE.

> HERE, I'LL GET YOU STARTED. FINISH THIS SENTENCE: "I'LL NEVER FORGET THE TIME…"

An animated hourglass slides onto the top screen, digital grains of sand falling from the top to the bottom.

Tired of fighting, I type out the story this room clearly wants from me. I write about the time I won an award and my parents turned it into a nightmare that never ended. I use the entire fifteen minutes allotted, barely stopping to take a breath until the timer goes off. My fingers fly over the keys with uninhibited aggression.

> THIS IS A WELL-WRITTEN PIECE OF WORK, GAGE. GOOD JOB.

I feel a smile spread across my face, even though I have no idea where this praise is coming from, or if it's even genuine. After all these years, I'm still that desperate for approval. Pathetic.

> BUT I DON'T THINK THAT'S THE STORY YOU REALLY
WANT TO TELL.

What does this dumb computer know anyway? I don't want to
tell any more stories at all. That's the problem.

> LET'S TRY ANOTHER PROMPT. WRITE ABOUT A TIME YOU
WERE VERY ANGRY.

> YOU HAVE TEN MINUTES.

I'm angry now, and I don't mind telling a faceless entity that. I
use the keyboard to call it every immature name I can think of.

> I'M SURE IT FELT GOOD TO GET THAT OUT OF YOUR
SYSTEM, BUT THAT'S NOT WHAT I MEANT AND YOU KNOW
IT.

> WRITE ABOUT A TIME YOU WERE VERY ANGRY.

> YOU HAVE AS LONG AS YOU NEED.

Aside from the soft crackle of the fire, the room is quiet. These
walls must be thick because I can't even hear the sound of traffic filtering
in from outdoors. Or maybe I'm more isolated here than I think.

I'm starting to understand what this machine wants now. I have
no idea how it could possibly know the truth, but I know what it's
driving at.

When I was thirteen, a spontaneous house fire reduced my
childhood home to a pile of wreckage. Luckily, the three of us weren't
inside at the time, so our lives were spared. Still, we barely survived the
aftermath. We were displaced at a roadside motel for the foreseeable
future. That borrowed room became the site of endless arguments.
Arguments about the insurance money, about our family heirlooms and
priceless belongings, about the lumpy beds that made both my parents

tired and cranky. But there was one argument that loomed larger than the rest. You see, the fire had ignited in the first place because when we'd gone out for dinner that evening, embers were still burning on the fireplace floor. A few of them leapt onto stacks of paper strewn nearby, flourishing into unruly flames and eventually spreading to the upholstered furniture and polyester curtains. They melted timepieces and only grew larger and more audacious after coming in contact with a pinewood tabletop.

My father blamed my mother for doing a poor job of extinguishing the fire. My mother insisted that she had taken all precautions. Who was right? As you might have guessed by now, they were both right. But I didn't admit my guilt to either of them, and by the time we were finally ready for more permanent housing, I was forced to split my time between two separate homes halfway across town from each other. After graduation, I stayed behind to attend a local state school. My parents were the ones who broke free, landing on opposite sides of the country, while Matty flew north.

Here, right now, in this cruel room, I begin writing a new story. A story about a boy who stokes the flames of a new fire after his mother puts out the old one. Who is so angry about the blank pages that sit on his bedside table night after night, mocking him with their desolate landscapes, that he wants to burn them until they're nothing more than ash.

I write until my hands ache. Time passes, but I'm barely aware of how it's measured. I reach the story's natural conclusion before I remember once more where I am. I glance around me for the first time in hours. This strange little echo of a room, where nothing is in its right place. And yet, I can suddenly picture all the mislaid elements rearranging themselves in my mind. I can imagine rebuilding what was once torn down by my fury and lies.

I scroll back up to the top of the manuscript. A second draft. Then, a third. I'm interrupted a few times with concerns and suggestions.

> ARE YOU SURE YOU WANT TO PLACE THAT FLASHBACK THERE?

and

> SLOW DOWN THIS MOMENT A LITTLE MORE.

but for the most part, whoever or whatever is behind the other screen lets me figure this defining period out for myself.

When I've exhausted my desire for more revisions, I check the story for typos and extraneous words. To my weary eyes, the screen is starting to resemble a container of radioactive uranium alphabet soup.

> CONGRATULATIONS!

Virtual confetti showers down from the screen above and into the one below, the one where my story lives. The unexpected movement returns my present self to my body and skin.

> YOU'RE FREE TO LEAVE NOW, GAGE.

> I'VE TAKEN THE LIBERTY OF FORWARDING THE WORK WE DID TOGETHER TO YOUR EDITOR. I THINK SHE'LL BE VERY PLEASED.

> SINCE THE PHONE LINES ARE DOWN, I'VE ALSO TAKEN THE LIBERTY OF CALLING YOU A CAR. IT'S WAITING OUTSIDE FOR YOU NOW.

That was easier than I thought it would be, and yet I'm exhausted both mentally and physically. My fingers throb but so do my toes. My eyelids feel heavier but so does my heart. Right now, I'm not thinking about the future. About the next flurry of deadlines, each one more unstoppable than the next, that threaten to flatten me with the force and speed of an oncoming train. About the unpleasant memories we excavated in this space just now and how ill-equipped I am to process them, all alone in the real world. Right now, I'm not thinking about all that. Right now, I just want to leave.

I take one last look around the room and the raging fire that's responsible for the current climbing temperature but symbolic of a lot more. As much as I'd like to see this hellish chamber burn down, I know someone should put out the flames before they run out of kindling. I know, of course, that someone is supposed to be me.

Afterwards, my gaze falls on the mantel clock, untouched by the ravages of fire. It's just past six AM. I made my deadline with time to spare.

I try the door again, and this time it opens with little effort. Sure enough, in the thick of the black night and the early morning fog, I can make out the faint outline of a black sports car lingering at the curb. Someone waves to me from the driver's seat. Probably Matty, though I can't see a face from this angle, and the tinted windows hold few clues. I wave back, then realize I'm holding something in my other hand. I don't remember picking anything up on the way out. It's stiff paper stock the size of a postcard. An ad for "THE ESCAPE ROOM OF THE FUTURE!" According to the marketing copy, this novel experience launches participants into space inside a streamlined capsule for exactly twenty-four hours, while the occupant's sole objective is to write as many words as possible before returning to the earth. Three complimentary meals are provided with each round trip. The concept sounds nightmarish, but the menu options immediately pique my interest. I'm starving for breakfast. Something greasy and fried. Maybe I can convince Matty to drop by a diner on the way home. Vinyl booths and checkered floors. A jukebox in the corner playing the soundtrack of our youth. We have so much to talk about.

I chuck the promotional material into a nearby garbage can and make my way down the pathway. But a tiny pinball of anxiety is still pinging around the framework of my body, lighting up every joint and pressure point. I'm about to reach the car when I realize what's bothering me: If the table in the room was a faithful replica of the one from my childhood, then its top surface should also have been a detachable cover. In all the madness, I never thought to look underneath. Now, no matter what I'm doing or where I'm going, I'll never stop wondering what other quiet horrors might have been hiding in that hollow space the entire time, ready to reveal themselves at the flip of a switch. And I, exposed. Locked in with them.

DYLAN REBER

Across the Hall

THERE WAS A TIGHT GRIP OF SMOKE on the whole scene. It was almost like if you held your hand out in front of you and made a fist, the smoke would ooze between your fingers like slime. I was walking side by side with my friend Mary, at midday. We were taking our lunch break in the courtyard commons, on a wide patch of yellow grass, centered in the roofless middle of a squat brick building with four tunnels cutting through each wall, leading back to the factories and work zones. We walked along the patch of grass, and when we reached the end of one side we turned and walked back down to the other. We didn't have much to talk about and the smoke would have stifled us anyway. I breathed through my mouth and it tickled the sides of my tongue when I inhaled. Mary had her chin pitched up towards the sky. She took shallow breaths through her nose, and her eyes watered at the corners. Tiny droplets hung on the ends of her eyelashes, balancing there until she blinked. She scrunched her nose and smiled with her lips only, still looking up at whatever it was she saw, her black hair curling into loops where it met the slope of her shoulders. A white band crowned the top of her head, and she looked nice.

   The work buzzer rang out in the courtyard—a shrill, angry noise like geese make—and we returned to our posts. I went through the north tunnel to the metallics factory and Mary went through the east to the textile manufacturing plant. Smog masked the sun, but I knew it was half-past noon and that I wouldn't see her for another five hours, on the ten-minute walk back to our apartment building. Mary and I lived across the hall from each other, only she lived a few rooms to the right of mine, and we had walked home together for some time now. We worked in the same factory complex, only in different sectors, and I saw her two times a day. I'd have walked her to work as well, but leaving a full hour before she did each morning meant twice a day was it.

In the factory, I stood at the hydraulic press and did my work. Every twenty-odd seconds, when the aluminum sheets slid into position, I'd push a button and down the press would come, loud and slow, to lay into the metal and shape it into form. I never paid attention to the form, and I didn't know what any part got used for. It was just what I did. Eight hours a day, Monday through Saturday, the metal would slide down the belt into place and rest until I entered the required command, and the other workers would stand at their posts and work as I did. The smoke never grew too dense where I stood, but other parts of the factory had it bad. We called it young smoke, the fresh discharge from the machines and furnaces. It was light in color, nearly invisible under the dim overhead lamps, but when it collected in a mass the factory would grow so hazy that even the machine in front of you blurred out of vision. But usually you didn't see the young smoke. It snuck up on you, parted your lips, slid down your throat into the lungs, and you wouldn't know it if not for the coughing fit that followed. There was old smoke too, black as pitch and jetting out from the stacks lining the factory roof. Old smoke had distinct curves that coiled over and over into each other like bundles of snakes, but the young smoke was what assaulted us inside.

I walked Mary home that evening, passing through the south tunnel and out to the street that led to our apartment complex, which was brick like the factory courtyard building and cracked all over. When we got there we climbed the grey stone steps to its entrance, then turned around and headed back down the street toward the plants. This gave us more time to talk and since Mary had a story to tell that night it only made sense that I walk her home twice. Mary cocked her head to the side and spoke about some workplace incident. She was looking straight ahead and I watched her face, its profile sharpened by the streetlights lining the curb behind her. Her mouth danced and her cheeks bunched up when she smiled. An automobile sped by and we stepped off the road and into dirt that squelched under our feet as we walked, passing a young couple with their hands in each other's coat pockets and their bodies pressed close together. A breeze came and it lingered a while, the air bitter and cool, and Mary swayed like a dancer because she felt happy that night. She didn't say it but her swaying did. She twirled and bumped my shoulder and laughed with her head thrown back so that her chin met the sky. To our left lay a railway, and Mary climbed onto its rusted tracks, balancing herself with arms thrust up into the night. She turned around to face me and we looked at each other for a while. Beyond the lift of her arms and the gleam of her eyes, the soft, monotonous *click-clack* of a running train whispered out to us from the dark.

I said goodnight to Mary at her apartment door before heading to my room to sleep. I hung my coat, turned on the overhead light, and placed my shoes in front of the bed. Through a small window on the far wall, I could see the dim row of streetlights and railway below. I turned out the overhead light and looked again through the window. The skeleton of a train station stood back from the tracks, with long grassless hills rising and falling behind it. Beyond these the frame of a distant factory could, if you knew to look for it, be made out against the horizon. Smoke swam out of its stacks, painting grey streaks on the black sky. My eyes drifted back to the train station. The *click-clack* of the train had gotten louder. A little ways down the track, the orange glow of two oval signal lights announced its arrival.

     A knock sounded at the door. It was Mary, asking me to join her for tea. I put my shoes back on and followed her down the hall. She wore a blue silk nightgown that spilled over her body. I kept my gaze on the corner of the ceiling as we walked.

Mary's room was a little smaller than mine but otherwise much the same. She had the same table, the same bed frame, the same dresser and the same desk, only hers were in better shape. And where the window in my room offered a look out into the night, Mary's offered none, as a newer, taller apartment building put up only a couple of yards away had blocked any view she might have had. If you peered through you could see the just visible impression of the neighboring wall, but it was so dark out there you may as well have been looking into nothing.

     Mary pulled a second chair up to a small table, and we sat across from each other drinking the tea she had brewed before inviting me in. A gas lamp centered on the table gave the room what little light it could. Its flame flickered and blew Mary's shadow up on the wall, the slope of her shoulders and the curled ends of her hair enlarged in silhouette. My eyes wavered from the shadow to the corner of the ceiling, to Mary's eyes, and then to the collar of her robe. She wore a chain with a golden crucifix I hadn't seen before. We spoke some about work and about whether that train we had heard earlier ever actually went anywhere. *Nowhere exotic* was Mary's response. She thought that if you boarded the train and stayed on all day and night it would just loop around to other factories before circling back on our own. She couldn't imagine it leading anywhere different from here, but it had been a long time since either of us had taken it.

Mary went to get more tea. I looked over her room again and saw a wooden cross hanging on the wall to the right of the window. It reminded me of the matching pair my parents had hung up on either side of their bed at home. Mary filled my glass and sat back down. I thanked her. She smiled and toyed with her necklace. The wooden cross was perched on her shadow's shoulder like a hawk.

"How old are you again?" she asked.

"20," I said.

"You know I'm 24, right? You probably think I'm old, but really I feel like I could have gone through school with you. And you've got that stubble—I would've guessed you to be my age." She paused, smiling. "If you shaved that off, you'd have a baby face, huh?

"I wonder," I said, rubbing my thumb along the edge of my jaw. When I spoke the words came loudly.

Mary whispered something I couldn't make out. It was almost just breath. I leaned forward to catch what she would say next. "Have you ever been with a woman?"

The lamp's flame wavered like it would snap and vanish. Mary's eyes reflected what was left of its light and they sparkled as she looked at me, right at me, without blinking or glancing down. She stopped toying with the necklace and her hands went beneath the table. Her mouth was parted slightly so that her teeth showed, but she was not smiling. I lowered my gaze and shook my head no and when I looked up she was smiling again, her body hunched forward, the necklace swinging back and forth through the half-light in an arc. My skin felt hot and my eyes shot around the room looking for something that wasn't her, waiting for something to break the long, dry, half-lit silence.

A muffled train whistle sounded from outside. It must have been leaving the station. I looked past Mary at the cross on the wall and thought of my childhood home, the dark-roofed red-brick house tucked back away from the road with all the trees in the world behind it. And I was there. And I stood in the yard under the morning sun and noticed the way the trees clashed against the sky, the thick green ceiling of branches and leaves spread out overhead like drawings of the nervous system I had seen in books, and the sky just above it, as blue as any blue could be.

I heard Mary speak my name and left the memory almost as soon as I had entered it. "You went away for a second," she said. I felt calmer now and looked back into her eyes. She was crying softly, but there was no smoke in the room. And so I wondered if she had felt it too, felt that longing when the train whistled. There were times before when we had talked about leaving, but I don't think we were ever very serious. Sitting in our rooms or standing at work, closed off from the world and from the dark, we could each scratch out a life, and for some time that had been enough. I told Mary I had been thinking of home and about leaving here. Then I asked her where she'd go if that train could take her any place in the world. *Anywhere exotic*, she said, but I was thinking I'd have liked to go home, and if I had asked her again that night I think she would have agreed.

Mary stopped crying and we finished our second round of tea. I didn't press her about the crying or about the question she had asked me earlier. She stood, took my cup, and went to the sink to rinse it off. I wanted to follow her and hold her from behind and press my head into the crook of her neck, but I stayed seated, looking down at my hands. When she came back, she skirted around the edge of the table so that she stood close to me and rapped her knuckles on the wood. I felt myself being pressed into the back of my chair. She was moving her jaw from side to side and looking past me, through me. After a few seconds she gave her head a little shake like she had snapped out of something. Then she took my hand and asked me if I would pray with her.

Mary and I knelt in front of her bed with our elbows resting on top of the mattress. Side by side, we closed our eyes and bowed our heads. Mary suggested we start with a personal, silent prayer, but I didn't know what to ask for so I just tried to breathe very quietly. The room was so still that a single cough would have sounded like a dozen windows shattering all at once. I turned and saw Mary deep in her prayer, her hands clasped and her eyes like they'd been sewn shut. We had never talked religion much before, but I could tell that she lived it. In that moment, at least, she must have been up there with God.

Mary finished and turned to me. "I'm going to recite an act of contrition," she said. "You can follow along if you know it."

I didn't, but she started anyway, reciting the prayer in a tiny voice that cracked a few times as she spoke. Still there was something in it that I could feel all through my body as I knelt on the floor. I thought I must have loved her, and if she had tied me to the bed, doused me with oil, and burnt me alive right then I'd have welcomed it. When she finished, I reached out and pushed her hair back behind her ear with my fingers, but she pulled away. On the table, the light from the lamp was dying, causing Mary's face to darken. Then the flame went, and the room went black with it, and the faint lines of her profile vanished. I leaned in close to see her holding her necklace with both hands and mouthing something inaudible. A thin shaft of moonlight shone through the window behind her, filling the space between our building and the neighboring one. It gave off a soft glow, so that Mary's cross gleamed a little and her face reemerged from the darkness.

Later, we sat on the edge of her bed talking. Mary seemed in good spirits. She had relit the lamp, so I could see her smiling and rocking softly back and forth as she spoke. She wanted to tell me a story from the Old Testament, and said that David, who was a king, had looked out from his roof to see a beautiful young woman bathing. His servants brought her to him. She said that David had then sent the woman's father to die in battle in an attempt to cover up his adultery. *Down and down the rabbit hole.* Then Mary talked about her childhood and life back home. She told me that her mother was Catholic and her father a Methodist, that Methodism had won out in the home, and about how much she missed having a place to go to on Sundays. I didn't say anything. I just listened and nodded my head every so often and tried not to think about how it would feel to sleep with her. Then she asked me what I was going to do at work tomorrow, so I made something up—a story about two workers who were fighting over the same woman and were planning on boxing to see who most deserved her. I said I would bet on the shorter, fatter one who looked like he had been in more scraps. Mary listened like she really cared, eyes wide as she grabbed my arm and made me promise to tell her all about who won.

I stayed for a while longer, until the lamp's flame waned again, then went to the door with Mary to say goodnight to her for the second time that evening. She hugged me, and I pushed her hair back behind her ear again and kissed her on the cheek. Then she smiled and wished me a pleasant sleep, so I turned and walked back to my room. Her door creaked until it clicked into place. I entered my room, undressed, and went to sleep.

I dreamt that I was with Mary in her apartment again. We had been talking like before when a dark grey carpet of smoke seeped in from under the door and began to fill the room. Mary and I were separated, and I wandered through the haze searching for her. A long time passed before I found her, and when I did I held her close to me so we wouldn't lose each other anymore. Mary and I made love somewhere in the smoke, but it got so thick that I couldn't see any part of her, feeling only her warmth. I woke in a sweat. The sun had not yet risen, so I sat up in bed and thought of David spying out from his roof. After a while, sleep came once more and weighed down on me like lead until morning.

Mary didn't show up in the courtyard for lunch the next day. It had rained early and soon after a damp, smoky fog settled over the ground. When you walked it looked like you were stepping through storm clouds. It had grown cold with the rain and those who took lunch in the courtyard stood huddled together under the tunnel arches. I looked around for Mary and asked a friend of hers if she had seen her, but she hadn't come in for work that morning. I spent the rest of my break leaning against the wall of the southernmost tunnel, listening to the whine of passing automobiles. If I listened closely, I thought I could hear a distant train running over its tracks: *click-clack, click-clack, click-clack.* The sound seemed to be growing louder, getting closer, striking out at me and filling the tunnel up like water into a sinking ship. When I walked back into the open courtyard the sound was gone. The rain started up again, and the world lay quiet and still as the fog began to clear. I stood beneath an awning and thought of Mary until the work buzzer rang out, then joined the throng shuffling into the northern tunnel and returned to my post.

Walking home that evening, alone, I turned over in my head the idea of leaving on the train the next morning. The ground was muddy with rain but the air had warmed, and I walked and thought about it. When I got to my apartment building, not a single light was shining inside or out. I stepped into the lobby, peeked over and around the front desk, saw no one, and felt my way through the dark to the stairwell. As I climbed the stairs something began to churn inside me, a pit at the bottom of my stomach that spread quickly upwards, snaking towards my throat. I climbed faster, two steps at a time, until I reached my floor and my room, passing Mary's on the way. I fumbled with the keys at the door—it was dark here too—and went in. Sweat had soaked through my clothes, so I turned on the overhead light and undressed, rinsing my face with water from the sink. Breathing heavily, I hunched over the toilet bowl until the sick had gone. When I went back into the bedroom, its overhead light flickered a few times, then died, leaving me in the dark again. I lit a candle and a cigarette and cracked the window to let a breeze in. Outside, the streetlights lining the road had gone out too. Power outage, I figured.

I lay in bed a while, watching the flame dance on the nightstand. I wondered if Mary might be sick and in bed as I was, by candlelight. But this, I felt, was wrong. So I wondered about where she had gone and if she would ever come back, and I knew that she would not. Above me the ceiling glowed with shades of saffron and yellow ochre. Outside the room, beyond the reach of my candle, everything was black. No light, not even moonlight, leaked in from the window. My stomach ached and I turned on my side away from the candle. Its light threw my shadow onto the wall before me. A lumpy, ugly shape, nothing like Mary's. After some time spent lying there, a breeze, carried in through the still cracked window, blew out the candle and I fell slowly into a deep sleep.

The textile manufacturing plant went up in flames the next morning and in its burning filled the air with thick, acrid smoke. The workers evacuated the complex and watched from across the road as the fire raged. Not everyone had gotten out, they whispered, people were still inside. I moved through the crowd. People still inside, they murmured as I passed. The smoke would spread for miles and miles, they said. And it did. And the sky became as black as Mary's hair had been when I saw her last, not long ago.

Shanghai Film Festival

TWO DAYS AFTER I was back in Shanghai, Tristan texted me, "Come to my house. Nobody's home."

"Sure," I texted back.

His house was so far away from downtown that most Shanghainese wouldn't even consider it part of the city. Getting out of the subway station, the first thing I saw were the construction sites, yellow cab drivers idling around, non-taxi drivers alluring you with their twinkly eyes to get into their cars. Flea market by day, gangland by night.

Tristan greeted me at the front gate of a cookie-cutter house, identical to the cohort of houses in the same neighborhood. This time he was still wearing his white t-shirt and grey sweatpants. I didn't ask if he never changed or if he had tons of those.

It was one in the afternoon, but nobody called him to lunch. In fact, nobody called him at all. He was roaming the house with its dark corridors and hidden rooms, with the shiny porcelain and the hideous imitations of Renaissance paintings and the mahogany furniture and the inevitable piano. He was chewing gummy bears, but not eating or drinking, casting a cold eye on every object I just mentioned, as if nothing in this house belonged to him.

Now Tristan led me to the second floor, where his room was, and there he forced me to watch all three of the original Star Wars films.

I didn't take in much of it, as I was still jet-lagged. Tristan, on the other hand, was riveted, tirelessly taking notes and sketching his own private storyboard.

"Epic," he kept murmuring, "epic."

I dozed off periodically, until noises woke me up. I saw Tristan smiling, and he said, "Oops, my folks are back."

I rose from his desk and said, "Well, I should go."

Tristan shook his head. "Let me investigate the situation first. You stay here."

He snuck out and I started investigating his room. His desk was surprisingly neat: *Georgics* by Virgil, a copy of *The Prince*, apparently unopened, the biography of John Adams, with a bookmark placed halfway. On the right side of the desk was a huge box of tissues and several post-its, an ostentatious contract for translating a book on Roman history, with a deadline two weeks from that day. Facing his desk loomed a huge mirror. I wondered if he ever saw himself aging in that mirror. Behind the jalousie window was a rectangular balcony. Jalousie, jealousy.

I sank back into his chair. A moment later Tristan opened the door, smirking.

"My little sister is back from school," he said. "I didn't realize it's a holiday."

"So?"

"I'm afraid you'll have to stay."

"Why?"

"It is almost eleven. I will have to explain to my sister why a girl is coming out of my room at this hour."

"When will they leave again?"

Tristan didn't know, or rather, he decided not to come up with an answer.

We talked about his sister. Tristan was a bit sad that she didn't speak much Chinese. I learned that she was a half-sister, thirteen years younger, so I didn't ask more questions. I was born into a generation of only children, to whom the mere concept of siblings was a taboo. Whenever I met someone of a similar age who had a sibling, especially when that sibling was more than ten years younger, I had the irrational fear that something must had gone tragically wrong.

Tristan also sensed my embarrassment, and he said, "Let's talk about something else."

So we talked about films, books, ancient Greek. We talked about the problems we created for ourselves as if they were shared by humanity. We talked about our greatest fears. The fear of being no good. The fear of destroying our bodies for unworthy causes. The fear of never accomplishing anything. The fear of selling out. But above all the fear of being no good. I asked Tristan how his translation had been going. He showed me some fragments that amounted to roughly two thousand words, careful but few. From time to time I suggested again that perhaps I should go. Each time he said no.

The next thing I knew I was sitting in Tristan's bed on condition that I should not be wearing any clothes. I agreed on condition that he should not be wearing any clothes either. Tristan was very thin. Looking at his torso I thought of Jesus, and I couldn't help but share this moment of sacrilege with him. He looked at me, from head to toe, and commented that I looked like a Renaissance painting. "You mean I'm fat," I said. "No," he said, "I mean, what's the word, voluptuous."

Tristan said, "You just lie there, and I will take photos of you." I said sure. He got up to fetch my polaroid camera, while I chewed my hair. I said, "It's confidential, right?" I said it just for the sake of saying it. In fact I didn't mind a bit. My body was as worthless as my heart. Tristan was saying, "Lean over, the light is better from this angle." He made a gesture. He said, "Put your hand on your hair." I said sure. He said do this. I said sure. He said do that. I said sure. I felt at ease. I didn't want to say anything else.

A moment later I desperately needed a smoke. I said, "I am already indulging you by being naked. You should indulge my vice too." He agreed and followed me onto the balcony. I only had two cigarettes left. I smoked one after the other, and hid the polaroid photos in the empty cigarette box. Tristan, with his arms dancing, was pointing at the stars and rambling on and on about astrology. It was obvious that he didn't know a thing about the stars.

We then went back to bed and talked about films again, the films we had loved as teenagers, the films we had ceased to love but would not tolerate criticism from idiots, the films we'd love to make but would never have the money to do so.

"Look at us, two losers, talking about films in bed," I said.

"Yeah, instead we should be talking about stocks and real estate."

We fell asleep from time to time, and woke up and continued talking, until our words ran dry, until the birds were chirping, until I forgot so many names. At one point, Tristan asked, "You wanna fuck?"

"Alright, let's fuck."

And we fell asleep again.

When we woke again, he said, "I still think we should fuck. Don't you agree?"

"Too European, too cliché," I said, "A man and a woman, in the bed, smoking cigarettes, rambling on about life and philosophy, and then they fuck. Too boring."

"Then let's do something un-boring."

"Such as sleeping."

"Such as," he said, "you go sit on the toilet, and I shave you."

We both laughed, and he turned to look at me, very sincerely, "Just for the record, I really want to."

We heard voices downstairs. It was his sister's private tutor. The little girl was taking private lessons in drawing, in piano, in calligraphy. The tutor was telling the little girl about the history and the future of our mother planet, while Tristan and I were talking about the history and future of ourselves. More of history. Less of future.

Tristan let me wear one of his white t-shirts, and it was then I knew as a fact that he did change. It was almost one in the afternoon. His sister finally left, as Tristan once again went downstairs to investigate the situation. While he was gone I hid his shirt in my bag and decided to keep it as a form of punishment, so that one fine morning he would run out of things to wear. Many months later, when the revenge finally expired, I kept it as a souvenir.

I went downstairs, and the maid, pretending that it was all very natural, asked me if I wanted breakfast. Or lunch? I politely refused and said I had important business to attend to. Tristan gave out a small laugh behind me. He walked me to the door and on the way I could see him rehearsing his guilty face. We were at the front door, now the guilty face. "Hey, I'm such a jerk."

"Yes, you are."

"You probably won't want to see me again."

"Actually I think I will." I said as I jumped into a taxi hailed by the maid and immediately fell asleep in the backseat.

Tristan texted me, "Do you know that the huge portrait of Mao on Tiananmen Square was replaced every year? I kept thinking, where did the old ones go? Isn't it a bit Dorian Gray?"

"You can take a stab at it to find out," I suggested.

When he texted me I was waiting for him somewhere near Julu Road, which literally means "giant deer." The street used to be called Rue Ratard, named after the then-French Consul-General to Shanghai in the early twentieth century. Today it was home to the Writers' Association and numerous bars and restaurants with English names, English menus, and American waiters. Tristan was late, as usual, so I lit a cigarette. While waiting for him under a streetlight, a couple of guys approached me for light, in English. For a while I thought I was still in America. I didn't recognize this Shanghai. The Shanghai that I remembered: sycamore trees, dust in the spring air, wonton soup from the street vendors, still hot and bubbly, the smell of watermelon in every small alley during the monsoon season. It was only when the sycamore trees were gone that you started to remember they were once there.

I was still thinking about the non-existent sycamore trees when Tristan arrived.

The first thing Tristan said to me that day was, "Give me twenty."

"What?"

"I don't have money for parking," he said. "Quick."

I gave him a twenty.

I don't remember exactly what we did that day. I remembered going with him into a jazz bar. We read the menu, and decided to wait for someone to get us food and drinks. Tristan, in his white t-shirt and grey sweatpants, looked decidedly out of place in this dingy bar imitating the Gilded Age. He was smirking again and casually eyeing all the girls.

There was a guy standing near us, swaying to the terrible music. He was extremely good-looking, but he was wearing a Harvard shirt. I had to laugh.

The guy turned to look at me and said, "What?"

"You go to Harvard?"

"Yeah, business school."

I said I would be going to the law school. We exchanged a few polite words and numbers, a prelude to the kind of life I was signing myself up to. The guy got me a drink. He started to talk about real estate and stocks, and as he mentioned the name Tesla, Tristan jumped in. "I drive a Tesla."

"What?"

"Yeah," Tristan repeated very seriously, "I drive a Tesla."

"O-kay?"

The guy looked perplexed. In his Harvard shirt his perplexity was almost impudent. Within a few minutes he regained his usual grace and said, "Well, it was very nice meeting you," and returned to his table.

As he was walking away, Tristan rested his elbow on my shoulder. "Fuck, whenever I see successful people like that, I want to poke him."

"What do you mean, poke?"

"Just poke," he said. "Literally poke."

He poked me.

Soon we were bored, bored with the nostalgic music, the guys with their business cards and the girls in little black dresses and meticulous makeup. We walked out into the night. Tristan was talking about the film festival that was opening in a few days. We agreed that we should get a cheap hotel room within walking distance of the cinema. The kind of hotel with a neon sign half-blind and mosquito nets, right underneath the highway. "You're paying, of course." Tristan smiled as he patted on my shoulder.

When we reached the parking lot, he took out his car keys and the lights of a silver Tesla, model S, blinked.

"You must be kidding me," I said.

We got into the car.

"Unbelievable. You drive a Tesla."

"I just told you."

"I thought you were poking that guy, whatever that means."

Tristan leaned forward, so close that his hair was almost touching my face. "I take my words seriously. When I say poke, I poke, with my fingers. When I say I drive a Tesla, I drive a Tesla."

He started the car. "You know what your problem is? Your problem is that you think everything is a figure of speech."

We drove past shadows of a city. We drove past high-end boutiques, pale mannequins posing with pale mannerisms, ever-present construction sites, bright yellow helmets and bright yellow hammer jacks. At a stop light, we saw again the girls with their little black dresses and smart makeup standing by the streets. Perhaps they were a different group of girls from those we saw earlier. But to me they looked exactly the same. Tristan pointed at them and said, "Hey, let's pick up some random chicks and give them a ride home." I said sure. He smiled and rolled down the window. I was thinking, these girls are like my city, my beloved city with its neon lights and elegant avenues, but underneath it was completely hollowed. Tristan said, "But you know, these girls, when they start to talk, you would think to yourself, shut the fuck up." He started to drive like a drunk person, though he never drinks, not then, not now. He always got a glass of tap water in bars. When we reached my apartment, he gave me a book. His Latin textbook. He had used it for seven years. I leafed through it and saw only light pencil marks. I imagined Tristan, an eighteen-year-old, jotting down these notes while daydreaming in his mid-west college town. He begged me to take good care of it.

That summer we booked a small hotel room for a week near the biggest cinema in town. I checked in early, lying in bed, waiting for the air conditioning to start working properly, waiting for Tristan. My favorite white dress was crumpled under my graceless weight and I didn't move. Little droplets of sweat seeped out of each of my pores and I didn't move. I had failed Tristan, I thought. I had failed to give him his half-blind neon signs and mosquito nets, and I was ashamed.

When he came in he was not disappointed, or he hid his disappointment. He sat down beside me and began to tell me a tale of love and darkness.

The first film we saw at the film festival was *Caravaggio* by Derek Jarman. Back to our hotel room, we talked about money, not art, not youthful dreams, not ambitions or betrayals. After seeing *Caravaggio*, we talked about money. Tristan was squatting in a swivel chair while I stood facing the only window. I asked Tristan, "What about your Tesla, you privileged little prick?" Tristan laughed and said he was just a driver for his sister. He got his license so he could drive his sister around. He said this in such a tone as if he was reading from a legislative record.

It was a rainy day and everything was a bit wet, like memories.

I mentioned that I had many rich friends. If I had gained anything from college it was my rich friends. I was hoping that they would settle down in New York, invest in an apartment, and invite me to live with them. I would iron their shirts, look after their kids, cook and clean, and read all their books that would otherwise only serve decorative purposes. I said this jokingly, but Tristan seemed thoughtful.

After a long pause, he said, "I always have this feeling that I'm living in an eighteenth- or nineteenth-century aristocratic family. I'm about the same age as the son, so we read together, hunt together, get girls together. Everyone in the family praises us equally. They talk about a splendid future. They talk about all the great things we are going to do. They even send me to the best schools, where I learn a couple of useless dead languages and pride myself on being cultured. It's only much later that it will occur to me that I'm but the son of the stableman."

He was saying this half-laughingly, then he stood up in his swivel chair and looked me in the eye:

"Fuck, I'm the son of the stableman!"

He then said, "I did all the right things, and in the end I'm still the son of the stableman!"

I couldn't remember what I said in response. I probably didn't say anything.

We had a three-hour break before our next film, so we wasted time on social media. I saw that an old friend of ours was graduating from the best university in the city—all her posts speaking of splendid futures and the great things she was going to do. I told Tristan about it.

"Great," Tristan said, "let's crash their commencement."

I laughed. "I didn't even go to mine."

"Me neither. I graduated with nothing but shame," Tristan said, "but I love seeing others graduate, people who are better than me."

"You are joking."

"I'm very serious." He turned to me, looking very serious.

We were already walking out of the hotel when he said this. A brief moment later, Tristan began telling me that these elite universities in China today were all total garbage. He asked me if I ever heard of St. John's.

"The St. John's College in Santa Fe?" I asked as we got into a cab.

He shook his head. "No. The defunct St. John's University in Shanghai. It used to be crème de la crème." Tristan made an arguably vulgar gesture and continued, "Everyone there was fluent in English and reading classics. I. M. Pei, Lin Yutang, Zhou Youguang, they all went there."

Tristan looked straight ahead. It was mid-summer, and the cold wind from the air conditioning pierced into my abdomen like a needle, as

I felt it patiently sewing up the unspeakable. Our cab was now squeezing itself into the little streets of the French Concession. Two of these little streets, in parallel, were once called Rue Corneille and Rue Molière. Today they were named after other cities in China. A morbidly self-referential country.

"What happened to St. John's?"

"It was gone," Tristan said, "it was gone, gone, gone, when our Communists started imitating the Soviets in 1952. All those former elite colleges, the best ones, founded by missionaries, were broken up and incorporated into the trashy state universities."

"I didn't know that," I said.

"All we have today is garbage," he said, "and that's the best they can do. We are all going through garbage for a little bit of nutrition. You have to remember this."

We reached the auditorium, just when the black ties and pastel gowns were lining up in circles ready for their faceless procession, the hope of my country waiting for permission. We spotted our friend in the crowd, dazzling the room. She was wearing a little black dress. She insisted that we take several photos together in the lobby, a lobby so bright that it felt like an operating theater. I was wearing white, and in the photos Tristan never once opened his eyes. A minute later our friend was taken away from us by her more immediate friends, by determined hands that would soon write down "live long and prosper," and "I wish that all your roads are straight, and all your tunnels leading towards light" on some huge board.

Tristan and I were left standing there at the entrance of the auditorium. It was in fact a huge soccer stadium, not an auditorium, so we were several hundred feet higher than the central stage. Directly in front of us was the red carpet, flowing down the stairs, down and down, until it reached the center of everything. To get to the center you'd have to continue going lower and lower, and to never look back. If you look back you'll either turn into pillars of salt or lose your sacrificial lover to the underworld. Either way it would be the beginning of an eternal existential question. At the center, in the blinding spotlight, were two student hosts crying things into their microphones, things like the beginning of *The Tale of Two Cities*. Tristan yawned, or he clapped. Either way it was all very sincere.

"I see the best minds of our generation destroyed by madness."
Tristan yawned again. "Weird. I never liked Ginsberg." He then
contemplated the signing board, picked up the marker, and wrote in the
very middle, stroke by stroke, very carefully, "Je suis poo-poo."

The second film we saw was really bad. An experimental work by a
young artist. I found it ridiculous. Tristan must have thought it kitsch.
After ten minutes he fell under his seat, literally. At first I thought he
left. As I looked around I realized he was hiding under his seat, face in
palms, like that famous Edvard Munch painting. I knew that if he started
screaming at that moment it would be really bad. In order to preempt
that, I lowered my head and offered my sincerest apologies, I apologize
for all the things that burn your eyes, Tristan, I apologize for all the
phony things that should not have existed, I apologize for my mediocrity
and that of others, I apologize for the ghosts and zombies you see
each day in the streets, I apologize for the daily humiliation you have to
endure worse than the two Great Wars and the starvation in between, I
apologize for history books without history, I apologize for those who
never apologize, I apologize for everything, really, until it was over, and
we rushed out.

The third film we saw was *Fight Club* by David Fincher. Walking out
of the cinema, I could tell that Tristan was in a better mood. We were
walking in the alley, three in the morning, and the streetlights above
flickered exactly thirteen times. Tristan finally spoke, as the first raindrop
of this summer fell into my eyes. He gave me this imagery of a night,
many years before I even went to college. That was a year when he was
really bad. Well, it was not particularly worse than the other years, but
still he went to Hangzhou to see a friend. He arrived at night. The friend
picked him up at the train station. They walked to the bus stop. Nobody
was lining up. They didn't have much to say, so they read out loud some
slogans. There was nobody else on the bus, and still they didn't have
much to say, so they read a couple of road signs and store names. At
night, Tristan was lying down in a hotel room, next to his friend's room.
It was a hotel with a half-blind neon sign, under the highway. He couldn't
sleep, so he started reading *Henry V*. We few, we happy few, we band
of brothers! He remembered that hotel room to the minutest details:

curtains, mosquito nets, fluorescent yellow lights, the scent of Florida water (I interrupted him, cut the details. He said, that's how I remember things.) He was thirsty the entire night. He went around the room to find water. There was not a single drop of water in the entire room. A while later he got up and looked again. Not a single drop. He was thirsty. His friend was crying in the other room, the entire night. He stood by the door for a while, knocked, hey, are you alright? The friend said, yeah, sorry. And then there was no sound. He said, okay. He stood by the doorframe. A while later, it was day. Both of them knew that they didn't have the right to feel sorry for themselves.

The fourth film we saw was Martin Scorsese's *Silence*. A guy sitting next to us started crying halfway through the film. Not crying, he was *sobbing*, so resolutely sad. Tristan glanced at him now and then. At one point Tristan mentioned the chapter of *The Grand Inquisitor*, but otherwise he was rather silent.

We started moving towards the exit, away from the man, still sobbing, and Tristan asked, "Do you know the last emperor of the Ming Dynasty was Catholic?"

"Really?"

He pulled out an article that he apparently saved on his phone:

"When the rebels were capturing northern China and the Dynasty was collapsing, the Portuguese sent out hundreds of men with their cannons, and helped the Emperor retrieve some lost territories. As a show of gratitude, the entire royal family converted to Catholicism.

"They all had Christian names. For instance, the Emperor's son became Crown Prince Constantine Zhu. This Constantine Zhu, now his name was chosen by the Emperor himself, as homage to Constantine the Great. Perhaps the Emperor was aspiring to the Roman Empire. I don't know. But this Prince Constantine Zhu only lived to the age of fourteen, when he was killed along with his father in the streets of Kunming by the rebels.

"Soon afterwards, the entire royal family was basically in exile. The Empress, now a devout Catholic, decided to dispatch a missionary named Chen An'de to Rome for assistance from the Pope.

"Now let me tell you about this Mr. Chen. He was probably the first diplomat to ever reach Rome, accompanied by a Polish missionary.

God knows what they went through to finally have a meeting with the Pope, Innocent X. But the Pope was suspicious about their claim of authority, and more importantly, the Pope really didn't like the French. Now that's a problem. You see, Chen and his Polish companion were able to get to Rome largely due to the help of a French diplomat. The Pope was unhappy, which might explain why nothing came out of the many meetings behind doors. Chen waited in Rome for three years. He was still waiting when Innocent X died, and Alexander VII became the Pope. Alexander VII was a bit better than his predecessor, but only a bit better. He wrote a letter showing some vague gesture of support, but did not say anything about men or weapons.

"But our Mr. Chen was a smart cookie. He knew that the Pope's words had weight. He traveled around in Europe, with the Pope's letter in hand, and finally managed to get the promise of military assistance from the King of Portugal.

"Chen tried to go back to China with the Polish missionary, but when they reached Siam, the Portuguese authority in Macau refused to let them in, because they didn't want to ruin their relationship with the new Dynasty, the Qing Dynasty. Chen and the Polish missionary had to skirt around to Annam, today's Viet Nam, and there they were lingering along the border and couldn't enter China. It was around that time that Chen first heard that the royal family had been exiled to Myanmar. The Polish missionary died a year later, with only Chen by his side. Chen buried him, and carried the very few letters, the only belongings he had, and embarked again on his journey to find the royal family. And then nothing further was ever known of him, and he disappeared in the so-called river of history."

I read through the story, as we were now standing in the scorching sun, as we forgot that we still had another screening lined up, as we forgot so many other things.

I asked him, "So, why do you keep this thing on your phone?"

"Don't you think it's sad?" Tristan said. "The three years in Rome. Their lingering at the border. Their precious, useless letters."

"Yeah," I said, "you just love those stories of the last emperors and their faithful followers."

"It's not necessarily the setting of the story, but…"

"The forgotten, the misunderstood, those who died in strange places…"

"... and those who have the wrong names," he said.

"I like your name," I said, "your Chinese name."

Tristan's name—his Chinese name—was taken from a dethroned king, today only remembered for the poetry he wrote while waiting for the order of execution from the new rulers. The other part of his name is a character which means "coldness." A dethroned emperor. Some cold poems. Such a befitting name.

"Oh," said Tristan the Cold, "but I don't like my last name."

"Why?"

"It means money, right?"

At the time we were standing at the gate of one of those Shikumen neighborhoods, with high brick walls and delicate houses abutting each other, all arranged along narrow alleys that we call "longtang," cemented balconies with pots of gardenia, grape vines meandering from one stone gate to another, and tiled roofs with traces left behind by pigeons who rose early. I wondered who still lived in those houses. Tristan lived in such a neighborhood as a kid, before the age of cellphones. I never did. The Old Shanghai. He sometimes talked about that Shanghai in vignettes, like someone talking about a victory that does not belong to him, or a love that is doomed to fail. The Shanghai I never knew.

The cinema for our fifth and sixth films, a double feature of *North by Northwest* and *Some Like It Hot*, was in a shopping mall. Before the films started we stood on the highest floor of the shopping mall, leaning over the railings. An extremely long escalator was transporting people from the ground floor to where we were. Next to where we stood was a little bookshop, the kind that called itself Sisyphus or Cervantes for no apparent reason.

Tristan said he finally found a job. He would start helping high school kids with their college applications to American universities. His job was to help these eighteen-year-olds tell their life story in the most promising light, so that one day, they would be able to stand in a shopping mall in Shanghai and speak English.

"Very nice," I said.

He asked about my future. "Well, I would be working at a law firm in New York for a few years, waiting for my green card. And then I would do whatever I want."

  "You will surely forget what you want while making all that money," said Tristan.

  "Perhaps," I said.

Between *Bonne and Clyde* and *Bambi* we wandered near the outskirts of town. An endlessly scorching summer afternoon. Tristan said he was thirsty, but neither of us had any money. As we were searching through our pockets, dark clouds started brewing overhead, soon to be followed by heavy rain. At first we feigned composure. We strolled leisurely, still bantering, while raindrops as big as pigeon poop were hitting my eyelashes and it was then Tristan asked me, "Why the fuck are you crying?" And I said, "Why the fuck did you not bring an umbrella?" At this point all I could see were the hazy truck horns rushing into my face. Tristan was a few steps ahead of me and I witnessed his hair slowly drenched by the clouds. Then I saw Tristan making some grand gesture of preparation, and the next second, one leg stretched out forward, he started to run. I felt betrayed. He burst out laughing. So obnoxious. I wished he'd fall, but at the same time I was so afraid that he would fall. So I ran after him, thinking that I should be able to catch him if he fell, not knowing that it was something I would do again and again.

  Tristan stopped abruptly. I couldn't tell if he was hesitating or simply tired. Then he walked into a store, a little barbershop/video games shop. I followed him and watched with amazement as Tristan started talking to the owner in a casual way, as if they had known each other for a really long time. Tristan, sitting in a wooden chair in the video games area, hands on his knees, suddenly looked very young, even younger than when I first met him, while the owner, a middle-aged, good-humored man in a white tank, was looking at him in such a way as if he were his prodigal son. As the owner turned back into the inner room, Tristan told me that he was here a lot as a teenager, those afternoons when he skipped school.

  The owner brought us two sodas.

  We were watching the rain. I fiddled with the straw, which now was soggy and superfluous after having served its purpose. For a while neither of us made a sound, as if we were waiting for the rain to stop. But it was hopeless, I thought.

  Tristan finally said, "You know, if I'm writing a novel, I would describe this moment as 'and then neither of them had anything to say.'"

"Which is true," I said.

"I'm just remembering," Tristan said, "when I was younger, walking with my dad, usually we didn't say much. I just followed him. I never opened my mouth. Neither did he. He was always brooding. You know, today it is rare that I keep my mouth shut when I'm with others, especially when we are walking. But sometimes, like now, it feels like if I open my mouth I will break something."

"I think I understand."

"So once, I was with my dad, both of us silent again. Perhaps he was taking me to my mom's place. I don't remember. My dad and I were standing on the street, silent. Then my mom appeared, in her pajamas. I don't know why. But I was so disappointed. I can still recall that disappointment to this day. I don't know why. Perhaps simply because she was wearing pajamas."

"Ah."

"But why was I disappointed? It was not her fault she was wearing pajamas. It's absolutely normal."

"Yeah it wasn't her fault."

"Too petty," he said, "things like these."

"And?"

"Nothing. Just, silence makes me sad. Anything that makes me feel I'm becoming my dad makes me sad. And it's not worth writing about."

We walked back to the hotel, collected our things, which took less than ten minutes, and proceeded to check out. We walked into the silent summer, striding in ashes of freedom. This night I saw pale fire on his face, and Tristan said, "I miss the Lincoln Center."

He started talking about a trip to New York he was planning, a crusade of retrieving something he had lost along the way. To put it less poetically, he had to go back one more time in order to ship back several boxes of relics he had left behind. At first it was just administrative, but as he started repeating to himself, "Well, I have to go back to America, I have to, I need to go back to America," the trip took on an almost mythical quality. The things he sealed in those three paper boxes were being sucked into some black hole named time, though Tristan could no longer remember what they were.

Tristan was saying, "Fuck, these films, for these films we booked a hotel, we actually booked a hotel room and we got up early to get the tickets and we rushed to and fro in the city. So undignified, running like we did earlier as if it were the end of the world. I'm not a fucking war journalist."

"Yeah. In New York we'd have Film Forum, we'd have Lincoln Center and Anthology and BAM. Even Quad and Angelika are much better than anything here."

"My only dream now is to open an adult shop in New York," Tristan said, "and use all the money for film tickets."

"Great. Then my only dream is for you to be in New York."

"Make money," he said. "I will count on you."

We were reaching the crossroads where I would take the bus, and Tristan would go on to the subway station. I stopped and looked at him. It always took him longer to say goodbye than what was socially acceptable. Each time, as we were parting, I could really see him making honorable efforts, though reluctantly, to peel something off, piece by piece, from his body. By the end of it, he would look like a lost object, not expecting to ever be found again.

I never remembered how Tristan handled the necessary goodbyes—usually it was a series of ill-defined expletives coupled with soul-searching questions such as "we are aiming for literature, right?"— but this time, I remembered him laughing and turning, waving once, with his fingers still holding the punched ticket.

That marked the end of my film festival.

The day before my flight back to America, Tristan texted me and said he wanted to jump off the building. I asked him where he was. He gave me the address of a cinema. It was not very far from where I was, but I ran all the way. When I saw him, he was standing by a camphor tree, the newcomer that had long replaced the sycamore. I saw him drifting in the wind, only for a few seconds, but that ghostly imagery stayed with me. I hugged him.

He told me that it was the intermission of *World on A Wire*. He asked me if I wanted to join him. I said I had to pack.

"The film festival is coming to an end," Tristan said.

"Yeah."

"Truly happy days like these are so luxurious."

"Yeah."

"If only I could just talk shit about people in different cinemas with you every day," Tristan said.

"All those sentences starting with 'if only' are all very luxurious."

"It shouldn't be that way."

"Yeah."

I asked him, "Is it only the film festival, or is there something else?"

"You're leaving," he said.

"You mean now, or for America?"

"Both."

We were silent for about five minutes.

"I don't know." Tristan laughed. "I don't know, maybe I'm just having so much fun messing around with you, and it triggers the defense mechanism."

"Fuck. I know exactly what you mean."

"Yeah, you said the same thing."

"Did I? How did I phrase it?"

"Oh. I was asking you why you'd never tell the other person when it hurts. And you said you don't deserve not hurting."

"Right, now I remember."

We were looking in the same direction. I saw camphor trees waving their leaves like drunkards. I did not know what Tristan saw.

"But, what are we protecting ourselves against, do you know that?" I asked him.

"Just the aftereffects of always being told, since a young age, that 'you will never get the best out of life.'"

"Ah."

"I'll say, it's not that we are afraid of pleasure. We are afraid of being happy."

"And we thought we were rushing towards some form of freedom when we left this country. And only later on did we realize that we were again being colonized, kneeling under the western gaze, speaking English, quoting the western canon."

"Now don't be dramatic," he said.

The film was about to start again. I walked back with him into the cinema. Placing the film ticket behind his ear, Tristan said, smiling, "I want to tell you a secret. A real secret."

"Yes?"

"It's very simple. Just one sentence."

We were in the lobby now, surrounded by scents of popcorn and colognes. I was still waiting for Tristan to say it. I could feel something thumping in my chest, like a group of marchers solemnly stepping on marble. I whispered to them, "Be quiet, be quiet, I'm trying to hear the secret."

In the end Tristan didn't say anything. He just kept smiling to himself. I dreamily followed him into the elevator. To this day I still can't figure out what Tristan was trying to say at that moment. Somehow I believed it touched the kernel of his being, or the ultimate theory of ourselves. But it was perhaps just my wishful thinking.

I said, "Tristan." He said, "Yes."

We were face to face with each other, in a small elevator. Some years later Tristan would tell me, "I used to think that the elevator is a bad touch. Now I kinda like the elevator." I asked him why. He said, "Because the elevator never waits."

We were in the elevator, looking at each other, and he nodded, once.

ZOEY BIRDSONG

Nails

WE SIT IN A CIRCLE of seven folding chairs in the middle of
Chestnut Park. I am the only one not wearing gloves, even though it isn't
cold. Parents whistle as children play soccer in the background. A couple
makes out on a picnic blanket six feet behind us. I am here because
Barney didn't want to come alone.

"I think we can get started," says the group's leader. "Looks like
everyone that's gonna be here is here."

He's got a mullet and a mustache and an overly large red t-shirt.

"Since we have some new folks, I think we should all go round
and introduce ourselves. My name is Chris, I run the meetings. I can
assure you that you're in good hands."

Nobody laughs. The silence is long.

"I can go first. I'm Marion, and I started picking over thirty years
ago. I'm part of this group because I'm trying to get closer with God,
you see, and nail-picking is another one of those temptations the pastor
says we ought to root out of our lives. Plus, it's just so bad for my skin."
She's waxy pale. Her gloves have rhinestones on them.

"Thank you, Marion. We appreciate you being here," says Leader
Chris.

Introductions continue clockwise. The next man's hair sticks
straight out of the top of his head. I can see a tattoo peeking up out of
his crewneck. He looks like he could teach me a few things about prison.

"I'm Grant," he says, "I picked for the ASMR content at first.
The scratching and the ripping, you know. But then I noticed that I
was doing it outside of the office, while watching TV, during intimate
time with my wife. And then, before I knew it, I was picking at the skin
around the nails, and then at my toes, and we all know what a bloody
catastrophe that can be. I'm here to mitigate the damage."

"Thank you, Grant. We're here to support you."

One woman plans to have the world's largest collection of hangnails. She's almost halfway to meeting the previous record, set by a Croatian monk. The man next to her, the last to speak, says he once thought he needed the nails to feed to his pet lizard, who is now dead. Everyone in the group expresses a strong desire to quit picking, despite their apparent passion for the sport. It makes me thankful for how normal I am, despite how I might feel sometimes.

"What about you boys?" asks Leader Chris.

"I'm Barney. I'm here because my mom says I have a problem, and uh yeah, I can kinda see where she's coming from. So I'm here to just get started, I guess."

Barney knows this is an understatement.

"Thank you, Barney. We admire your courage. And you, son?"

"Oh," I say, "My name is Todd, and I pick." I'm comfortable lying, especially if it helps me blend in. I slide my hands under my thighs.

"And?" Leader Chris gestures for me to continue.

"That's about it."

"Thank you, Todd."

We sit on the plastic-covered floral couch in Barney's living room, eating carrot sticks and drinking whole milk. His mother, Carol, has not redecorated since she inherited the place over forty years ago, in 1979. She says she doesn't need anything new when the things she has work fine.

My mother and Carol met in birthing class. They took to each other quickly and were certain we would too. Barney and I went to the same daycare, the same elementary and middle schools, and now we go to the same high school. We're not besties, but we're solid. I'm larger and smarter than him and I'm allowed to drive. I've always felt a duty to protect him that I can't quite explain.

Carol protects me, I suppose. Ever since my mother's accident, she's always made sure to make herself available as a mother figure. My father works nights at the hospital and doesn't have time to cook like Carol does, and I'm not sure if he knows how much I go to her house.

Carol pops her head out of the kitchen. "I'm eager to hear about the meeting but give me a couple minutes to get these puppies out of the oven."

She's making her signature pigs in a blanket to thank me for accompanying Barney, even though I said it was no trouble at all and that I was trying out vegetarianism, neither of which is true.

We stare at the wood-paneled walls and half watch Jeopardy. Carol has a strict no-cell-phones-downstairs rule. Her sage incense makes my throat tighten. There's some burning in every corner of the house. Barney still wears his gloves, which Leader Chris calls "PunishMitts." Beginners wear lightweight, knit PunishMitts while they adjust to the decrease in dexterity.

She emerges with two plates and one fork for Barney, so he doesn't accidentally ingest any of his glove fuzz. She sits in the armchair that matches the couch.

"Make sure to blow on those first."

There are a lot of awkward silences at Carol's house.

"So?" She leans forward. "How was it?"

"I thought it was helpful," says Barney. "All the people seem to care a lot, and seem really dedicated."

"Yeah," I say, "it seemed like a nice community." Carol is easy to lie to.

"Oh, baby. I am so happy to hear that. Marion told me it changed her life."

"You know Marion?" I ask. Carol never really talks to anyone except her son.

"She's in my water aerobics class. That's how I learned about the group. She was just *raving* about it, and then I thought of my Barney. He's had that obnoxious habit for years, and I'd always been trying to get him to cut it out."

Barney leans over the side of the couch, fishes through his backpack, and hands the handbook to Carol. It's thick, bound with a wire spiral. Mine is still on the floor of my car.

"Wow, they've really got a plan for everything," she says while flipping through it.

"Yeah, Chris came up with it all himself," says Barney.

Carol reads through the table of contents, "New Member Guidelines, Meeting Structure, The Seven Steps, Norms and Expectations, Glove Tiers and Rules, Group Traditions, Personal Journaling Recommendations, Emergency Relapse Protocol."

"The only thing is," says Barney, "the membership fee is two hundred dollars, and I don't know if we can afford—"

"Don't be silly. I've got quite a bit saved in the cookie jar." She means this literally.

"Thanks, Mom." Barney smiles.

Carol sits beside her son on the couch and hugs him.

"It is just so reassuring to know that you're not alone in this, and that there are people out there who are ready to help you."

"Yeah, it is," he says. Unbelievable.

"What about you, Todd? Will you join?" Carol looks at me, still embracing Barney.

"Well, I don't really pick, so I don't know, probably not. I just came today to make sure Barney got started okay."

"Oh." She's disappointed. "Right. Of course. Thank you, Todd."

Carol sends me home with my Jell-O in a plastic tub. She tells me I'll get a tummy ache if I eat it too soon after dinner.

Barney's glove wearing becomes the talk of the school within days. Some people say he has hand lice, some say he was crucified, and others guess what unfortunate tattoo he must be hiding. I'm afraid people will find out that I was initially involved. I choose different seats in Biology and French, our shared classes. I redirect when I see him in the hallway.

The thing is, Barney starts avoiding me too. He knows what people are saying about him, my friends included. He knows that I'm participating in the banter to save my own ass. Carol asks me to stop giving him rides and starts doing it herself. On Tuesdays and Thursdays, she pulls him out early for meetings, and then it starts happening on Mondays after a while.

Carol calls my father, asks what happened, says that Barney is upset. My father says he doesn't know. They both offer inaccurate guesses, thinking we can't hear. My father lectures me about how important it is to include Barney. He says he doesn't know what's gotten into me. This happens several times.

And I feel bad about it, I do. All of this starts to make me realize how much I value Barney. He's annoying and loud, but it feels quiet without him. I consider letting up and reintegrating myself with Barney, but I'm only a sophomore and I can't afford to lose the little social credibility I have. I wouldn't be able to withstand the mocking and torment. He's stronger than I am.

Things are beginning to return to normal when I see Leader Chris at the grocery store. He stands pensive in front of the canned ravioli.

I turn my cart around and try to dart in the other direction.

"Todd?" I hear.

Shit. I look over my shoulder. I should have kept going.

"Todd."

He parks his cart next to mine and gives me a non-consensual hug. He smells like Taco Bell and incense.

"Hi, Chris."

"Long time no see, son."

"Yeah, I'm just doing some grocery shopping for my mom. She's, uh, waiting for the pasta sauce, so I have to get back." Which I guess isn't technically a lie, if it's true that loved ones wait for you in the afterlife.

He hooks a couple of fingers onto my cart so I can't pull away. He's wearing heavy-duty ski gloves, indicative of a relapse.

"Can I ask you a question, son?"

"Uh, sure." I make a show of looking at the time on my phone.

"What's your *pickin' situation* been these days?"

"I don't pick," I said, "I was just there to support Barney."

"But you told us all that you were a picker."

"That was a lie."

Leader Chris shakes his head. "That may have been what it was to you, but you don't know what's underneath."

"What?"

"Has anything been bothering you lately, son?"

"No, I'm—I'm fine," I say, looking around me.

"See, you're still thinking of pickin' as a literal thing, which it certainly can be," he says while glancing at his gloves, "but we also like to think about the pickin' you can't see."

Manager to aisle three. Manager to aisle three.

"Anyway," he says, unhooking his puffy fingers from my cart, "I'm having a little get-together for the group on Saturday afternoon."

"I have practice."

"Oh, well that's a shame. I know it'd mean a lot to us—Barney especially—if you came, but that's fine."

I pull my cart away before he can say anything else and do the fastest self-checkout job I've ever done.

Barney calls me late that night as I'm finishing my geometry homework in bed. I know it's him when I hear the phone ring–he's the only friend I have that doesn't text. I put the phone on speaker so I can continue working on my equilateral.

"Hi Chris–Todd, I mean Todd–Hi Todd."

"Barney."

"Yes, man. It's Barney," he says. He's never called me "man" before.

"Is everything okay?"

"Todd, I have a favor to ask."

"Shoot," I say. My ruler slips out of place.

"Chris is having this casual thing at his apartment on Saturday afternoon."

"Is he?"

"Yeah, it's just like a thing for group members and our supporters. And since you're my biggest supporter, we thought–"

"Saturday afternoon? I have practice," I say.

"Did you get on a sports team?"

"No, I'm, uh, picking up violin again."

"Oh," he says, "That's really great."

Silence.

"Do you think you could practice another time?"

"No, I don't think so, my teacher has a crazy tight schedule."

I hear scuffling on Barney's end of the line. It sounds like he dropped the phone and is fishing for it under the couch. I hear voices that aren't his.

"Hi baby, it's Carol, hold on a second."

She takes the phone into the bathroom. I hear her close the door and turn on the shower.

"Baby, listen," she starts, "can you hear me?"

"Yes."

"This party at Chris' is more important than it sounds."

"Mhm."

"A big step in Barney's healing is maintaining a network of support, which you know from the handbook. It's vital that Barney knows he has people he can rely on, and if you aren't able to make it, then that might make healing a lot harder."

"I really—"

"And, honestly, he's just so fragile. We're afraid he might, you know, regress."

"Carol, I don't know if this group is…" I trail off. I don't know what word to use.

"Please."

"I'll think about it," I say, and hang up the phone.

I stare at the ceiling fan. The chassis wobbles as the blades spin. That thing is going to crash down onto my bed one day.

Leader Chris' apartment complex is made up of several three-story buildings connected by well kept paths and landscaping. Children play on the jungle gym in the common area.

I find building E, climb the outdoor stairs to the third floor, and stand in front of the only door. I listen at the door but hear only silence. I knock and Chris answers the door too quickly.

"Come in, come in."

Everyone from the meeting is there, deep in conversation with one another even though the room was silent when I listened through the door. They sip something red and sticky from plastic cups. Grant says something and Marion emits a laugh only dogs can hear. She plants her gloved hand on his beefy bicep.

All the shades are drawn, but Leader Chris has a candle on every surface. The furniture is pushed up against the walls and the carpeted expanse looks freshly vacuumed. A satin-covered hammer sits in the middle of the room. The curved television screen shows static.

Barney runs over and hugs me.

"Todd, I am so glad you came."

I see Carol over his shoulder. Leader Chris has his arm around her like he's Danny Zuko in *Grease*. They exchange a quick, toungey kiss. She wears gloves now, too. I pull away from Barney.

"Can I get you a drink?" he asks.

"No," I say, "I mean, no thank you, maybe later."

"Come here," he says, "Grant's telling this incredible story."

I follow Barney across the room and exchange rote greetings.

Leader Chris walks into the living room ringing a cowbell, one I remember from Carol's house. The group arranges itself cross-legged in a circle around the hammer.

"Welcome all," says Leader Chris in an unfamiliar mellow voice. "Let's begin by taking a deep breath together, inhabiting this space as a collective entity."

Everyone closes their eyes and inhales, synchronized.

"We extend a special welcome to our guest of honor, Todd," he says.

They stretch their gloved fingers towards me. Leader Chris hums a low note and everyone else matches it.

"We are here together as one, amidst the excess and chaos. As one, we inhale. We exhale. One being. One heart."

The group chants: "*Et nos unum sumus. Extra strages sumus. Ut unum agimus et amamus.*" Their voices get louder every time.

I can feel my heart beating. I am dizzy. My feet fall asleep.

"I have to go," I say, "Sorry."

"We're sad to hear that, Todd," he says, "But we certainly understand."

Something within keeps me stuck to the carpet.

"I can't–"

Laughter. "We understand the feeling."

"We *pickers*. We harbor the compulsion to pick away at the excess–our nails, our skin. We scratch. We rip. These motions become us. We destroy ourselves."

They hum again, faces pointed upwards.

"But what else do we pick at? What else beyond flesh?"

I see my mother sitting in the circle next to Leader Chris, but she's gone the next second.

Leader Chris makes eye contact with me. "The worst part is what we can't see."

"How do we take back what we have been picking away?"

They remove their gloves and extend their hands, palms facing out. Their wounds match: nail-sized holes in the center of each of their palms. They rotate their wrists. The wounds follow through to the backs of their hands. The gashes have healed and scabbed over, except for Barney's and Carol's. Theirs are fresh.

Memory fails me. I must have run away. I must have gone to the police and they must have taken me to the hospital. Maybe somebody saw me running down the street with blood dripping from my left hand. I must have escaped before they nailed the right. It's an optimistic theory but it's the one I'm going with.

In the hospital, people ask me lots of questions. I know they're speaking English, but it doesn't feel like it. I give a television interview, drugged up and incoherent. I hold my bandaged paw up to the camera.

I'm back at school now. Some people are afraid of me; they saw me on the news and cross themselves whenever I pass. They ask if I'm still "one of them," and I guess I have no way to prove that I'm not. But everyone calls me Michael Jackson. It's better than the names they'd call me if I didn't wear the glove. Perhaps I'll dress up as him for Halloween and pretend it was all on purpose.

The Hunted, the Haunted

IT WAS HIS EYES that caught her. Familiar deep eyes that drew her in and held her there.

As Mahmoud poured tea into fluted glass teacups, Angeline's nostrils filled with the smell of mint. She chased a silver strand of memory but it escaped her.

She gazed at the façades of the buildings around them, lower floors blue and upper levels white, terracotta rooftops and a pale marble sky. She heard the coo of pigeons and the flutter of wings.

"Are you searching for something?" asked Mahmoud. He wore a black leather jacket and along his smooth jaw was a thin, jagged scar. It bothered Angeline that she could not tell his age.

"Yes, myself." Her hand shook as reached for her glass.

The eyes watched her.

Urgency rose like a tidal swell as Angeline wound through the streets of Chefchaouen. There was one point she sought as a marker, a place to orient herself. The Clock Café. But the blue streets of the *medina* seemed to twist in on themselves, the scent of spice mingling with smoke, until everything became too familiar and she realised she was walking in loops.

Colour shifted on uneven walls. From the pale blue of the sky to the cerulean of the sea to the purple-tint of a desert bluebell.

She passed men in *djellabas*, long hooded robes of made of heavy coarse wool and women in kaftans, ankle-length and shapeless, gauzy head-scarves fastened beneath their chins.

Pausing at a blue archway, she saw canvas sacks rolled down to reveal apples, in a two-toned yellow-red. Her fingers twitched and she longed to take one but refrained. From a hook on the wall hung sheets of henna designs printed with a pair of red hands.

On the arch above were loom-woven belts in shades of sunset. It led to a passage where azure arches stretched endlessly, lined with cobalt doors. As if diving underwater, she plunged in.

At a blue wall hung with mirrors she stopped. The mirrors were cut into diamonds on thick wooden frames painted aqua and accented with reds and yellows.

The reflection caught her. Her own. A moon-pale face with jutting cheekbones and hollowed eyes. Coal-black hair straggled past her shoulders. Dark clothing hung loose from her gaunt frame. She could see the pain in her own eyes, and how it layered over her, distorting the essence beneath.

She squinted as she tried to remember her younger self: eyes brighter, chin higher, face bronzed with sun and vitality. She attempted a smile. Saw thin lips turn up, crooked. The smile faltered. She tried again, stronger, wider, but the smile did not lift the blue mist within her.

"I seek the self that was smothered by someone else. That got buried in the sands of time, eroded by arguments and compromises. I want to dig her out, to climb back into her."

Mahmoud frowned. He twirled a teaspoon and dug it into the sugar pot. Piled the spoon high and tipped it into his tea. "Do you think you could ever truly return to your past self?"

The silver thread of memory pulled her forward. The sights were familiar but it seemed as if everything had been shuffled, and she could not understand where to go. She began to feel like the hands of a clock, circling a centre-point that was ever out of reach.

She passed red hanging carpets like swaths of fire against oceanic walls. Leather bags embossed with geometric patterns, woven hats in the Rastafarian tricolour, a man wearing one sitting in the shop entrance, crochet needles flying.

As she walked down a powder blue alley, a pair of eyes watched her—and they belonged to the white furry body of a cat in an alcove. Angeline reached out her hand but the cat jolted up and darted along the alley.

Unsure of the way, she followed it.

Angeline pulled her lips inward and pressed them together.

"Not fully, no. But I'll try to resurrect her." She took a bite of *chebakia* and a shower of pastry shards fell to her plate. Honey and sesame seeds coated the flower-shaped fried dough. It had been her favourite but now the sweetness seemed so sickly she did not understand how she had liked it.

Mahmoud leaned forward. "And what was she like, this past self of yours?"

"She was filled with hope that carried her like a balloon through rough situations. Until her life was taken over by love and a relationship bound her."

"But you chose to be bound."

"I did." A shadow flitted across her face and she looked down.

"So what went wrong?"

She told how his cynicism seeped into her, infecting her. Till bouts of melancholia bloomed like blue flowers, and she sank into them. How he took over her life and the things she loved fell away without her noticing. Until, years later, the love ebbed away and she realised but it was too late.

The white cat led her down a covered passageway, thick stone in a soft shade of twilight. It slipped past the ankle-length robes and flat slippers of passersby as Angeline followed, down a cobbled street of pale blue walls and periwinkle doorways, to a stairway leading upwards and curving out of view.

She paused.

She had been here once. She remembered the cold, how it crept through the thin cotton of her jacket, cropped short and hooded that hardly kept her warm. How she'd pulled the hood low but it kept flying back, exposing dark hair that was shorter then, chin-length.

The ice-blue stairs were lined with potted plants—bright orange, pink and lime that stood out like gumdrops and jutted from the walls on wrought iron supports.

She looked up the stairs and the cat had disappeared.

She began to walk up, passing archways leading to blue walled-courtyards, vines curling out of the pots fixed to the walls. She paused, absorbing the scene with her eyes, catching at the traces of what had been before. Of running for the joy of exploration, filled with the thrill of the new.

She walked faster, around a bend as the stairs curved upwards, and there was the cat, sitting on a step, licking its paw.

"My past self is like a ghost I chase through the streets. Around each bend I hope to catch her but she is gone. I lose myself in the smells of spices. I catch her scent and it stirs a memory, of clove-infused coffee, drunk on a golden afternoon as a pigeon flapped its wings above a square..."

"So you were here before?" His tone sharpened.

"Yes. Nine years ago."

"Interesting."

"And you?" She had barely grasped the edges of him.

"I passed through once and now my routes keep looping back here. The Blue City holds me in its thrall." Mahmoud let out a short dry laugh. "But I never stay long."

Angeline leaned forward. "Why not?"

"Business calls me away."

"What kind of business?"

He gave an elegant shrug. "Import-export."

"Are you a collector?"

"Yes," he said, and she saw the way his eyes glinted.

"So how did you get that scar?" she asked, eyeing the jagged white line along his jaw.

Mahmoud turned away from her. "By doing something that someone did not agree with."

"Someone stopped you?"

"Yes."

"I see. Is it a knife wound?"

"Yes."

"You do not need to tell me the details."

"Good."

Already she felt and imagined too much, a knife flashing silver, the blade scraping bone and his scream. When she looked up, Mahmoud was studying her, his eyes sharp.

"Shall we stroll?"

"Sure." Angeline stood and slipped on her jacket from the back of the chair. When he hooked his arm into hers, she did not wrench it free.

There. Down a slim lane lined with windows and Aegean blue plant pots.

Mahmoud watched as Angeline's face broke into a smile. She was gazing at a vertical banner with the red letters: *clock*. The Clock Café.

At a marble-topped table against a wall of cerulean blue, they drank tea in tall glasses turned green by floating mint leaves. While Angeline smiled, her gut twisted with uncertainty.

A waiter set a clay dish on the table and pulled aside the triangular cover to reveal a mound of slow-cooked vegetables, orange-tinged with paprika: *tagine*. Beside it he placed a stack of *khobz*, hot flour-dusted flatbread. Tearing off chunks, they scooped up sauce till the bread disintegrated and the spice stained their fingertips.

When they had eaten, Mahmoud paid the bill despite Angeline's protests. Before she could leave, he took her hand and led her up a stairway.

An indigo doorway led to the rooftop.

Angeline walked to the ledge and gazed, at soft violet buildings interspersed with white like a carpet of flowers. Broad dark mountains loomed above like horns, as brooding clouds sank into the dip between them.

She pictured her past self winding through the streets below, with a joy she could no longer capture.

"Did you wear a purple jacket?"

Mahmoud's words jarred her out of her reverie.

"Excuse me?"

He repeated the question.

"Yes..." she began, her mind piercing the haze of years. She saw her younger self walking up a blue stairway, rubbing her arms against the cold.

"And your hair was shorter, yes?"

"It was."

Mahmoud's dark eyes drew close to her. "Then I've met you."

"*Where?*"

"You were lost. Your hands were pulling at the sleeves of your jacket as you bit your lower lip. You asked me for directions and I invited you for mint tea."

Angeline frowned. *Another life, another self.* "But where was I going?"

"You were searching for the path up the mountain. I told you it was far but you said it didn't matter."

She looked to the mountains but the drifting mist gave no answers.

"Don't you remember?"

Angeline pressed her hands to her temples and closed her eyes.

Hot breath on her cheek and he was beside her, too close. Angeline stepped back.

"There's something I never got a chance to tell you."

"What's that?" she asked, the threat of his proximity driving her heart-rate.

"How beautiful you are."

Angeline froze.

Mahmoud took hold of the side of her jaw and leaned forward, till Angeline smelt the *tagine* spice on his breath.

She shook her head and the grip tightened, vice-like.

"No," she said, wrenching her head free.

She ran down the stairs and out to the alley, turning at random while the steps rang like shots behind her and a voice called, "Cherie, come back!"

Her feet beat the cobbles like drums, every footstep a *no*.

She ran down cerulean streets winding like a maze. Rain fell in cold stinging drops that sent shivers down her arms.

She pulled her shawl low and glanced over her shoulder. A hunched man in a *djellaba* shuffled down the rain-slick cobbles. His hood was pulled forward, face hidden in shadow.

As the rain stung and the light faded, the walls became jewel-toned and a chill crept into her. She darted through an archway.

Angeline had been chased before. A memory flashed in her mind. Feet slapping stone, heart pounding, lungs sucking in cold air. But it had been a game that time. Her paramour had caught her, laughing, and she had laughed with him, in bright short bursts like a flickering streetlamp.

She raced on, straining for familiar details as the streets became a blur. The flame-bright carpets and sacks filled with apples had vanished. Electric lamps threw out pools of soft light.

At the top of a flight of stairs, a doorway was open. The warm glow drew her forward.

A rounded archway led to an orange-walled room with high ceilings lit by an electric chandelier. She dipped a spoon into a bowl of steaming hot *harira* that warmed her body and bones but could not warm the ache inside, the ache she carried with her.

Angeline sat at a table in a plaza, alone. A descending sun stretched rays of light across the blue walls as shadows thickened.

She could remember small vignettes but not the parts that joined them together. The feelings as she wound through tangled streets, but not the conversations. Like water in the desert, they had vanished.

The sound of footsteps on flagstones. She kept gazing at the walls but the footsteps grew closer until she realised they were beside her.

"Madam," said a male voice.

Heart racing, she lifted her head up. The man wore a uniform the blue of a midnight raid and an officer's cap. Police.

"Have you seen a man with a scar along his jaw?" He showed her a picture.

It was Mahmoud.

"Why do you ask?"

"He is wanted for the theft of a valuable antique."

Angeline froze. "I saw him at the Clock Café..."

Angeline raced down streets sunk in shadow, past keyhole-shaped doorways and up curving stairs. A pair of cats curled like commas at the base of a door.

She turned a corner and she was standing at the archway of her *riyad*. A wave of relief washed over her.

She slipped in and pulled the heavy door behind her.

In the blue shadowed darkness she regarded the mirror. Gazing beyond what she had become, she saw the past that Mahmood had unlocked. The shards retrieved on her route came together to form what was lost.

A love like sunlight spreading across a blue alley. Believing in it so fully she allowed it to infuse her. It was not fully gone, but lay buried within her. Like uncovered treasure, it glimmered in the light.

A shaft of light shone on a blue wall and Angeline followed it. She carried her luggage and the gathered shards of memory, out of the labyrinth of doubt and reminiscence to a smooth shining road and the blank walls of the new.

ROSARIO SANTIAGO

Meet Me in the Universe

WE TRAVEL THE SPACEWAYS in space canoes. There is no need for maps when we have the stars. I have oceans in my blood, but I'm not too sure about spacedust. Something about it just feels off-balance, like a fish taking to land for the first time. I don't remember what a wave looks like, but I can see the Sun's corona right outside my window, tiny particles of plasma radiating from that giant red star, peppering the sky all around us. When it gathers enough power, it's a great big wind of light, streaks of it in seafoam, crimson, and cerulean.

Sometimes, I tell my mother that I want to go space-sailing in my father's canoe, a simple wish dressed in a hypothetical question.

She looks at me without looking at me, a firm and facile no, and walks away.

My mom doesn't know what it means to grow up amongst the stars. I was young when we left home, the image of the water surrounding my little island blurring as I got older. I forget what the color of an ocean looks like, or what it feels like to dip your toes in warm, wet sand. I have a photo of my parents getting married in Las Picuas, two young people so desperately in love that, to make an eternal promise, they let the water officiate for them. My father, ever the poet, wrote on the back of the photo: *Hasta que el mar se seque.*

I take this photo out when my room is lit up by the solar winds outside, one phenomenal thing against another in my hands. I see my parents looking at each other, enamored, the bright blue sea and sky behind them. This is as clear as I can remember what home felt like, just a memory from a time before I was born.

I don't think space is all that bad. I've made something of myself here. The atmosphere of my planet is so clear and true that our sky isn't really sky at all, but the galaxy itself. Back home we'd need a telescope to

see Jupiter, but that's just another Tuesday afternoon here. I have friends
on our little floating rock, a life that feels semi-rooted and comfortable.
I've lived here for over five years now. I've come of age in space. Of
course it's important to me. I just want to know more about where I
came from, what it would feel like to be somewhere that doesn't feel
so far-away. I look at this photo of my parents, where Puerto Rico isn't
shoved in the back of a drawer like this picture was, and I start to taste
the saltwater in my mouth, the sound of the sea in my ears. It visits me in
waves, leaving just as soon as it comes. My mom doesn't even let me ride
in the space canoes. It reminds her too much of home.

"Gatita," I hear my mom call for me. "Dinner!"
        Every now and then my mom makes my dad's favorite dishes and
sets out a plate for him. There are no words about this. These are the
small, mercurial actions she takes, a lighthouse shining out into a deep,
dark sea, waiting for a ship that will never come to harbor. Sometimes
she makes these dishes and calls me down to eat in a sing-song voice.
Other times, I can feel that heavy weight in her words.
        "The yuca tastes really good, Mom. I remember Dad loving this
stuff," I say, my mouth filled with food. Any mention of my dad makes
my mom tight-lipped and ashamed. She mumbles a response, and we go
back to the sound of forks scraping on plates.
        "I think I want to go away for college," I tell her, the bravery
bubbling up in me. "Maybe I even wanna go back down to Earth."
        "I don't think that's a good idea, Catalina," Mom says, using my
real name. She swallows her thinly cut vegetables without chewing.
        "Lilah and her parents are going on a trip to visit schools next
week, and she really wants me to come. I am going with them."
        "No," my mom says, finally looking up at me after all of this
time. It is a short word tinged with finality.
        "I'm almost eighteen. I can't stay here with you forever."
Sometimes, cutting tension is the swipe of a knife in the air.
        "What would be the problem with that? Have I not taken care
of you your entire life?" She is red and splotchy in the face. The unsaid
things are braided around us. *What if you disappear like he did, and I can never
get you back?*
        I wonder if this is a fight we can keep having. I've learned there

is no getting through to her. Is there any way to get through to someone who has lost everything? I am still my mother's daughter. She stares at me, a look that is stained with regret, and I know we are living in two different universes. Even if we are both here, on this tiny floating rock in space, she looks at me and remembers everything she's lost.

"Look at me!" I say, dropping my cutlery. "Do I look so much like Dad that you can't even look at me? Are you even seeing me?" My mom is dumbfounded, startled, frozen in place and for a moment, I wish for her to meet me in some universe where I'm not only my father's daughter, but her's, too.

"I'm not Dad. It's not 2017 anymore."

I get up and leave the dinner table, those few words digging up a grave my mom would rather keep buried. I don't want to keep showing up to her cemetery of memories. I leave like the child she treats me like, the child she needed to take care of before we left the island. When we left without my dad. I don't look back to see if my mom follows me to my room. Time is still, suspended in disbelief.

These fights happen. Now, with increasing frequency, the fights are what lead me to keeping secrets, little things I can keep to myself without worry of her tainting it.

It started just after we moved to our new house on this space colony, millions of miles away from home. I was twelve, sneaking out into our backyard and taking what she thought she'd keep hidden forever, our shed an archive of grief. First, it was the photo of my parents in Las Picuas. Then, my father's diaries. I had so many things that my mom had kept hidden, including scrapbooks dedicated to our little family. Sometimes I flip through those pages, looking at photos of a little girl with my name and my face. I don't recognize her. My favorite photo is one where I am covered in birthday cake, surrounded by balloons, streamers, and my parents by my side. Below it, in my father's looping cursive, says *Primer Cumples de Catalina*. It was my father who made the memories. My mother lays them to rest.

After our last fight, I managed to take the huge oars that belonged to my dad's canoe from the shed. They were wrapped up in a heavy cloth in the back, but being oar-shaped, it was hard to miss them. At night when it's quiet, not even falling stars outside my window to make a sound, I would bring the oars into bed with me, rubbing my hand against the soft grooves of wood. I know what I know about seafaring from my father's diaries; a lot of it is dreamy stuff, Dad taking this little handmade boat out into the ocean and looking up at the stars. It takes millions of years for a star to form, and even a million more after that for them to die. I just know that those twinkling little stars I wish on at night are the same ones my dad saw in Rio Grande.

My father was an inimitable oceanographer. He didn't need college to learn about the ocean around him; he lived and breathed it. His diaries are filled with sprawling notes about the sea, information on native flora and fauna, the ebb and flow of the Atlantic Ocean and the Caribbean Sea, what it meant to travel by water. There are portions about tsunamis and hurricanes and earthquakes, too, all things relevant to what it means to live on an island. Those parts of the diaries are faded and smudged from water damage. I imagine my mother when we first moved to our little planet in outer space just after Hurricane Maria, flipping through these pages, her tears staining the diary with love. She was seeking the same answer I was: a way to travel back in time, a way to save him, a remedy for grief.

When the water takes, it takes. Space feels like something entirely different. It's given me stars to believe in. Though I've never touched them, their light shines through my window, illuminating me in their soft glow. The stars let me dream. From what I read in my father's journals, a galaxy isn't so different from an ocean. These oars that waded through water are equally capable of wading through low-gravity, plasma, and solar winds. Seafaring and Spacefaring are two-halves of the same coin.

I look through the objects I've taken from the shed, imagining the spirit of my father inside of them. I talk to them like he's in the room with me.

"Why's Mom such a pain in the ass, huh, Dad?" I ask out loud, "Is this really the woman you fell in love with?"

I stew in my anger, asking my dad the same questions I ask him every time my mom and I get into a fight. These questions slowly turn into wishes, into dreams.

"I wish you'd stayed…" I say to him, which feels unfair, but I try to let myself have what I want. I imagine a life where my father is alive, where the hurricane didn't happen, where I live my life as a happy island girl.

I look back at the oars next to me, feeling the wood one more time. With the oars comes the canoe, right? I look out into our backyard to see it covered in tarp, lonely. I have the sudden urge to see it, to sit in it just once, to feel what my dad might've felt when he was in the ocean. It's late enough that my mother's gone to bed, so I prepare myself in the way my father taught me in his journals. I bring my life vest and my pack, filled with all the essentials needed for a journey out into sea. I'll dress up the part and play a role if it means I can fall into an imagination. I love my little floating rock, but I feel like a cut-out pasted into a picture I shouldn't be in. My leaving is not an escape, but a homecoming.

I'm quiet as I walk through the house, my arms carrying the pack, Dad's journals, and the oars. I know I'll be safe as soon as I get outside, because sound doesn't really travel in space unless you're really trying to make some noise. Sound can only be heard when an object breaks through space's airless vacuum, like when a rocket is landing to bring more citizens, or a satellite is being launched into orbit. This is the kind of place where playgrounds filled with children are silent, their sprightly screams and cheerful laughter being swallowed up into a voiceless background.

When I get to the canoe beside the shed, I can tell my mother has done all she could to bury it into oblivion. There is the tarp that I can see from my bedroom and underneath is a clump of heavy blankets. When I finally get it all off, I drag the canoe to where you can't see it from the house, the small boat rickety and old. There is a port nearby, I remember, where I've seen Lilah and all my friends drift off in their own canoes, these lovely objects of water taking to space. I decide to go there, heart bursting and excitement thrumming in my bones.

It's easy to see my way as I make it to the dock, and I realize it's because there is an aurora borealis forming. I walk with my head to the stars, as much as the canoe allows me, since I'm carrying it on my back to keep from making noise and raising suspicion. As soon as I get to the port, I take a second to breathe in all that the Milky Way is gifting me. Living in a place that is ever-filled with night gets tiresome, the rays of the sun only coming in small particles of radiance. This night is beautiful, the aurora in its grandest splendor, shades of lilac, indigo, and juniper coloring the world around me.

I take the canoe just far enough to the edge without worrying
of the solar winds coming to nip at me and send me swirling in air. I
barely fit the life vest, fastening it to where there is just a sliver left of the
buckle, and I take a seat in the canoe, my oars beside me. As I inspect
the inside, I see a small engraving, something I wouldn't have been able
to see without the aurora's light. *J+V para siempre.* Javier and Valeria, my
parents, forever. I take out the photos from their wedding and my first
birthday, placing it just beside the engraved words, a small ofrenda I'm
creating in honor of my dad. He loved my mom, and he loved me, so
maybe having both of these pictures in the canoe will let him know that
I'm here.

I close my eyes and face the aurora, which is getting brighter and
brighter in front of me. There is no Catalina at this moment. I become
something just as wonderful as the galaxy.

It's bright and bright and so, so radiant. The wind begins to pick
up, the smell of plasma and solar particles in my nose. I feel it in my hair,
on my cheeks, and I open my eyes to a sky filled with stars. The aurora
is huge, huger than I've ever seen it, and my heart is racing in my chest.
Mesmerized by its beauty, it takes me a second too long to realize the
wind has picked up, tiny pieces of the sun swirling around me, whipping
my hair in all directions. The photo of my first birthday and of my
parents' wedding day fly out of the canoe, and when I reach out to grab
it, I am tipped into the air, caught in what I can only think to call a gyre.
It's starting to become too much, and I know it's dangerous when I start
to hear the disaster alert sirens blaring, throwing my head back against
the current to look back at my small hometown. There are flashing lights.
Everything is illuminated.

In times when there is too-huge phenomena, like a geomagnetic
storm or a spacedust tornado, the emergency system picks up the
electricity in the air and warns all the residents to find shelter and safety.
I'm not in the pull of my planet's orbit anymore, and I start panicking.
I can barely move my head or my body against the strong forces in the
gyre, the aurora forcing me in the directions it wants me to go. I hear the
crackling of magnetic energy, and I'm suddenly lifted up high, so much
higher than I've ever been, my body riddled with excitement and fear and
something indescribable. I grab the oars out of sheer terror, rowing the
same way I see others when they get caught in space currents, but I'm

just not strong enough. The oars rattle in their little wooden hooks, my arms failing to move them in the way I want them to, and I'm suddenly turning, spinning out of control, caught in a dance with the aurora that is pulling me deeper and deeper into its core. I look out into the deep dark space and I see it, something fictional, something I had only read about, something scientists say is mythological. Giant amounts of plasma are formed at the center of a vortex, its funnel-like shape concentrating an abundance of dark matter.

I know Earth hurricanes are real. It's what took my father away from me. But my mom brought us here out into space to escape those disasters. We left home so that we could be safe.

And yet, here I am, hurdling into the eye of the storm.

"Catalina!" I hear a familiar voice screech. I am spinning so fast that I can only see my mom in bits and pieces as she runs towards me, rope in hand, attempting to throw an anchor out to me to hold on to. *It's too much*, I try to yell out, and I hope she hears me.

"Mom!" I'm screaming, the sound of a thousand little thunderbolts in my ears. "It's too much! I can't stop it!"

"Catalina, it's going to be okay! I'm coming to get you!" She runs as fast and as hard as I've ever seen her.

It's too late. I watch as it becomes dark all around me, swallowed into the being of this vortex, my mother stopped dead in her tracks, watching. She's tear-stricken and weeping, and I can't help but scream. *I love you, I love you, I love you.* I look at my mother, wrapped in the auroras I thought were so beautiful, and I cry. I am nothing like my father. I felt silly, like a little girl, and I wanted to be back in my mother's arms. I succumb to whatever is inside that black hole, my mom the last thing I see before I fall under. It is dark, so dark, the whirlpool slipping me out of consciousness for forever, and then some.

Under an infinite blue sky, the sounds of waves ahead of me, I wake up, spurtling out ocean saltwater.

MICHELLE D'COSTA

Your father has caught you watching porn

YOUR FATHER HAS caught you watching porn. Your mother is at church; she will be home anytime now. Your father sits in silence across from you. His feet are almost touching yours. The disappointment he is experiencing almost touches your toes. His toenails need trimming. You feel disgusted. You live in a one-bedroom apartment in the suburbs of Mumbai. You have no privacy.

Your father is a pastor. Your parents weren't this obsessed with Jesus when you were still Catholics. It's only when Mother Mary's photos disappeared from the house that you realized your parents would never be the same again. A man had spoken to both of them and since then they weren't themselves. 'Maria Pitache' starts playing from the ground nearby. Someone is getting married. Dance, booze, sex. Lucky groom, he is going to have some fun tonight. You smile, thinking about this. Your father slaps you.

You are ashamed of yourself. Especially because of the type of video he has caught you watching. You want to justify to him that it was only your curiosity that led you to watch it. He starts talking about the ways of evil and how Jesus is constantly there to protect you from temptations. Do you have a conscience? Do you? You look at the picture of Jesus Christ on the wall opposite you. You focus on the crown of thorns above his head and the blood dripping from his scalp. You want to wink at Jesus. He was born as a human; he would definitely understand.

Your father is still talking. He's doing the talking, but your throat is dry. You pick up your favourite cup, holding it gives you some comfort. It's a gift from your girlfriend. When you miss her a lot, you let the rim linger on your mouth a little longer than necessary. There's some water in it. You take a sip. Your father yells, 'YOU… IDIOT… LOOK AT JESUS! HE DRANK VINEGAR! HERE YOU ARE SIPPING AWAY AS IF… DON'T YOU HAVE ANY SHAME!'

'Oh my God, dude, chill, it's not wine, though I would really like some now,' you want to say but you know better. You look at Jesus, hoping he will hear your thoughts: 'Where are your skills when I need them? I need some wine. There's still some water left in my cup.'

Your father interrupts your conversation with Jesus by saying, 'It's all my fault,' and pushes the cup from your hand. It slips and shatters on the floor. It takes all the energy you have to not explode into expletives. Your father doesn't even apologise, all he says is, 'See that? That's how your mother's heart will break when she finds out. God, save him! You are a D'souza. How can you do this?'

D'souza. My foot. He spent his whole life at the mercy of the Catholic convent when his parents died and now he's changed paths. He claims he has given you a life of comfort and luxury and that's why you are ungrateful. 'Look who's being ungrateful' you want to say. People find him inspiring for the way he has built his life from scratch. But you're sick of him. You have taken advantage of your privilege, he adds. You want to say 'shut the fuck up, you old loser.' The words bubble inside you. You look at Jesus, you relate to the pain and anguish on his face. It's almost as if Jesus is willing you to say these words to your father.

You get up suddenly, startling your father and yourself, the table in front of you shaking from your sudden movement. He looks at you like you are possessed, you can almost read his mind, he is planning to call an exorcist. You pick the nail cutter from the shelf behind him and hand it over to him. He is confused. You tell him about his toenails. He gets up, knocking the plastic chair slightly off-balance, and slaps you, again. This time it's on the left cheek. No, I didn't agree to turn the other cheek, you want to tell Jesus.

The chair falls back in its original position. The only reason it didn't topple over is because of the lack of space in the living room. Your cheek feels numb from the slap. The doorbell rings and you almost pee in your pants. Your mother has arrived. You don't move. Your father takes your mother to the bedroom after she has taken off her shoes and has kept her handbag on the chair. They shut the door, leaving just you and Jesus in the living room. The flap of your mother's bag falls open,

as if on cue. Her prayer book slips out of her purse, onto the chair, as
if nudging you towards it. You sit down, in defiance. You bend down
to pick up the pieces of the broken cup and keep them on your table as
if exhibiting evidence of your father's crime. 'Crucify him, crucify him'
you whisper. You think about what would happen if your parents knew
you had a girlfriend. Jesus is looking at you, you want to ask him, 'Did
you date Mary Magdalene? C'mon, I won't tell anyone. You know what it
feels like right? It's natural, right?'

The door clicks open; you straighten up in your chair. Your
parents sit on the divan and make the sign of the cross. They pray for
you. Their eyes are closed, they ask Jesus for forgiveness and for you to
find the right path. When they are done, they open their eyes, their eyes
meet and they smile at each other as if harbouring a secret.

'Come with me,' your father tells you.

You wonder where he is taking you. Maybe to the church. He
shares another confidential look with your mother. They do that often
as if they can read each other's minds. You want such a telepathic bond
with your girlfriend. You are happy that your mother is content with your
father but you often think she deserves better. She would have led a very
different life had she not been with your father but you never dwell on
that for long because then you wouldn't have existed.

When your father leads you up to the terrace, you are frightened,
will he push you from the parapet? Your parents' increasing piety has
made you worry about their sanity more than once, and your resistance
against that has made them worry more than once. It was only the other
day that you read the news about two children who were slaughtered by
their parents in the hope of resurrecting them moments later. What if
your father pushes you off the terrace and expects you to resurrect in
three days? What if Abraham has possessed him? What if the sacrifice
needs to happen now, in present-day Mumbai?

You reach the terrace. You are panting. Your father walks straight
ahead; you don't want to follow him. He looks back and orders you,
'Come.' He is definitely going to push me off the terrace, you think. Your
father almost reaches the parapet, you follow him, slowly, your short life
flashing in front of your eyes. This is it, you think. You think of your
girlfriend; you wish you had told her that you couldn't afford to lose her.
She has been the only one keeping you sane.

Your father looks like a loser from behind. His pale trousers are high on his waist. His half-sleeved shirt is tucked in it. He has no ambition. If he had had ambition, he would be living in Bandra and not in the suburbs. Or he would have at least gone to the Gulf. You envy migrants in the Middle East. They make a fortune for themselves and then retire. You have not travelled at all until now, Mangalore doesn't count as it's your native place. Let alone another country, even a different city or state is beyond your father's comprehension. What if you push him off the terrace? You don't have the courage. You can see there are some labourers bathing in the dark corner of the terrace. They will be eyewitnesses.

'There are some construction workers bathing there, I wonder how they can see in the dark,' you say loudly, hoping this will change your father's mind. He pulls you closer, telling you to look below the building. Both of you look at the large sprawling slum. He tells you to look carefully, you are blessed for having everything in life, and what do they have? You sigh in relief, so this is what this was all about. You listen to his lecture and then both of you walk back down. Did he change his mind on seeing the labourers?

On your way down, you think about the slum kids. How do they learn about porn and sex? They must have seen their parents do it, for lack of privacy. If you barely have space in your one-bedroom house, what do they have? How did your father learn about sex? He is behind you this time, you can feel his eyes burning holes into your back. When did he first watch porn? When did he lose his virginity? You will never find the answers. Your father is not your friend.

When you reach your flat, you tell your parents you have learnt your lesson and that you need to take a shower to cleanse yourself of the dirty thoughts. They smile at each other and say a small prayer. You look at Jesus; he winks at you. I got you, his wink seems to be saying. While bathing, you think about your girlfriend and you feel like an idiot for having been so well behaved all this time. The next day in college, during the break, your girlfriend is sitting beside you, she's having an ice cream. The way she licks the strawberry scoop gives you ideas. You look at her eyes, trying to tell her that both of you should take things to the next level.

She says, 'What? Why are you staring?'

That breaks the spell. You wonder when both of you will reach the point of telepathy. You flick a strand of hair away from her face and you tell her how pretty she looks while she's having ice cream. You lean forward, whispering in her ear. She smiles, pushing the cone towards your face. You try to dodge it, but the scoop finds your nose.

On your way back from college, you stop by the pharmacy to buy a condom. Your girlfriend is waiting for you at her house. When the pharmacist, an old man, who looks just like your father, looks you in the eye, you buy a bar of Fa soap instead and slap your forehead when you cross the road. You fucking idiot, will you ever move on from soap? You tell yourself that you deserve to have been sacrificed. You decide to head home instead of your girlfriend's home.

No, you're not a loser like your father, be a man. Be a man. Be a man. Jesus carried out his father's calling despite the difficulty. He just did it! Be a man. You chant this until you reach your girlfriend's house. You are on her bed; her room is bigger than yours. Her house is a two-bedroom apartment. She has privacy. She wants to move outside Mumbai for her Master's. She wants to go to Bangalore. She is ambitious, unlike you. Will she outgrow you? If you stay the way you are, she definitely will.

'So, did you get it? I hope you got the strawberry one.'

'I'm sorry. I… I bought soap.'

'What?' she snorts, 'Soap?'

'Listen, I'm sorry—'

'I actually wanted to tell you something.' She adjusts herself on the bed, moving slightly away from you.

Her left breast moves slightly above her right one because of her position, you want to reach out and play with it. She has changed into her pyjamas, she looks cuter in this, the grey and pink combo suits her. You are still wearing what you wore during college, a black T-shirt and jeans. You want to strip and lie naked beside her.

'What happened?' you ask, your heart beating really fast.

'Nothing,' She shifts on the bed again, now resting her stomach on it. Her fingers fidget with each other.

She does that, she shifts a lot when she's about to address something that makes her uncomfortable.

Your voice is a whisper. 'Tell me.'

'The thing is my parents want me to date a Goan only ya…'

'What?' You sit upright now. 'C'mon, what's the difference man?

Mangalorean Goan same thing. We speak the same fucking language, if it weren't for the bloody Portuguese, we wouldn't have left Goa you know. We are the same. And honestly, I don't even know, we could be Goans. I don't know my grandparents…'

'I don't know…' She cleans the tips of her right hand's fingernails with her left nails.

'Are you breaking up with me? Is it something else? Is it my crazy parents? I know they can be a little too intense… especially Dad… you know what happened yesterday?'

'What? What happened?' Her eyes widen.

She will think you're a freak. You run your fingers over the red check pattern of her bedsheet to avoid her eyes. Should you tell her about it? Will this information make her retreat from you even further?

'Dad caught me watching porn,' you say and lie down in defeat, staring at her ceiling fan.

'Whaaat?' She sits upright and starts laughing. 'What were you watching? Don't tell me…'

She looks at your eyes. Both of you are thinking the same thing; you can bet on it. You hold her neck the way you held your favourite cup, sliding your fingers around it slowly and then holding it firmly while you bring your lips closer to its rim, drinking from it like it's the last drink you will ever have.

Once you're done kissing her, you ask her if she's still in the mood. She says yes. You jump off the bed and tell her you'll be back in a blink. Small steps like these are all it takes, you hope. You will outgrow your life and conditioning. She has pushed you out of your comfort zone and that's the only way to grow. If your girlfriend doesn't break up with you, you will follow her to Bangalore, no matter what it takes. Your mother moved for your father. You will not be your father.

NEETHU KRISHNAN

Night Of The Butterfly

THE CLOCK HANDS REFUSE to budge past six, probably paralyzed by my drilling gaze. Both the house and I are sparkly and ready for Robin who promised to be home by seven, and I'm out of things to occupy myself with.

For someone who's lucid dreamed about this day for the past eight years, I'm a nervous wreck.

The last message from Robin was two hours ago, a selfie of him frowning at a tray of cucumber sandwich triangles in the hospital cafeteria captioned *Will be ravenous tonight*, followed by a string of winking emojis. It'd sent shivers through me the first fifteen times I read it. However, my anxious shudders transmuted to anticipatory flutters as soon as I admired my reflection in the cupboard mirror.

I look perfect, the way I'd projected in my mental rehearsals.

The soft waves of my brown-streaked black hair and minimal makeup—a flourish of eyeliner and a dab of clear red lip gloss—make me look like a dream, if I may say so myself. The ethereality of my dress, the colour of Nabokov's Blues, intensifies with the constellating graininess of the evening, its gauzy fabric giving the illusion of transferability. Admiring my gruelly-worked-for slender middle—accentuated by the flare of pleated gathers ballooning into an open umbrella, its hem stopping short of my stocking-clad knees–I imagine Robin's face at the door when his eyes lock with mine. Will he be shocked speechless? Stumble back, disoriented? Or will he be nonchalant, draw me into his arms?

The wait for the priceless reveal, though sweet as honey, is also viscous.

Silhouetted in this delicious dress—wispy cap sleeves framing my neck, sweetheart neckline snug at the swell of my chest, the gossamer, shapely stretch of feathery fabric teasing at just the right spots—I am a Common Blue butterfly about to take wing, but my insides are a torpedo of adrenaline.

Will Robin be mad when I inform him of Sarath joining us in an hour? Would my plan B ever have to see the light of day? And how long into our charged encounter until Sarath realizes and admits the obvious: his love for me? Most importantly, how buzzed would Srishti be at the confetti of surprises raining on her tonight?

With every limping second, I'm closer to witnessing true magic. While I've always scoffed at the glorified law of attraction, tonight, as my phoenixing nears, I can't help but wonder if I've manifested it through sheer single-minded focus. Because what were the odds otherwise, in an unmanipulated universe, for any sequence of events culminating into this moment of my becoming?

I swipe through the albums on my phone, the four of us reverse-ageing in real-time, filters and polishes fading to non-existence at our earliest photos, low resolution smears of baby faces in a class of forty uniformed kids.

For as long as I've known them, I've always wanted to be friends with the three—Sristhi, Robin and Sarath. Even in school, when they were ordinary, individual entities. Even when they only ever noticed me to chuckle with the rest of the class as the popular kids bullied me. I don't blame them; I was a walking invitation back then.

More armadillo than girl, my painful shyness and radio silence that could've passed off for cool in another body or face definitely didn't in mine. While my black caterpillar eyebrows, knit in a permanent scowl as if offended by the world in perpetuity, softened nothing of my demeanour, the metal braces, overbite and beady angry eyes on my egg-like face weren't exactly inviting to friendships or self-esteem boosters either. There was also the stutter, zero eye contact, faring poorly in academics and extracurriculars. And not to forget the crowning glory, the wisdom everyone made sure to pass on to every new joinee in school: the warning to stay away from the girl who wet herself during morning assembly prayers so many days in a row, she'd be banned from participating.

It was true for a month in fourth grade, after which my parents pulled me out of school for a year, enrolled me in therapy to remediate my lack of control and convinced the principal into promoting me into fifth grade the next year. When I rejoined, the school lore still circulated hot and humiliating; a permanent, wet bull's-eye punctured with darts of snickering gazes.

In college, there was respite from the familiar hounds. I was an upgrade of my earlier self with straighter posture, clear braces, eyebrows threaded down to thin curves like Srishti's, the trend then, and feathery layers on my thick mass of black hair. I was an optimistic blank slate until I spotted the three in the admission queue of my college: Robin, scarily attractive with his filled-in frame and angular brown face; Sarath, with his one-cheek dimple and floppy grown-out hair; and Srishti, with her gentle eyes, non-condescending smile and bear hug that aspired to sponge off all sadness of the one in her embrace. While I secured myself with a safety net of a humble group of four moderately popular girls, I had constant nightmares of the three remembering to inform everyone of my shameful past. But as time breezed by, I realized I could relax. They had more important things to fret about than the non-issue that was my past.

I longed to be included in their little circle, watching them grow entwined roots as if in a time-lapse. I almost made it in, but also didn't. I padded in and out of their lives so inconspicuously, I doubt if any of them ever noticed the cords criss-crossing among us four, squaring us in. Srishti was my favourite of the trio, whom I aimed to mirror, be best friends with. She always smiled at me like we shared a secret—the connecting truth and warmth of which I craved and savoured. For her, I was happy to oblige as Robin's on-demand delivery service. When his gifts, letters, apology notes, house keys and cheesy one-liner Post-its found her at the most unexpected of places, she was child-like in her glee and wonderment as if Robin was supernaturally omnipresent, never once suspecting I was the sneaky smuggler. When Sarath was in shards, which was often, and which the other two almost always never noticed, I hovered nearby silently commiserating, until he learned to seek me out to sit out his angst in peace, by a kindred ear, a patting hand.

My threads with each of them then were gossamer, visible only to me. But tonight with the four under the same roof once again, the first time since graduation night, our chrysalis will no longer be spun of invisible silks. Pulled tauter and closer together than ever before, we'll be a nest of live wires forever bound.

My phone pings. It's Sarath. My chest ices over. He was to pop in at eight at my go-ahead. He cannot, by any means, ruin my evening. I eye the time at the corner of the screen. 6:20. I want to delay the inevitable by not reading his text, but I'm running out of breath with the hail in my ribs. I tap on the message.

Boarded the train to Delhi. Personal stuff. Sorry for excusing myself at the last possible minute. I appreciate your tireless advocacy for this evening, Tia, I truly do, but I'm not ready yet. If it's any consolation, I've dropped a truce approximation at Srishti's, the most I could bring myself to. The signal's chalky, not sure this message'll even reach you in time. Will talk later when there's better reception.

I'm trying to belly breathe, hug myself, smooth the dry stretch of dress across my middle; none of the self-soothing techniques easing my despair. Where's all the air when you're gasping for it? I cannot, for the life of me, believe this. Sarath ran over me not once, but twice.

At first, I naively thought his bailout via text was the most devastating and ruinous thing he could do to me. Then, at about a hundred re-reads, my brain cells fired enough to flash the mention of his "truce" like a hazard light in my head. Racing to the door with a free-frothing anger I never knew I was capable of, I lashed it open. Wedged behind the door latch was a thick violet envelope. I didn't have to open it to know what it was. The sandalwood scent, the holographic Ganesha, the gold-embossing on the face of the card were enough to hack the realization through me. Through the furious flood in my eyes, I didn't register the girl's name below Sarath's. It was Priya or Riya, or an inconsequential variant, one I've never heard of from the selfish blabbermouth.

The wedding is in two days. *Personal stuff.*

I have the urge to tear something to irreconcilable shreds. My hair? His chicken heart? The invitation card?

With each violent rip of the glazed, glitter-spewing cardboard, I address myself in the third person to distance myself from the meltdown, just like my therapist suggests. I'm not sure it's easing any of my helplessness or shock. Try as I might, I cannot control the hammer in my chest echoing the one of the night that led me here.

When Robin and Sarath lunged at each other that night—as they were prone to at the slightest of scrapes to their egos — I was trapped in a dark corner of a stranger's kitchen with no exit, walled in by the violent two, sipping unholy amounts of fizzy drinks alone as my friends

meandered off for refills. I'd have waited out their juvenile fist fight
to slink out unharmed, but Srishti tried breaking them up using me as
scare bait. She hissed at them to stop their intoxicated punches, warning
them if I got hurt in their scuffle and my family demanded explanations,
I could get them in serious peril not only with their strict families but
also with the local societal authorities if I even hinted at the illicit drugs
circulating in the room and their systems, at which Robin eased his hold
on Sarath's collar, turning to face me.

The moment his burning gaze landed on me, I fled my frigid
body and floated, a numb spectator. He scanned me head to toe like I
was vermin. He manic laughed, summoning the crowd to attention, his
eyes searching the air above heads for a punchline. Hovering at the other
end of the room, I watched the hatchet of his words descend, misting
the blood of noise in the house to a wine-red vapour.

Yes, I should be afraid, very afraid, he screeched, mock-shivering,
his eyes glazed with madness, *of her soaked diapers exploding on me,* he
cackled, palms cupped into a megaphone at his mouth, vomiting the
pungent yellow of my worst fear into the receptacle of my college
community—the one with my four wide-eyed friends, mouth agape,
frozen mid-stride; the one where my peers considered me normal, not a
sick freak until then; the one where I'd sought sanctuary, reconstructing
myself painstakingly as an amicable, resourceful human and for once was
accepted at face value.

Having lost all physical sensation when I dissociated, I scanned the
vista of faces for cues, trying to settle on an estimate of how long before I
could kill myself. I studied Srishti's red-rimmed eyes bulging with a mixture
of fear and disgust as she approached him, slapping away his protesting
hands, straining to dam his running mouth with her tiny palms. I watched
him shake her off like lint, his eyes roving hers, like she was the one out of
her mind. I was impressed at my body still maintaining itself upright, hands
clutched with a death grip on the glass bottle of Sprite, eyes vacant, face
splotchy, as he seared it with his despicable gaze.

Why do you even care about this dumb muppet? he barked at Sristhi,
gesturing vaguely at me. The flat was a single entity, a massive lung
ballooning with a held-in breath. Even Sarath, who was so hammered he
seemed to have forgotten his rabid fight with Robin, watched with pity
and forced concentration.

Because she's my friend, Srishti mumbled, planting herself before me like a human shield.

I'm not sure which irked him more, her declared alliance with a lowly being such as me, or her resolute, protective stance as if anticipating physical violence. From my bird's eye view, the flint in his eyes and the murderous tensing of his muscles was obvious, but the eyes on my body stared unseeing and unflinching as he swatted Srishti away with one arm, swiped the island of drinks in a bulldozing sweep with his other.

My bad, guys, it's just booze, not piss, for now, he shrieked, convulsing with laughter, pointing at the dripping middle of my pink tunic, stained like a weeping sunset clinging to the shivering shape of me. With that, he segued out the room and my life.

What followed was a numb blur of being gurneyed in and out of psychiatric wards. The only thing of clarity glowing bright through the scalding haze of it all, a small mustard seed of promise, the source of which I still can't place. It luminesced with the promise of a rewriting of history, of a rebalancing of the universe, of being seen, loved, included.

Srishti's betrayal a few days later only helped cleave open its cotyledons. For reasons I still don't comprehend, she broadcast to everyone I was a closeted lesbian who preyed on unsuspecting straights like her. It took a couple of days for the few residual peers from my alumni, who occasionally checked in, to peter out and be wiped off the planet thereafter. Even if it wasn't a baseless rumour, even if I was into girls, which I wasn't, my ostracization'd still have been the same.

Years piled. Ablated from the world of the living, I meandered virtual corridors, whenever my sanity allowed, as Tia, an alias not only much cooler and confidence-exuding than my given name, but also one that never got me blocked.

I had no agendas or strategies in my lurking. I only wished to watch the world that had abandoned me from the sidelines. The greening of my seeds was organic, unplanned. The manure fell into my lap, or at my feet, to be precise, in Robin's case.

With no stigmatizing history or qualifiers of weirdness, Tia was friends with everyone. Her profile picture on Facebook —a lazy click of my feet, nails painted siren red, crossed over a pile of throw pillows— was all it took to lure Robin in. He was, apparently, lacking a good friend,

as he'd lost his best friend and childhood pal, Sarath, over a minor
financial tiff that escalated to an irreconcilable split a couple years back.
Then, he dove to the real point.

Whoever knew my feet could turn him putty? He never asked
for headshots or to meet. Easily dehumanized without a face or a touch
of real flesh, his guilt was conveniently walled off, his prized marriage
preserved spotless. His infidelity wasn't cheating if the IVF hormones
turned "the wife" into a chaotic mess driving him into seeking release
elsewhere, if he wasn't technically with a human woman, if the one
spinning him in pleasure circles was a headless photo reel of body parts
or a disembodied, sultry voice dripping down earphones.

For Sarath, going by her melancholic quote reposts, Tia was a
mysterious, occasionally sad damsel, who could divine his every twitch
and mood like magic. The next best thing to "the girl he loved" in his
words. In a few swipes, he was addicted to her salves. He swore no
person could substitute the way she understood him. Screens, being
the treacherous invisibility veils they are—illusory safe voids where
boundaries blur and dissolve, the darkest, most intimate coexisting with
the mundane with no threat of repercussions beyond the virtual—
honey-trapped Sarath into unspooling every secret. Sparing no detail, his
fingers tap-danced what his tongue was forbidden from rolling out.

The year her fiancé left for a one-year diploma in Australia, "the
girl he loved" rekindled ties with Sarath. He swam with Srishti in the
fantasy until she started dragging him onto land. He thrashed out her
cupped hands. Already two strides ahead of his predictable slipperiness,
she speared him with the indisputable proof of their creation. He lost all
sense of self with the news. He wasn't ready, won't ever be. She called him
spineless, but yielded on the condition he'd take his failure to the grave, not
cross paths with her ever again. He, of course, fled with his life.

Tonight, he was to reunite with both his ex-friends for Tia. With
no reason to disbelieve the benevolent sorceress when she told him how
her neighbourhood friends Srishti and Robin sorely missed their dearest
friend Sarath, he promised her he'd make up with them. After all, it was
the least he could do to impress her on their first ever in-person meet.
She'd only to text him the cue to surprise-visit Srishti's.

The neighbourhood part wasn't a lie. I've lived in the flat below
Srishti's ever since graduation. Not once has she ever noticed my

existence. I, however, know everything about her past eight years: the first four with her parents, the unfortunate one with Sarath, the recent three with Robin. Thanks to mental health stigma, my parents aided in the stealthy, unpeopled escorts to and from the psychiatry visits and admissions with such expertise and finesse, I could pass for a stranger in my own building. Every time Sristhi deposited her house keys with my grandmother for our common maid or for emergencies as spares, I was always around, recuperating or working, albeit in the cave of my bedroom. Like a nocturnal creature, I'd perfected scaling darknesses to my advantage. But, never, until today, did I ever use Srishti's keys to let myself in.

Tonight was my night of magnificent bloom. A perfect square awaited. A pair of couples, two pairs of friends. Tonight, I wouldn't be a footstool. I was to be an equal.

Sarath loved Tia for her essence, or so I thought. He had one job. To reconcile his love with the physical form of me. Without Sarath, what remains? Robin was to meet Tia for a first-time rendezvous at his at seven. Post his recovery from being catfished, he was to make up with Sarath on my insistence. After, we three were to surprise Robin's beloved wife Srishti at the hospital, where she was under observation for Braxton Hicks contractions.

What use for my ammunition of Robin and Srishti's infidelities if I have no Sarath to threaten them back into friendship with? Despite wielding all the power to derail Robin and Srishti's life as they once did mine, I choose mercy over revenge and yet, what good has it done?

The ping of Robin's message on my phone circuit-breaks my mental treadmill. I shudder with the jolt back to reality. It's 6:50. Violet slivers, like dead aster petals, fly around me. I am numb, except for the sting of paper cuts slicing through my fingers as I hold the button to turn off my phone. I stare unblinking at the red criss-crosses until they yawn and bleed. In its first ever resurfacing since the night, the clarity of the memory is visceral, life-like.

I'm under a stranger's showerhead. I hear Srishti apologizing through sniffles, her incessant chants sprayed down to unintelligible prayers by the tepid water. I see her eyes flood every time she plucks out soda glass from my arms and feet. I smell the rust of the snaking threads of red on the ice-blue bathroom floor, hers intermingled with mine. I taste but one grain of companionship, and in its leaving me yearning for more, keeps me from dying.

Feathery lavender ruins spiral up and about my folded butterfly wing as I hoist myself off Srishti's floor. I race out the door, shutting it behind me.

As I dash down the stairs, a monstrous bouquet of roses on a man bounding upstairs whacks the side of my head. I don't stop; neither does he. The gargantuan flower arrangement and our hurries are excellent barricades. He belatedly calls out an apology from upstairs. The muffled *Sorry* floats in the air between floors. I whisper it's okay, that all of us are forgiven, as we key ourselves into our separate worlds.

Doctoral Daddies

I HAD SIGNED UP for the Philosophy of Science class thinking maybe it would give me something to talk to my dad about. It was a 500-level class, for graduate students. I had to get the professor's signature to sign up as a senior. I assumed it would be pretty boring and was surprised Professor Johansen returned my final paper with "Have you considered a PhD?" in the margin. I'd written about the metaphysical implications of the many-world interpretation of quantum mechanics, which even I had to admit sounded like pretentious gobbledygook.

Metaphysical questions, questions about the way the world is, were the most interesting to me. But in general they were the hardest for other people to understand. It made it really hard to explain what exactly you studied to strangers on an airplane or, as it turned out, your own father.

Professor Johansen had arranged a little end of semester celebration for the class, which was a nice gesture, a recognition of the hard work of the semester and a chance to exhale instead of just marching on. I'd enjoyed the small upper division classes where we talked directly to the faculty in circled chairs so much more than the giant anonymous lecture halls of freshman year. You kind of couldn't help getting to know everyone when there were only fifteen people in class all semester. Laura, from my dorm, and I were the only undergrads in the class.

The atmosphere in the classroom wasn't quite a party, but it was festive. The desks and tables had been shoved to the side of the room and one table was laden with plastic cups, a couple bottles of wine, some beers, and a plastic bowl of pretzels. It was my final Friday night of college, which was a weird thought. Parents, including mine, would descend on campus tomorrow for graduation weekend. I still needed to pack up and clean my room. If my mother saw it in its current state, she would have a heart attack.

Will had just shared a self-aggrandizing anecdote about his childhood and I swore Professor Johansen caught my eyes for a split second. Will was Laura's minorly scandalous grad-student boyfriend. She was the reason it even occurred to me that I could take this class. Professor Johansen had a dry humor in class. A few times he'd glance my way as I'd silently grinned at some joke he'd made, my fingers on the keyboard in the midst of taking notes, while he waited for the rest of the class to catch on and laugh. I imagined he was slyly saying to me *I tolerate all my students, some are just more intolerable than others.*

"I was a weird kid," I said, the impulse to be contrary was one I'd always struggled to suppress. The group of my classmates laughed, and people shifted from foot to foot.

"How so?" Professor Johansen said.

"I didn't really have a lot of friends, so at recess I would just make up challenges for myself. Like I had to swing every other bar on the monkey bars five times in a row with no mistakes. I liked to pretend I was training for the Olympics."

"Curious," he said. He didn't say it in a bad way though, and he didn't look away from me either. It was strange to see him like this, chatting casually instead of teaching, even weirder that we were all holding drinks. I was pretending to be accustomed to talking to an adult while sipping alcohol.

"One day I decided I wanted to swing the whole way skipping every two bars. My imaginary strict Soviet coach's disapproving expression egged me on. Skipping two bars required maximal stretch of my little arms," I said.

"Wait, you had an imaginary Soviet coach?" Will asked bemusedly.

"I was kind of obsessed with Nadia Comaneci. I kept waiting to be discovered on the playground doing cartwheels like she was. I didn't understand America doesn't work like that."

Will didn't say anything out loud, but his face said a lot.

"I don't remember the actual fall. I just remember lying on the ground. Other kids and the gym teacher were looking down at me. I looked down at my arm and then looked away really fast. Mr. Monroe, the maintenance man, came and they carried me on a stretcher to the nurse's office. It took forever for my mom to get there. I kept waiting for the nurse to ask me what year it was or who the president was. I kept rehearsing my answers in my head, but no one ever asked me."

I switched my plastic cup full of cheap champagne to the other hand, and I rolled my wrist until it cracked.

"You can see the scar. Where the bone broke through the skin."

The faces in the circle squirm and twist and the circle disintegrated into small clusters. No one wants to think about that, Natasha.

"Let me see." Professor Johansen stepped forward. Ever so lightly he traced the faint reddish scar along my forearm.

I looked up at him. He was still standing barely the distance of my forearm away.

This little moment would stick in my memory. My memory feels like a mosaic of tiny moments encased in amber and colored glass, organized next to each other in a pattern that can only be discerned by someone else, further away, by God maybe? This is a flawed, very human conception of time—utterly unrelated to what time probably is, a fourth dimension that exists in the physical world.

I had learned early that you could ruin something in an instant, the wrong decision could destroy a moment before it fully crystallized. My earliest memory of learning this was desperately having to pee while playing tickle war on the floor with my uncle and his two wiener dogs. I was squealing in laughter. He was lifting me in the air with his feet, airplane style, and tickling me until I couldn't breathe. I was having so much fun the dogs were jealous, barking at me. I waited as long as I possibly could, but eventually the burning need to pee and all the laughing was unignorable.

"Wait, I'll be right back!" I said. I ran to use the bathroom as quickly as I could, cutting off my pee before it was even finished, as soon as I was just a bit less desperate. But by the time I ran back into their living room with the thick cream-colored shag carpet and the glass-topped coffee table that had been shoved to the side for our roughhousing, my uncle was on the phone and my aunt was chopping carrots. I don't know if I comprehended this in one long glance or if I begged my aunt to have my uncle come back and play. But I know we didn't play or have fun like that for the rest of the weekend, and then my parents were packing me back into the backseat of the car. The trip was over and the moment never came back.

My life felt like a never-ending series of missed moments. Maybe that's why I wrote my final paper on the many-worlds theory, the idea that quantum theory requires that a multitude of universes exists, that for every significant decision someone makes there is a branching, one world where they said yes and one world where they said no. One world where my uncle waited for me to come back, and one where he didn't.

But this moment wasn't over yet—Professor Johansen was standing there looking at me. I could still feel the warmth of his finger lingering on my scar.

"My mom loves to tell the story of when the nurse put the IV of pain medicine in my arm. Apparently, I looked right at the doctor and said 'Hip hip hippopotamus. They don't eat people, but you can't pet them. I feel great!' I tried to say it like the Tiger on the kids' cereal. *Grrrrrreat!* And jab my arm in the air. Which then caused me to faint. She told me they were concerned I was going to end up addicted to drugs," I said.

"And did you?" His mock serious tone hinted at his amusement. I didn't know why I couldn't stop talking. I realized no one ever asked me questions, I was always the one asking.

"No, not at all, but I was also obsessed with reading the cocktail menu at Applebee's as a kid. I loved all the colors. Swirling blues and purples with colorful straws and umbrellas. They looked like wizard potions to me. That also worried my dad."

Professor Johansen reached out and touched my lower back lightly as he stepped forward. I realized he had effortlessly moved me out of the path of a few students cutting across the room to get more drinks. He dropped his hand back to his side. I looked down at the cup of bubbling liquid in my hand, up at his face, and down again.

"You mentioned your father has a PhD as well, when we talked about your future, I mean possible future, as a philosophy doctoral student. What's his specialty?" He smiled when he corrected himself.

I tried to physically will the blush off my face with the force of my mind, imagining my blood draining away from the surface of my skin. I had hesitantly visited Professor Johansen's office hours after his comment on my paper. He was younger than I ever imagined a professor could be, or at least he looked that way. He exuded a calm thoughtfulness, a genuine curiosity about the world, that set him apart from the posturing graduate students.

"Dad studies fish," I said. "His 'office' was a lab with tanks and tanks of these small boring-colored fish. It always smelled weird. It made me think of dead things and chemicals. I also used to think that incense in church was the smell of decaying bodies, so maybe that's just a me thing."

"And this death smell has ruined PhDs for you? As you know, my office does not smell." His eyes twinkled and glanced off mine as he put undue concentration into swirling the cheap red wine in his plastic cup.

"Perhaps you were more persuasive in a different branch of the many-worlds," I said. I bit my bottom lip to staunch my smile.

"Perhaps," he said. My stomach fluttered.

Metaphysics is the most abstract and theoretical of the branches of philosophy. People understand ethics. They can even understand what epistemology is, the exploration of knowledge and what is knowable, if you mentioned deductive reasoning, geometric proofs, probabilistic inferences, those kinds of things.

But most people don't know how to even begin to examine the nature of the world around them. It's like a fish not knowing what water is. I smiled to myself at the thought of this fish failing to live up to the Socratic ideal that *an unexamined life is not worth living*. It was an absurd notion, fish are almost certainly not conscious in the way humans are, we had explored this at length in my Consciousness class last semester, but something about the idea still tickled me.

Fish made me think about Dad again. The fact I was graduating hadn't sunk in. I doubted it had for my parents either. I was sure they would still treat me like a child when they arrived. Even though graduation was tomorrow, college didn't feel quite complete.

"My dad, he built me a birdhouse when I was little," I said to Professor Johansen. "It was clear plastic on one side and he put it against the window. I could watch the mom bird build the nest and see the baby birds hatch out of their shells. It was neat. But mostly he never had any idea what I was talking about. He seemed perpetually confused that I was his child. I was always asking things like who came up with the word red? Was it always called that? How did he know that I saw the same color he did when I looked at the grass or the sky?"

Then Professor Johansen got interrupted by a student asking

about a recommendation letter. As I turned to leave, he told me he had a book he thought might be of interest to me and to find him later.

I wandered on the outskirts of the party, listening to snippets of conversation as I walked by. I heard the words Kantian, GPA, kegger, oppressive, and rhetoric. It was funny, I'd sat in the same room as these people twice a week for ten weeks and yet in this moment they felt like strangers. I wondered what fears and hopes they harbored about life, how they had felt when they were graduating college, what Laura was thinking now. I was still thinking about the conversation with Professor Johansen and how it ended. I had felt grown up for a moment while we were talking, but now I felt itchy and restless.

When I was younger, my brain was always itchy. I used to imagine a hamster scratching around inside my head. It would get especially itchy during read aloud time in fourth grade when it was little Charlie's turn. He was the slowest reader in the whole class. I'd have read the page five times before he got through the first paragraph. But if Mrs. Matthews caught me reading ahead, she'd reprimand me in front of the whole class.

I stroked my scar. I remembered waiting impatiently for the doctor during the final visit. I was fidgety, sitting on the metal exam table going kick, kick, kick against the side until Mom said something exasperated. My arm was so itchy inside the cast. I had never wanted to scratch anything that much. I would try and stick my finger down inside it a bit, but it didn't go far enough, and I was sort of scared that the bone was still sticking out and I would accidentally touch it, even though I knew that wasn't possible.

"Everything is looking good! Time to get out Mr. Buzzy," the doctor boomed when he opened the door. He pulled out a turbo-charged pizza cutter. I remember he told me it wouldn't hurt and so I tensed my whole body because even then I knew that doctors lied. I was terrified of sneezing and him cutting into my arm. I remember the vibrations made the roof of my mouth tickle. Like having to sneeze but worse.

He cracked the cast open with an alarming crunching noise and unwrapped the gauze. I stared at my arm. It was pale and kind of wrinkly. Soft and unused. Like a dead baby bird whose egg broke open too early. That happened to one of the eggs from the birdhouse. When I scratched my arm, my other hand came away with lumps of dead skin under the nails. I couldn't believe this was part of me.

"How did you make the bone go back under the skin?" I asked. I don't remember what the doctor said.

My brain had felt less itchy in college, at least most of the time. I walked out of the classroom, down the hallway and into the big impersonal bathroom. The stalls were that nondescript beige-gray that only airport, college, and department store bathrooms are painted. I sat down to pee and pressed the back of my hand against my forehead. My hand felt cool. I wondered if I was still blushing from talking to Professor Johansen. I grabbed one of the toilet-seat covers and blotted the oil off my face. I had walked in on a girl in the dorm bathroom doing this once during freshman year and she'd sheepishly explained that they work just as well as the fancy rice paper blotters you can buy at Sephora, but they're free. She was right.

As I looked in the mirror before I left the bathroom, I thought about the rays of light traveling from the light bulb, reflecting off the mirror, to the receptors in my eye. One aspect of studying metaphysics is reasoning about the relationship between the physical world and our perceptions thereof. Perceptions can never quite be trusted; I can never be absolutely certain I'm not hallucinating or experiencing some other distortion (like from the champagne I had been drinking). I thought of this whenever looking at my face felt like an agony of what ifs—what if I was a little prettier, what if my nose was a little smaller, what if my chin was a bit less pointy.

Reentering the classroom, I sidled up to a cluster of people talking. Will and Laura were there. The cluster was discussing some work of Kierkegaard's. I'd never read him so I stood quietly on the side, listening, trying to arrange my face into something inscrutable. I liked my classes, but I didn't read philosophy books outside of the assignments. This was one of my unarticulated hesitations when I thought about a PhD. I wondered if everyone else did, or if they just skimmed a few pages and were pretending.

When there was a lull in the conversation I asked quietly, "What exactly does he think is the relationship between existentialism and the individual?" But either no one heard me, or no one had an answer.

While I wasn't paying attention, Will and Laura and the other couple they were talking to had formed a little knot and I was standing too close, but not included. I headed out the big front door of the

Social Sciences building, onto the steps flanked by columns. I walked to the far edge of the cold, gray cement. The walk back to my dorm felt daunting. Leaving the party that early, that day of all days, felt pathetic. I had nowhere to go but back to my dark room and spartan twin bed. So I sat. The warm spring day, the excitement of impending graduation, felt drained away.

The perfect weather had made me think of Senior Skip Day back in high school. I didn't go to school that day, but I didn't go with my classmates either. I had stayed home and binge-watched a stupid sitcom. The kind where the kids are played by 25-year-old actors and the show makes high school into an endless stream of hijinks, glamorous parties, and gossiping in the hallway between classes no one ever attends. I remembered the sun moving across the bright blue sky outside the window as the hours passed, as I watched the TV raptly. The pretty blonde lead paired up with the pretty blond boy, then switched to the moody dark-haired boy to add tension and intrigue. I was angry that no one including my parents could or would ever answer my questions. And I was just as angry at myself for being full of questions that felt like they were always getting in the way of getting invited to sleepovers and kissing boys and whatever songwriters meant about *having the time of your life.*

I wondered if there was a branch of the world where I went with the rest of my class to the Six Flags, where I had the time of my life, where I kissed a boy on a rollercoaster and ate caramel apples with sweaty, laughing kids I'd known since first grade. But I was not in that branch of the many-worlds and there was no point wishing I was.

My butt was cold through my skirt. It was amazing how quickly the cold seeped and spread. I looked down at my toes in my sandals and at the mysterious smudgy stains on the stone steps. My earliest memory was of my dad giving me a bath. I remembered sitting in the lukewarm water staring at my toes. They poked out above the water, and I'd thought they looked so funny, like pudgy little aliens. I liked to wiggle my toes and watch the water tremble. I remember Dad poured a cup of water over my head to wash the shampoo out of my hair. I scrunched my eyes shut and squeezed my lips as tight as I could, but the smell-taste of the shampoo would still get in my mouth. I could read the shampoo bottle. I could suddenly read words when I saw them. And any time I looked at words, they would repeat over and over in my head. "No more tears no more tears no more tears." I didn't tell anyone I could read. I loved my bedtime stories. The words in my head weren't the same as when Dad read to me. When I read, the words went faster and sort of mushed together. "Nomoretears."

After my bone healed, I started taking swim lessons to help my arm get stronger. The shock of jumping into the cold pool made my face clench and my mouth gasp and it never got better no matter how many times I did it, in fact it got worse. The dread of the cold shock grew from repeated exposure. I'd swim back and forth, back and forth, staring at the painted black lines. Sometimes Coach would tell us to dive down and I'd touch the rough cement at the bottom of the pool.

While swimming, my ears were full of noises, swishing, murmuring sounds, almost like words. But I could never understand them. Maybe it was the swirl and wash of the water moving from the motion of our bodies, or the water lapping, gurgling, and glugging in the drain. Maybe it was the distorted echoes of parents chatting in the bleachers or Coach shouting from the deck. But it really sounded like words. And the days this happened most, I'd get out of the pool with a headache. My brain would feel exhausted, as prune-y and puckered on the inside, from trying to decipher the words that weren't words, as my fingers and toes were on the outside.

A group of four or five classmates, or maybe just students, I didn't recognize them from the backs of their heads, walked out the building and down the steps. There were giggles, scampering, heads tilted close together. A girl rose on tip toe to speak into a boy's ear. She touched his shoulder to balance herself. All I heard, floating back to me as they faded into the night air was, "and then she slapped Courtney across the face with the pillow." If I'd studied anthropology instead of philosophy, I'd have written my thesis on the mating rituals of college students—the bright lipsticks and shiny jewelry reminiscent of flamingos and magpies. How happy my dad would be if I studied birds instead.

"But Dad, what if the color I see for the ketchup is what you see for mustard!" I said.

It was breakfast, and Mom was quick to point out both bottles were supposed to have been put away by me the night before when I had been told to clear the table. We were learning about color blindness in biology class which had reawakened my long-standing questions about the perception of colors, something I had been bothering my parents about since I was a little kid.

"We know dogs see color differently than people, for example," I said.

Dad sighed. He lifted the remaining part of his bagel to his mouth and took his plate to the sink, more an excuse to stand than a need to rush.

"Why does no one ever answer my questions! Or even acknowledge when I'm talking. I might as well not exist! Did you even want a child? I thought parents were supposed to love and adore the fresh eyed curiosity of their offspring. Not my parents!" And I stormed out to wait for the school bus in the cold, jacket stuffed uselessly in my backpack.

Professor Johansen walked out the door and down the steps. My chin was resting on my hand. I had been watching the flickering light above the emergency intercom attached to a blue pole. They were sprinkled across campus, and you were supposed to use one if someone was harassing or following you, not that anything that dramatic had ever happened to me.

"Ah, Natasha. Had enough of your peers for the evening?" He'd donned a tweed jacket with elbow patches that I'd never seen him wear before.

"Is that your professor costume?" The champagne lubricated the words right out of my mouth before I had time to think.

He looked down at his jacket and laughed. My head felt floaty, like this couldn't be real life. Like I was lost in a daydream, the universe merely a creation of my mind.

"The book?" he said. I nodded and stood, brushing off my butt and smoothing out my skirt.

We walked across the dimly lit sidewalks, a diagonal traverse across a lawn we would have perceived as green in the daylight, then through a parking lot. He scanned his badge at the entrance to another large stone building. This one held the offices of many professors and a small social sciences library on the ground floor.

"Stairs or elevator?" he asked. I picked the stairs because I was not in the mood to pause or wait or stand still. I wondered about the other Natasha, the one not walking next to Professor Johansen. The

Natasha still sitting on the cold steps. But she was not me. Or I was not her, not anymore.

"So, your father didn't engage your precocious etymological inquiries and now you're here. Like this." He trailed off because I had popped open the final button on my skirt. In my mind, I was pretending to be the pretty blonde girl from the TV show. Imagining what she would do off screen, in the bedroom, with her handsome co-star.

I let my skirt drop to the floor. The gentle smirk slid off his face and I could feel the shift in power. I had never had power before.

It wasn't sex. We didn't go all the way. I didn't know what to call it. He was on top of me, he had one arm cradling the back of my neck, and the other arm gripping the back of the couch for leverage. My ear was pressed against his arm, and as his motion moved my body slightly up and down, my hair becoming staticky against the throw pillow, I heard those murmurs. Maybe it was the blood in my ears, pressed against his arm. The susurration was not quite words, as much as I tried to make them out—far away murmurs echoing down a marble corridor. The whole thing wasn't unpleasant, it was just all faster than I had expected.

I knew my parents would be appalled by this. They'd blame Professor Johansen. My dad would blame my not fully developed prefrontal cortex, and my mom would blame celebrities and pop music, and other inane things.

If you asked me why I did this, I'd cite high school, existential nihilism, and the many-worlds theory. If some version of me was going to say yes to going to Professor Johansen's office, if some version of me was going to unbutton her skirt, then for once I wanted to be that version. But no one ever asks me. I can imagine the fight without even needing to have it.

Mom: What were you thinking! [*Not a question, a statement*]

Me: When you met Dad, you were his graduate student!

Dad: Things were different back then.

Mom: Shut up, David! How your father and I met was unfortunate, but it turned out alright. And anyway, I was older than you are now. Did you do this because of us? Was it to get back at us?

Mom under her breath to Dad: She's never really grown out of her teenage angst.

I wanted to scream *It's not about you, Mom. It's about metaphysics!*

And while that sounded satisfyingly dramatic, I knew it would come out sounding childish. Which was exactly what I didn't want to be, not even in this imaginary fight.

I wondered about the branch of the many-worlds where Professor Johansen said no instead of yes. I wondered what that would have been like, how I would have felt—rejected, relieved, misguided? I imagined my seductive powers overcoming the rules of quantum mechanics, making it impossible for him to say no. I think I'm glad he said yes. I think no would have felt worse.

I didn't realize you could do these things with a man and still have so many questions racing around your brain. I imagined the enormity of it would wipe my mind blank, but it hadn't. I was going to tell Professor Johansen, *I have questions about the objective versus phenomenological perception of color in objects*. But I also had questions about whether this is something I was capable of, whether anyone would want to do this with me, when my life would really start. I've always had a lot of questions. I wonder for the first time if a PhD might answer more of them than I thought.

MICHAEL AGUGOM

The Happiest People in the World

OUR NAAMU HASN'T BEEN OUT of her blue striped uniform for twelve days now, since she was brought back into this facility, into this solitary dark room; her yansh on the floor, her back pressed to the wall, her thighs pressed to her breasts, her arms wrapped around her legs, her brow on her knees, she has been in this posture half the night.

Our Naamu hasn't known fear in this room. Outside, the sun hasn't risen yet; the moon has been cowering behind thick dark clouds throughout the night.

Our Naamu hasn't known sleep throughout the night: has been envisioning herself as redeemer of the people. Doing so even now, she lifts her head. Her gaze on this darkness she's drowned in (even though directed at the steel door facing her), she intones, *I swear, Abu, today you'll see that the beauty of fire is at night.*

This room, dark as devil's heart and whispered all over the country as Devil's Heart, has no bed. No furniture. Just the thick walls, the concrete floor and ceiling, and the piss-stained bucket at the corner for Naamu's body-wastes. She's breathed long enough under its cloud her sense of smell is dead to it: the pungent pong of piss in this room.

These walls have intricate patterns of scum, scum left behind by us from losing our minds—we were daughters, mothers, grandmothers, once alive and gainfully employed as professional mourners, all thirty-seven of us. Six Supreme Court judges had, before Naamu's turn, condemned us to this room. Our crime? We refused to laugh, we refused to be counted among the happiest people in the world. Naamu is different from us only in how she intends to end this day.

The beautiful thing about her being locked up here: this room doesn't have a mirror so that she hasn't beheld her disfigured face—a reminder of her mother's cruelty. Even in this dark Devil's Heart she can still—in her head, that is—see the scum on the walls clearly: she's been in this room as long as she's been in that prison uniform. The walls, the floor, the ceiling, and the bucket are what her eyes have had to feed on that long, as long as this room is served with daylight; ten feet above her head is the miniature window that serves the room daylight every day.

A weight she can't wait to throw off: her body, has become deadweight; a few hours from now Naamu's decision will get a hand from the government. Aai... when the sun rises outside today, Naamu will be set free to join us. She'll hear the warders tramp through the corridors to this steel door. They'll throw it open. Cuff her. And drag her out through the corridors into a washroom. They'll shave her head moromoro, not a strand of hair left, and wash her clean—will doll her up to look acceptable to death.

But before Naamu is executed she'll get her wish. This country's new constitution entitles her to one last wish, provided it isn't that she be absolved of the crime that fetched her this death sentence. Also, Naamu is by law entitled to the blessings of a cleric moments before her death.

Her last wish: she has demanded that her execution be live streamed on all media platforms in the country (and this already-granted-last-wish has already gone viral and made headlines); in place of a cleric, she has demanded for her brother to be seated across from her, face to face, in the execution room—*There'll be plenty of time to discuss my disappointments with God after I'm dead,* she had mused: she doesn't need Him present at her moment of death.

The people don't know this yet: at the moment of Naamu's execution, she'll do exactly what fetched her this death sentence: cry—yes. And Naamu will enjoy doing it, unperturbed by death.

Her many deaths began with her name. Her name became Naamu because her people couldn't pronounce Naomi without their native tongue getting in the way, not even her mother who had picked out the name from a basket half filled with foreign names.

Amrika's husband had returned from his travels. Joyfully holding his infant daughter for the first time, he had asked Amrika, *Why oyinbo name?* Wearing a frown, Amrika bawled her response, *You no see am yourself? No pikin ugly like you deserve our fine names.*

Amrika had also been denied a native name. Her name, a corruption of America, was her first abuse by her father. He named her America hoping the gesture would influence a favourable response to his family's application to the American Visa Lottery, back when this country was still eligible for the program. He wanted desperately to abscond to America with his family, to flee from a choking debt.

Amrika grew up feeling like a worm thread to a hook; the day she saw the end of her first period, her father cast her into sea: he offered her up to his creditor: an old bachelor Amrika despised not just for his age but his scorched-back-of-a-cooking-pot skin colour… and his dirt-face as she thought of his face. The rusty bachelor accepted Amrika in exchange for the old debt.

Amrika (as long as she lived with her husband) allowed him only between her legs, never into her heart, while fervently praying for early and childless widowhood on herself. But Naamu came and took all the physical characteristics of Amrika's husband; Amrika's son followed before death finally relieved Amrika of her husband. It pleased Amrika that her son didn't take any physical feature of her husband—her son was her carbon-copy. But it churned Amrika's stomach that she'd have to raise a replica of her husband: her own daughter.

Amrika would insist, *Woman no suppose black and ugly like this, my daughter. I wish, like your brother, you no resemble that dirt-face*—as if it was Naamu's choice to make whom she's to resemble. To cleanse her daughter of *that dirt-face*, Amrika bleached Naamu's skin with a concoction of imported and locally made creams and chemicals. Her effort left Naamu with an amalgam of skin colours: a patch of Fanta here, a patch of Coke there; different shades of skin burns and irritations in-between. This disfigurement (Naamu's second death) made Naamu a brutish and resentful daughter.

At fifteen Naamu's resentment towards Amrika grew hands and feet. She got pregnant having sex on Amrika's bed with the most infamous drunk in the town. She fled from home barely a week before her newborn was due for a name, leaving the infant to die nameless on Amrika's old breasts. She returned two years after and kept her head down—even gave Amrika a hand at Amrika's cassava farm (Naamu who despised farming). Like a hawk, Amrika watched her daughter, expecting another act of spite. Six months passed, nothing happened. Amrika let her guard down, convinced Naamu had become reasonable. But Naamu was only taking her time to find a suitable accomplice. She found him: the town's most notorious burglar whose charcoal-skinned colour reminded Amrika of part of what Amrika hated about her late husband. She brought him home to Amrika as her boyfriend. Amrika's jugular veins almost burst open from vehemently rebuking Naamu for having an affair with *that thief!*

She responded to Amrika's rebuke: she got pregnant with the thief's child even though she had no feelings whatsoever for *that thief*.

She had the baby. Again, before the baby was due for a name, she fled (the thief had been shot dead on his first highway robbery attempt). Amrika named the infant even though she feared the infant wouldn't survive. She didn't pick out a name for him from a basket of foreign names. She didn't give the infant a native name. She named him the first word that came to her mind when news of *that thief's* death reached her ears—Justice, hoping he'd grow up guided by his name. But for the remainder of Amrika's life Justice remained her *penance for her sins* against Naamu.

Justice survived. Amrika raised Justice. If raising the replica of *that dirt-face* gave Amrika headache, raising the son of *that thief* gave her heartache, but the heartache did an excellent job of mellowing her into acknowledging her earlier parenting-errors, especially that of bleaching Naamu.

Justice and an old-age of constant musings brought painful remorse to Amrika. She sent messages to Naamu begging for forgiveness, pleading with her to return home. But holding a grudge had already become a source of nourishment to Naamu. In fact, she replied to Amrika with a video of her humping a kinsman. The shock of the taboo of the sex with a kinsman and its impending consequent curse upon their family, shot up Amrika's blood pressure, causing her to suffer a severe stroke.

Naamu found holding a grudge poisonous after she survived a car crash that left her in a dark space between life and death for two months. But by the time she had decided to return home and saw the evidence of the love and devotion Amrika had put into raising Justice despite his black-as-shadow skin, Amrika had crossed into the otherworld while sleeping. And Naamu suffered guilt that was as paralysing as her mother's stroke.

Bereft of reasons to run away from home, Naamu stayed back with her son and fended for him and he became her major purpose for existence. Adept at nothing but faking emotions, she became a professional mourner; happily crying at funerals for income for more than nineteen years until she found herself out of work—no thanks to a heinous law drafted by her own brother.

Her brother had just returned from abroad with a heart as cold as Russia, where he had studied for an engineering degree. He had learnt from phone calls with Amrika what Naamu had put Amrika through. Naamu had hoped for a warm closeness between her and her brother, but he avoided her like Covid—avoided her for more than forty years. Once, he allowed a phone conversation between them. He made it clear, *I swear on Mama's grave, you and I will never ever see face to face. It's best to assume I'm no longer your brother!*

She tried: Naamu bah. She begged. She pleaded that they see each other. She wanted him to hear her side of the story, to see her remorse. But he stuck to his words and blocked her on all channels of electronic communication. He made money. He made a name for himself in politics. He made sure no one knew he had a sister. At first it depressed Naamu, then it infuriated her. Then the fury dissolved into indifference until that heinous bill drafted by his own brother became law, and Naamu's mouth bulged with venomous words to say.

She initially found no platform open to her to express her disgusts for that law. But after her son's tragedy, she found a way to have her say.

Our Naamu has been dragged out of Devil's Heart—dragged in handcuffs by two male warders through the corridors into this washroom, where two senior female warders order the men to uncuff her immediately, howling, *She no be dog,* and the men obeyed and shuffled out of this washroom grumbling like broods scolded by their mother.

Our Naamu has, in this washroom, been gently stripped naked by the female warders in front of a well-polished human size mirror—she has seen in the eyes of these female warders the compassion she had sought all her life from her mother.

Our Naamu has been allowed a moment before the mirror to take stock of how she looks—has seen that the naked woman in the mirror before her isn't the woman she had known. This woman has in the past twelve days aged but not into her mother as she had feared. She smirks, recalling how she was called *ugly* by her brother.

One harmattan morning that year, Naamu's brother, Distinguished Senator Abudu Amam, a.k.a Senator The Genius, a.k.a Socrates of Our Time, a.k.a Senator Sharp-Sharp, a.k.a Abu, stood before his colleagues on the floor of this country's National Assembly during a plenary session and argued in favour of a bill he had carefully drafted with support from this country's president. *Crying-room*, he had cried, *my distinguished colleagues, crying-room is the singular solution to all the economic problems bedevilling our country.*

His primary argument? That citizens of this country spare no expense throwing ostentatious funerals; that they hire professional mourners to showcase grief. He insisted it's become imperative the government take advantage of the potential economic gains from *this frivolous behaviour.* He sneered, *Tradition asks us to perform our grief when we're bereaved. That's not bad. Now, my distinguished colleagues, consider for a moment the benefits that will come from providing our people with a conducive space where they can mourn or shed tears in private. At a time like this when our crude oil reserve has depleted—and what's left of it has become cheaper than an old woman's rag—as a responsible government we are called upon to be innovative in our fight against economic recession. That is what this bill is about. Our only means to economic recovery is the provision of crying-rooms all over this country.*

Abu. He had done his math on how much revenue the government could generate from charging every citizen a fee for the use of his proposed crying-rooms. And the numbers looked even better than what this country had made from crude oil sales. *But for this to work*, he cried, *this house has to pass a law that prohibits any public and even private display of grief in this country. No one is to shed a single tear for whatever reason outside the crying-rooms. Grief and all other related sad emotions must be milked of their economic benefits. Whoever can afford professional mourners in their numbers to toss and wail on the ground at funerals as a way of giving their deceased a befitting burial can as well afford a crying-room.*

He concluded strongly, *When you consider the amount of grieving and crying that goes on in this country, you'll see the irrefutable potential of my proposed crying-room.*

There was a challenge though: funding the construction of such rooms all over this country required huge sums. *Our treasury is empty*, a Senator took the floor to remind the house, *we haven't been able to service our Chinese loans. Need I remind this honourable house how China lined our testicles on the floor and trampled on them the last time we went begging for more loans to build more mortuaries for our people? And say we could finance these... these crying-rooms and pass such law, think of the impossibility and impracticability of policing our citizenry on such emotional displays outside these supposed crying-rooms, much less how they're to be prosecuted...*

Abu hadn't come to the senate floor unprepared for objections: *My distinguished colleague, impossibility died with Covid more than a decade ago! Technology, I promise you, is the key! Our tech boys have assured me they can in a heartbeat create an app capable of identifying emotional changes in humans. This app when created will be rolled out. And revenue from its compulsory download and use by our people will be enough to fund the building of crying-rooms all over this country. It would also serve as digital police: no phone or any other electronic device user—by that I mean everyone in this country—would be able to cry outside the crying-rooms whether in their homes or hidden public spaces without being detected, caught, and prosecuted.*

What was not openly mentioned and agreed amongst Abu's colleagues that day was that, just as the revenues from crude-oil sales ended up in their pockets, so too would revenues from the use of these crying-rooms. The app was developed. Everyone in this country was compelled by law to download and use it. It became a crime in the country, a crime to shed tears or express any form of sadness both in private and in public. A five-year imprisonment crime. A capital-punishment crime for two-time offenders. *You're not to infect others with your grief,* the lawmakers insisted. It came to be by December of 2037. The same way mobile phones arrived and every hand you glanced at on the street was clutching one, so did crying-rooms. All over the country. Every street you walked into there was at least a crying-room for you to cry yourself to dehydration or mourn or do whatever you do whenever life shoved you into tragic days.

Given the many social classes and the classless classes of this country, there began to emerge crying-rooms for different pocket sizes; even crying-booths for the many of the classless classes—remember how *pure-water* was packaged for the masses in small nylon bags back in those days?

They became a basic necessity: crying-rooms. Their demand broke every economic chart. It appeared there wouldn't be a point of equilibrium between their demand and their supply. Because only the government is versed in defying the law of gravity—that whatever they toss into the air never returns to the ground, and like everything else in high demand in the country—it rose and continued to rise: the cost of using crying-rooms.

Crying-rooms became luxury spaces. Their prices went so high only the rich could reach it. The rich meaning the politicians and a handful of wealthy businessmen. They even conceived the notion of Exclusive Crying-Rooms, the way you have VIP lounges in bars and clubs. In fact, they began to build private crying-rooms; awarding themselves the licences to use them. Some had multiple crying-rooms: one in their countryside villas, another in their city estates. In less than a decade, crying-rooms became a mark of affluence. You couldn't be called *big-man* or *big-boy* if you didn't own exclusive crying-rooms.

Women in the country, especially the poor ones, suffered the brunt of this law most. A poor girl couldn't even cry in her shack from her first sudden breakup without being arrested and prosecuted. A poor mother couldn't burst into tears in front of her kiosk at the sudden news of her son's death without being arrested and prosecuted. A poor grandmother couldn't mourn at the grave of her murdered grandchild without being arrested and prosecuted. Women couldn't tear up from watching a sad soap on TV without being arrested and prosecuted. Women needed to cry. Like the rest of the poor of this country, women couldn't afford the supposed cheap crying-booths. On behalf of the poor of this country, we the dead thirty-seven professional mourners, before our death, began to protest.

The government didn't see the downturn coming. But animated by the international applause and the attention their "ingenious crying-rooms" garnered, the government responded to the protests in the egocentric manner typical of this country's government for generations now: they passed another law censoring all social and traditional media content capable of eliciting tears from viewers and listeners. *Crying-room has come to stay*, they insisted, *those who can't afford it will have to learn to laugh over their tragedies*. By those who couldn't afford it they were referring to more than eighty-five percent of the country's population. They insisted that the masses rise above their tragedies. That the mind is a powerful tool. That the masses can harness that power to laugh even in the face of their grief. That genuine happiness can't be affected by external factors, not even the loss of a loved one. They even employed teachings from obscure religions that extol strength in adversity. They put their feet down: *You can't laugh over your tragedy? Use a crying-room.* They had the power. They silenced the protest.

Indeed many of the masses began to laugh over their tragedies. Almost everyone began to compartmentalise and value tragedies the way real estate brokers value properties. Grief came at the top: it required long hours, even days, in the crying-rooms, hence too expensive for any sane person who could barely afford to feed. Everyone, except the politicians and the few rich businessmen, lived figuring out ways of dancing around grief. We professional mourners, including Naamu, soon found ourselves out of jobs. No one would hire mourners at funerals. Comedians were hired to crack jokes at funerals instead. They were cheaper, compared to hiring mourners and having to book crying-rooms for them and other guests to use. So, it became commonplace to find the people at funerals laughing over their loss.

The country soon took on the look of a wildlife reserve of raucously chortling animals. It fetched the country international laurels. Go to WHO headquarters. Check their records. It says this country has the happiest people in the world. Check the pages of the Guinness Book of World Records. This country holds the number one position of the happiest people in the world. You may have even seen the government's pathetic ad on CNN or Aljazeera where footage of her peoples' beaming faces invite tourists to the country for its hospitality and exotic crying-rooms—how gross?

Nowadays, you'd see Abu on TV gloating, *In the past we were a country infamous for financial fraud, but today we're a country famous for our phenomenal crying-rooms.* For more than two decades now the people haven't shed tears, the people haven't seen tears. Of course you can cover faeces with plastic to spare the eyes, but can that spare your nose? The people hid grief like landmines, watching and waiting for someone to trigger it. But not the thirty-seven of us convicted before Naamu's turn—we just couldn't hold or hide something so tsunamic in us. And for our public show of it we paid the ultimate price on the same chair Naamu is about to sit on today.

Imagine! The thirty-seven of us even fooled ourselves thinking
if we feigned laughter at the hour of our execution that we might be
pardoned by the government. How laughable we must have seemed. Our
executions went quietly. We wish we had done differently—wish we had
done what Naamu is about to do today.

However, it must be said that Naamu isn't doing this for just the
people but also for Justice. If Justice inherited his father's thievery, he
never exhibited it. Thanks to Amrika: all the mistakes she made raising
Naamu and Abu she righted raising Justice. But despite her best efforts
Amrika couldn't rid Justice of his wilfulness. Yet if you asked Naamu why
she loved Justice so much, why she would die for him, the first reason she
would offer with a grin would be (aside the fact that she had come to love
him dearly and found him her purpose for living), *He's stubborn like me.*
What she loved him most for cost her enormous pain when Justice found
work at the biggest construction site ever seen by the people.

The government had embarked on a monumental project: the
would-be biggest crying-room in the country. A twenty-thousand-room
capacity crying-room. It would be the country's Eiffel Tower or Statue
of Liberty or Taj Mahal: the government's priceless gift to her people.
Naamu forbad Justice from working on a building that she regarded as
the landmark of the government's oppression and mental repression of
her people.

But Justice couldn't be stopped. To him it was just an honest
labour with a decent pay—a pay they needed if he and Naamu were
to survive. That afternoon, two months after he started work, Naamu
walked to the site with a lunchbox for her son. She was ten paces before
the yellow-tape barrier into the site when Justice missed his step on the
scaffolding and fell from fifty-feet high. Naamu dropped the lunchbox
and ran to the spot, holding her breasts tightly to prevent her heart from
falling out. It took her half a minute to process the reality of her son's
remains on the ground. She fell on her knees. She wailed, right there.

Hours later Naamu was arrested, prosecuted, and convicted. She
served the full term of her five-year sentence. But a week after walking out
the jail-gate, she shambled to the front gate of the Supreme Court building
and wailed at the feet of the gigantic statue of Lady Justice there.

Our Naamu has been shaved moromoro, washed clean, and dressed up nicely. She has been led to the execution room where the masked executioner is at work by the chair (this executioner who wakes up every morning wishing he had a different job). There's a plexiglass wall between this room and another. Legal witnesses are seated in that other room.

Our Naamu has been strapped to the chair, has glanced at the white switch on the wall (a flip of the switch will do it: a painless freezing of her brain). Set on two tripods are two cameras, strategically positioned at different corners of this room.

Our Naamu has leaned into the chair, taken a deep breath, and let it out slowly. She now puts on a smirk as the executioner straps patches, tubes, and wires to her shaved head. The green lights of the cameras are on: her last moments between her and her brother are streaming live. He's sitting across from her; her brother, a foreboding presence in this room.

This childhood memory has been a leech on Naamu, sucking her blood dry: Naamu is fourteen and stout, Abu is thirteen and lanky, basking in the euphoria of having just passed a scholarship exam that would take him far away from home for secondary school (same exam Amrika never gave Naamu a chance to write, insisting, *Like your papa, you no get head for book*). They're at Amrika's cassava farm, making cassava mounds and burying cassava stems in them; Abu makes an impressive dome-shaped mound, and Naamu is filled with rage watching Abu get an encouraging nod and grin from Amrika (a gesture Naamu would never get no matter her best efforts at impressing Amrika). Abu, lost in the rapture of Amrika's attention, teases Naamu, *You can never make a perfect dome mound*; Naamu loses her temper and wallops his face. The blow sends him crashing onto his mound; Amrika pounces on Naamu, pinning her to the ground to strangle to death; passersby dash into the farm and pull Amrika off her. Much later, at home in their room when you'd think the incident at the farm had been forgotten, Naamu is preening in front of a mirror, behind her is Abu; she turns towards him enquiring how she looks, hankering for the tiniest compliment from him; Abu stares her in the face and blurts out, *You'll always be ugly no matter what you paint on that your colour-riot dirt-face. You'll remain ugly. You'll grow ugly, even die an ugly death!*

That was the last time she saw her brother face to face; his last words, her third death.

Outside, the people are glued to their phones and TV screens, in their homes, in the markets, in the bars, on the streets, everywhere. No live coverage has drawn more viewers than Naamu's execution, not even the grand opening of the monumental crying-room early in the year, not even the country's first ever victory at the FIFA World Cup the year before.

Inside, the executioner allows Naamu her last words with her brother. Even though he's masked, he's jittery. He had periodically executed women in this same room (still sees their faces in his nightmares) and none had requested live coverage—much less a sibling present. He's never had to perform his duties on live coverage before.

She sneers at Abu. *Good to finally see you again, small brother.*

Motionless in his chair, except for his trembling hands clasped on his thighs, his jaws clenched, he doesn't respond, her brother.

She scoffs: *Why your face like shit wey person shoot catapult? Relax. Shey I'm the one about to be executed, not you. You're supposed to be laughing. Is laughter-in-the-face-of-tragedy not what you've been selling to our people?*

Stop it, he blurts out, struggling now to hold in the tide building inside him, his heart palpitating with guilt. He wanted her hurt for their mother's death, not dead. He would have gotten up and stormed out of this room if it wouldn't amount to breaking the law, if those goddamn cameras weren't streaming these moments to the people.

Again she sneers. *Stop it? Why? Don't tell me you're heartbroken your sister is in this chair. Or too ashamed to hear me out before your 'fine' law kills me, bah? Ah, the corpse of a stranger is indeed firewood. How many have died in this chair for the same reason I'm in it now?*

Still holding in the tide, his eyelids heavy and drooping, he attempts a defence, *You killed her. You killed mama with your scandalous behaviour. Oh, so you want sympathy now?*

Flush your sympathy down the toilet! Who's asking for it! I see. But wait o! Let me oil your rusty memory a little. Take a look at me very well. She killed me first. She kills me every time I look into a mirror. She killed me on that farm. And you bah! Is this not your prophecy come true… now I'm only giving you a gift: the last memory of me you'll have will be of me in this chair, of how you completed the killing you and mama started. You wouldn't—

He can no longer contain it: the tide, it breaks free; with the crook of his arm, he wipes the tears and whimpers, *I was only thirteen,*

Naamu. I never meant those words… I'm sorry, Naamu… I'm sorry I swear… I just couldn't—

She cries, *Aaah abeg abeg.* And words become rocks lodged in her throat as she sobs: *You're sorry? No you're not. You just couldn't stand the monster you and mama turned me into. You're never sorry, you attention-crazed selfish goat, only good at ruining the lives of others. Look at our country. You've made a population of puppets. For what? To get back at me? Poor masses can't even mourn their loved ones as they want without paying for it with their lives…*

Now, if the executioner wasn't having an emotional moment under his mask he would have spared the people any more of this dismal scene by turning off the cameras. But turning off the cameras now would be pointless: the people have already seen enough to uncork more than two decades of bottled emotions. They sob. They weep. Some even wail. In their homes. In the markets. In the bars. On the streets. Everywhere, but in the crying-rooms. As their mouths empty their hearts of grief and their tears wet their stony cheeks, they feel clearheaded enough to summon courage; their first step toward repossessing their lives.

Contributors' Bios

Michael Agugom is a W. Morgan and Lou Claire Rose Fellow at Texas State University, where he's also an MFA candidate. He is a recipient of a 2018 Iceland Writers Retreat Alumni Award. His works have appeared in *Prairie Schooner, The Cantabrigian Magazine, Queer Africa 2: New Stories,* and other places.

Timilehin Alake is a Ph.D. student at Washington University in St Louis from Lagos, Nigeria. He studies comparative literature in the International Writers Track where he is currently working on a debut novel. He has been published in *The Florida Review, Kalahari Review,* and *Contrary Magazine.*

Alex J. Barrio is a political consultant and progressive advocate living in Washington, DC. He is a Cuban-American who grew up in New Jersey and spent most of his adult life in Florida. He can be found on Twitter for poetry (@1001Tanka) and fiction (@AlexJBarrio).

Zoey Birdsong, originally from Taos, New Mexico, is a third-year Creative Writing major at Oberlin College.

Michelle D'costa is a writer, editor, and creative writing mentor from Mumbai. She co-hosts the author interview podcast Books and Beyond with Bound. Her poetry chapbook *Gulf* was published by Yavanika Press in 2021. Her work can be found in *Litro UK, Berfrois, Eclectica, Out Of Print,* and others. www.michellewendydcosta.wordpress.com/

Malina Douglas conjures rich imagery by the encounters that shape us. She was awarded Editor's Choice in the Hammond House International Literary Prize and longlisted for the Reflex Press Prize. Publications include *The National Flash Fiction Day Anthology, Typehouse, Wyldblood, Opia, Ellipsis Zine, Back Story Journal,* and *Consequence Forum.* She is an alumna of Smokelong Summer and tweets @iridsecentwords.

Neethu Krishnan is a writer based in Mumbai, India, who holds postgraduate degrees in English and Microbiology. A 2022 Best Of The Net poetry nominee and recipient of the Creative Non-fiction Award in *Bacopa Literary Review* 2022 contest, Neethu's works have appeared in over a dozen literary journals.

Kimaya Kulkarni (she/her/hers) is a writer and editor living in and being constantly inspired by her hometown, Pune. She is an editor at *Bilori Journal*, *Spooky Gaze* and *decoloniszing our bookshelves (dob)*, and holds an MSc in Comparative Literature from the University of Edinburgh. Her prose has appeared in *Wizards in Space*, *Honey and Lime*, *Cobra Milk*, *Lily Poetry Review* and *ROM Mag*.

Anna Lapera is a middle school teacher by day and fiction writer in the early hours of the morning. She is primarily a Young Adult fiction writer but loves writing short stories for the grownups. Her forthcoming debut upper middle grade novel *Mani Semilla Finds Her Quetzal Voice* is scheduled to be published in Spring 2024 through Levine Querido. She is a 2022 Macondista with the Macondo Writers Workshop, a *Kweli Journal* mentee, and a 2021 mentee with the Las Musas Mentorship Program for unpublished Latinx kidlit writers. You can find her on Twitter @WriterOfCuentos.

Susan L. Lin is a Taiwanese American storyteller who hails from southeast Texas and holds an MFA in Writing from California College of the Arts. Her novella *Goodbye to the Ocean* won the 2022 Etchings Press novella prize and is available to purchase at susanllin.wordpress.com.

Sienna Liu is a writer of prose and poetry based in London. Her work has appeared or is forthcoming in *Cotton Xenomorph*, *A Velvet Giant*, *HAD*, *Lit 202*, *Occulum*, among others. She is the author of the poetry chapbook *Square* (Black Sunflowers Poetry Press, 2022).

Sam Moe lives in Normal, Illinois. She is the first-place winner of *Invisible City's Blurred Genres* contest in 2022. Her chapbook, *Heart Weeds*, is out from Alien Buddha Press and her second chapbook, *Grief Birds*, is forthcoming from *Bullshit Lit* in April 2023. You can find her online as @SamAnneMoe.

Dylan Reber is a writer and graduate student. He resides in the Atlanta metropolitan area, where he is finishing up his thesis and working on a collection of short stories in the company of his dog and four very dusty bookshelves.

Kris Riley is from Houston, currently residing in New Orleans. They are a co-editor for *Scar Tissue Magazine* and work with Upturn Arts as a teaching artist. They have works featured in *The Ember Chasm Review*, The *Raw Art Review*, *Beyond Words*, and *HUMID*. Visit them on Instagram at ampersand_ anyway.

Rosario Santiago is a queer Boricua writer. Their poetry has been published in *mag 20/20*, *celestite poetry*, and the *OutWrite D.C 2022 Festival Journal*. "Meet Me in the Universe" is their first published short story.

Previously published in *The Acentos Review* 2020 December issue, and the *Big Muddy Journal* 2021 issue, **Christian Vazquez** is a 26-year-old gay writer from Brownsville, Texas. Today, he is a professor at Houston Community College. Also, he is cohost of El Unnamed Podcast on YouTube. His Instagram: christian77vazquez Twitter: @christian77v.

Severin Wiggenhorn has worked as a Senate staffer, software engineer, and technical writer. She has degrees in classical ballet, philosophy, law, and is an MFA candidate at Randolph College.

Ashley Wolfe is the author of *Pachamama*, and has published work in *Superstition Review*, *Parentmap*, *IRLS* and the London Centre for Interdisciplinary Research Narrating Lives Conference. She holds a BA in journalism from Arizona State University and will soon complete an MFA at the University of Arkansas at Monticello. www.ashleymwolfe.com

April Yu is a young writer from New Jersey with an affinity for language, running, and human anatomy. Her work has or is slated to appear in *Milk Candy Review*, *The Aurora Journal*, and more. She is a graduate of the Alpha Workshop for Young Writers.

Ivelisse Rodriguez's debut short story collection *Love War Stories* was a 2019 PEN/Faulkner finalist and a 2018 Foreword Reviews INDIES finalist. She has published fiction in the *Boston Review*, *Obsidian*, *Kweli*, the *Bilingual Review*, *Aster(ix)*, and other publications. She is a contributing arts editor for the *Boston Review*, where she acquires fiction. She was a senior fiction editor at *Kweli* and is a Kimbilio fellow and a Las Dos Brujas and *VONA/Voices* alum. She earned an M.F.A. in creative writing from Emerson College and a Ph.D. in English-creative writing from the University of Illinois at Chicago.